Also by Kate Cann:

www.katecann.com

Possessing Rayne

Kate Cann

SCHOLASTIC

To Jeff, Hester and John,
with love

First published in the UK in 2008 by Scholastic Children's Books
An imprint of Scholastic Ltd
Euston House, 24 Eversholt Street
London, NW1 1DB, UK
Registered office: Westfield Road, Southam,
Warwickshire, CV47 0RA
SCHOLASTIC and associated logos are trademarks
and/or registered trademarks of Scholastic Inc.

Text copyright © Kate Cann, 2008
The right of Kate Cann to be identified as the author
of this work has been asserted by her.

ISBN 978 1407 10246 7

A CIP catalogue record for this book
is available from the British Library

Printed in the UK by CPI Bookmarque, Croydon, Surrey
Papers used by Scholastic Children's Books are made
from wood grown in sustainable forests.

1 3 5 7 9 10 8 6 4 2

This is a work of fiction. Names, characters, places, incidents and dialogues are
products of the author's imagination or are used fictitiously. Any resemblance to
actual people, living or dead, events or locales is entirely coincidental.

www.scholastic.co.uk/zone

Chapter One

Rayne sat on the end of her narrow bed next to Jelly's cot, painting her nails. It was the end of August and the heat was vile. She'd pulled the blind against the sun to cut the glare, but it made no difference. She'd just had a cold shower, but she was sweating already, her make-up melting off her pretty, pointed face like wax. Her cheap electric fan had broken yesterday and now there was absolutely no movement in the stifling air.

She checked her watch – ten to seven. Damian had said he'd call for her at seven but he was always late. She couldn't stand it any longer, trapped in the flat like a rat in a lab cage. Everyone had their windows open, and the evening was full of pounding music, television sport, shouting, swearing, babies wailing. . . She had to get out. It would be no cooler out there and there'd be sirens and screeching cars on top of all the other noise – but at least she could move and *breathe* out there.

She picked up her bag and went to the front door, past her mum, who was flaked out on the sofa, mouth open, snoring softly. Her little brother, Jelly, was fast asleep beside her, on his stomach, quiet for once. Jelly was really Jeremy, which was a weird name for a kid around here, but he couldn't pronounce it, it was always "Jelly wants more!" and "Jelly come too!" and soon everyone else called him that too.

Their flat was four floors up and the lifts had broken down again, but Rayne never used the lifts anyway. They trapped you. If someone rough got in on the second floor, you'd be easy meat. And running up and down the stairs was some kind of exercise, it made you feel better. Even though the stairs stank of pee and had rubbish all over them.

She met Damian as she was halfway down the last flight of stairs to the ground. "What's up?" he said indignantly, his heavy forehead creasing in a frown. "I'm not late!"

"No," she said. "Just I was going mad in there, Day. I couldn't stand it."

They collided in a kiss. "I don't like you going out on your own, babe," he mumbled. "I told you – it's getting dodgy out there. The police've been round already, loudspeakers and everything, going on about not congregating in groups and threatening everyone with *dispersal* orders. . ." His voice was full of relish. He loved it, he'd loved it in the long freak spell of hot weather they'd had in April when there'd practically been riots on the Estate, he loved the drama and the battles.

"Don't worry," Rayne said. "I'd've waited for you by the door."

"You look great," he said, scanning her thin body, her short, glossy black hair, her cheap but stylish dress and high-heeled sandals. Then he pushed open the great heavy glass doors to the flat entrance hall, and ushered her out. It was even hotter outside than in, but the sun was sinking, and that would bring a bit of relief. Although not much – the air stayed hot because the layer of pollution in the sky from all the traffic trapped the heat underneath it. She'd read that somewhere. She stared down at a tuft of dusty grass that was forcing its way through a crack in the concrete. "It must curse when it finds out where it is," she thought. "Some bits of grass get to come up in a meadow by a stream, but *this* bit. . ."

"Get a bus, shall we?" said Damian, happily. "Go down the canal?"

Groups of teenage boys were hanging about, leaning up against garage doors and perched on broken benches, waiting for the night to start, waiting for a chance to vent, let out all the stuff inside them, but no one started on Damian as he swaggered by, Rayne's hand in his. He wasn't that big but you didn't start on him. His older brother was inside, done for knife possession after two warnings, and everyone knew that Damian Hunter could carry himself.

They headed for the main road, jumped on a number 471 and rode past great concrete walls made vibrant with graffiti, down to the canal with its pubs and wine bars. It was more upmarket here than the Estate, but it was even more crowded. The air smelt of beer and sweat. Damian elbowed a place for them on a bench in the pub garden, went and got the drinks, and sat down again, dumping his hand on her bare leg.

Rayne had been going out with him for six weeks now. She'd been dazed with success when he'd first asked her. He was three years older than her – he was nineteen, she'd just turned sixteen – and he had such status on the Estate. He was black, like her dad – her mum, also thrilled at her daughter's success, went on about him being a daddy-substitute.

But now – now she wasn't quite so blown away by it all. Now she sometimes thought that the main thing about Damian was she felt safe with him. When there were other people about, that is, people who might threaten her. She didn't feel so safe with him on her own.

"So," he said, "what's up? Your mum been getting on your nerves again?"

"Yeah," she answered, grateful for the question, for his interest, "big time. It's like – the more I help her the more she expects. She's like some bottomless needy pit, honestly. . . She thinks I'm there just to help her out, now."

"You need a job."

"I know. I wish I could get one. She says there's no point if I'm going back to do A-levels, but I don't know if that's what I want. . ." She moaned on but she could tell he wasn't really listening. His eyes were swivelling to everyone who went past, taking stock, assessing the girls for looks and the men for danger. "I wish we could get away, Day," she wound up. She hated the sound of her voice, it was whining and powerless – when had it got like that? "I wish we could just – *go* somewhere. Right away from here. Just for a day, even."

"Me too, babe, but you need money for that. But look – I

4

was talking to Sly last night, and *he* reckons there's some work coming up Mead Estate way. . ."

It was her turn to switch off. His plans to make money never came to much. Just got him enough to live on, buy stuff with; well, maybe that was all he wanted. . .

"I hate it here," she suddenly burst out. "I hate how you have to watch your back every time you go out. I'm on edge all the time, I hate it. I hate how it's never quiet. I hate the way you can't go out without seeing *people* all the time and cars and it's *never quiet*. . ."

"*Heeey*," he soothed, and put his arm round her. "Listen, babe, we'll sort it out. We'll get away, I promise. We'll go on holiday. Two weeks on a beach – that's what you need. We'll do it, I swear."

She knew it wasn't going to happen. To say that would get him sullen and angry, though. Bleakly, she picked up her glass and finished her drink, thinking. Two weeks on a crowded beach with Damian – it wasn't what she wanted.

But what *did* she want? Whenever she thought about that, all she could come up with was: space. Silence.

Some kind of gap, a chance to slip out of her old life, and make a different one – make a different her, maybe.

Which wasn't much to go on.

After two more rounds of drinks they left the pub and walked hand in hand to the bus stop. Rayne felt slightly drunk but it didn't lighten her mood. The night was heating up, coming to the boil, like it did every Friday night, and the air seemed to shake with pollution as streams of cars roared past, never ending, never stopping. The noise hammered in your head and you could taste the poison in the back of your throat, all the time.

On the bus back to the Estate, she thought: "If I stay here much longer I'll go mad, mad like Mrs Chrysler on the second floor who never leaves her flat and has food delivered and talks to social workers through the bolted door."

Chapter Two

Damian tried to get Rayne to go back with him to his place. He kissed her, then muttered into the side of her mouth that his dad was out. Sex hung over their relationship like a great bird of prey, waiting for its time. Damian didn't talk about it but increasingly made it clear it would happen soon. Rayne's friends told her how patient Damian was being – how much that meant he must respect her. Rayne's mum had bought her a packet of condoms because "she needed to be prepared".

Whether Rayne actually wanted to sleep with Damian had somehow got lost in among all of this.

She thought she did. Sometimes, when they were kissing, when he held her close to him, she'd definitely feel something. But it was always chased away by panic. The whole thing was too much, too soon – heavy, invading, pressing.

It made her feel a bit like the Estate made her feel.

She told him she was feeling ill, because of the heat, and long-sufferingly he said he understood and took her back to her place and promised again that they'd get away "and that would sort her out".

She ought to be happy, she thought sadly, as they kissed goodbye at the door of her flat. Damian was great. Look at now – he'd seen her all the way up to her door, and he hadn't minded too much when she'd refused to go back to his place with him. Maybe her friends were right – he did respect her. Loads of girls would give their right arms for a boyfriend like him. What was wrong with her? Why didn't she like him better? Why couldn't she just go along with it, *be* Damian Hunter's girlfriend?

And she ought to be happy because she'd done all right in her GCSEs, and now she was free, freer than she'd ever been before in her life – she had all these opportunities before her, she could decide whether to do a course, whether to do A-levels, whether to go to work. . . But it didn't feel like freedom.

And she wasn't happy.

She crept through the living room, and into her room, trying not to wake Jelly, who slept in her room because Rayne's mum had an occasional boyfriend. He was called Dave and he seemed nice enough. He'd turn up out of the blue and take Rayne's mum out for a drink, for a meal, to the cinema . . . she deserved a bit of fun, her life was boring enough otherwise. He'd always stay the night afterwards, and because you never knew when he was coming, it worked out better for Jelly to share Rayne's room. Jelly was nearly three, after all, and sleeping through the night now. . .

Except Jelly didn't sleep through the night, not in this heat. He woke at around one and roared with misery, smashing his feet into the bars. Yanked out of sleep, fuddled and sick-feeling, Rayne thought, "He's too big for that stupid cot now. Bet he feels he's in a cage too." She hoisted him none-too-gently up to lie beside her. They were even hotter side by side and he kicked her, twice, but she gritted her teeth and stroked his back and soon he went back off to sleep.

"*I can't bear it*," she thought, desperately. "I hate having him here in my room, in my *bed*. . ."

Music from the flat above came through the ceiling like a pile-driver, *bam, bam, bam*. The couple next door started one of their fights and outside a car blared its horn and drove off with a squeal of wheels. "It never used to be this noisy," she thought. "Maybe it just seems that way because school was so noisy, it wasn't too bad in contrast. But now. . ."

A shop alarm went off half a mile away, screaming into the night, and then two police sirens answered it, screaming back even louder, and she felt so claustrophobic, so trapped, she thought she'd start screaming alongside it all.

And then something cracked in her mind and she resolved there and then to get out.

Just . . . go.

Chapter Three

The next day, Rayne set off in the slightly fresher air of the morning to go to the town library so she could use the Internet. They didn't have a computer at the flat – Rayne's mum said she couldn't afford it. Damian had one, he was always on various chat rooms to his friends and she'd sit and watch him, when she was round. But it never seemed like real talking, more like faking and bragging. Like the endless texts she got and sent – *where r u, what u doing, who u with* – some days it drove her crazy, some days it felt like madness, all that chatter and checking up and linking up, it just wasn't real.

Inside her head she was calm, determined. Last night she'd lain awake sweating and plotting and around dawn she'd decided that the only way to get away was to get a residential job of some sort. She'd tell Damian and her mum she was taking a gap year, so she could work out what she wanted to do with her life. If she had a job all sorted, ready to go to, she thought she could stand up to them. Maybe Damian would finish with her, everyone would think she was mad – maybe she *was* mad. But she couldn't think about that now. She had to get away.

She searched *Service Jobs*, *Residential* and all the variants on that, then ploughed through the vast lists that came up, following any leads that looked good. She told herself it didn't have to be the perfect job, just one that allowed her to escape. But by one-thirty she was starving hungry and apart from the vast number of hotel jobs that sounded like bigger traps than the Estate – like they'd really prefer robots if they could get them – she only had three possibles. A dodgy-sounding amusement park, waitressing at the seaside (*our season doesn't end when August does!*), and a strange-sounding appointment in a stranger-sounding place – Morton's Keep at Marcle Lees, Herefordshire.

Marcle Lees – it sounded like a little backwater village. The sort with one church, one school, one village hall. It sounded . . . *empty*. The kind of place to let your head out of its clamp, where you could breathe deeply with no one and nothing to make you choke up. . .

She checked the details again. Morton's Keep, it said, needed someone in its tearoom. It was an ancient, independent manor house that opened its doors to the public but was very unusual in that every room in the house was still used by the owners. Mostly at weekends, which is why it was shut then.

Shut at weekends! That would be a real sweetener for Damian, wouldn't it? She could tell him he could do his stuff in the week, and she'd come home on Friday night . . . it would shut Mum up, too, if she was back at the weekends, when Jelly was most likely to need a babysitter.

A pop-up appeared in the bottom left-hand corner of

the screen. She just had time to see a double H, heavy and heraldic – the sort of thing kings had inscribed on their silverware – when it disappeared again.

Weird, she thought, and went back to scanning the job information. Hours were moderate, and as staff you'd be living at Morton's Keep "sharing the beauty and grandeur of a bygone era, and the delights of isolation from the stress of twenty-first-century life. . ."

Isolation. It was a charm-word for Rayne, it lured her. But she feared it too. She sat back in the worn library swivel chair and thought about taking the job, thought about having silence all around her, silence and space . . . it would be like floating in the sea, suspended. . .

The strange, heraldic pop-up appeared again, and this time she zipped the cursor over and caught it. After a long pause, it opened up an amateur-looking website called *Hidden History of Marcle Lees*, run – she clicked to the *About Us* page – by two geeky-looking girls. Geeky enough to know how to fix their pop-up on to any page mentioning Marcle Lees, at any rate.

What interests us, their introduction self-importantly announced, *is the history that doesn't make it into the history books. This can be for all kinds of reasons . . . political, social, economic. . .*

"God, *boring*," Rayne murmured. What was it – some kind of school project? She clicked to the *Pictures* page, which showed grainy-looking photographs of a church and a wall with two towers behind it. Then, on an impulse, she hit the *Contact Us* button and tapped in an email:

I'm sixteen, I'm thinking of taking a job in Marcle Lees. What's it like there – is there anything going on? Love Rayne

Those two might be sad-looking but they might have some better friends. All she could think of *now* was silence – no one nagging at her, demanding her attention and her time – but if she got the job she'd need *some* human contact down there.

If she got the job.

She took a deep breath, applied for the position of waitress at the seaside and at Morton's Keep, and went home for lunch.

Chapter Four

Rayne left it for forty-eight hours before going back to the library to see if she had any emails. She reasoned if she didn't have any, she'd have to go back to square one and start job-trawling again, and she couldn't face that two days running. And besides, Damian had turned up the next day with a car he was thinking of buying – a little blue Citroën. He'd get, he said, an amazing deal on it. They'd driven around for a while, calling on people, doing his deals, which must have gone well because he'd treated her to a pizza. Maybe she was mad to think of giving this up, being his girlfriend, living her life on the outskirts of his. Except for the flashes of panic she'd feel, as though her real life was somewhere else, and she was missing it.

The next day she was at the library by ten a.m. She logged on and discovered she had two emails waiting; one from the agency handling the seaside job (telling her that that post had gone but there were plenty more opportunities around if she'd like to register with them for a small fee) and a reply from a Mrs Driver at Morton's Keep, inviting her for an interview at three in the afternoon in four days' time.

She sat back on the swivel chair, heart thudding, staring at the screen. It seemed so real – so definite – Mrs Driver had even given her directions.

She planned her journey online; two changes on the underground to Paddington, then two connections out to Marcle Lees. It was a long trek.

She replied, saying she'd be there.

"I've got an interview, Mum!" Rayne called out when she got back to the flat. Jelly was gawping at the noisy telly in the living room, toys all around him.

"What – for college?" her mum called back. She was in the tiny kitchen, pulling clothes out of the washing machine and draping them on the airer. "What course d'you want to do?"

"No – not for college. For a job."

"But the new term starts in a couple of weeks – you've got no time to do a job!"

"I want to take a year off, Mum. I want to work for a year so I can get some money together and be sure what I want to do."

Her mum turned her head to look at her, still hanging clothes. She was thin, like her daughter, with dyed russety red hair. "Good idea, Rayne. Make sure you really *want* to go to college. I know you got good grades in your GCSEs but that's not the be-all and end-all. Some of those teachers – they're only interested in ticking their boxes, saying they got kids into further education. . ."

"The interview's for a residential job. In Herefordshire."

" *What?* That's near Wales, isn't it? What d'you wanna go all the way out there for? What's it for anyway?"

"It's in a teashop. In a . . . in a stately home."

"*Wha-at?*" Her mum had stopped hanging clothes. She was standing there looking horrified. "You'll be bored stiff."

"No, I won't. There're other kids working there." Rayne was inventing as she went along. "Working in the gardens and stuff. You're always going on about what fun you had working as a chalet girl in Centre Parks – how it was like being on holiday yourself when you'd got through your work—"

"Centre Parks was a bit more fun than a bloody *stately home.*"

"Look – I need to get away for a bit – work out what I want to do with my life. And I . . . I need to get a break from Damian, too."

"Why?" demanded her mum, sharply. "What's going on?"

"Nothing, nothing – we're fine. Just – he's getting really possessive."

"You could do a lot worse than Damian. He's a good lad. If he's possessive it's just because he loves you."

"Maybe. But I really need a break, Mum. I just. . ." To her horror, she'd started to cry. Putting it into words – she wasn't prepared for the power of it.

But it was the best thing she could have done. In seconds, her mum was at her side with her arm round her, saying, "Hey . . . *Rayne!* Come on, tell me what's wrong."

"I'm just . . . all screwed up and *confused!*" she snivelled. "I dunno *what* I want."

"I know. I was the same at your age, love. It'll sort out."

"I'm just gonna go for the interview, OK? See what it's like there, see if I like it."

"You do that, Rayne. Go and see what it's like."

"I'll probably hate it."

"Probably," said her mum, and hugged her again.

It was easy, Rayne thought, to manipulate people. If you were really focused on what you wanted from them, it was easy. And what she wanted from her mum and boyfriend was a kind of approval, a backing, for her leaving the Estate. She knew she was too much of a coward to cut her ties. She had to keep everyone sweet, so she could run back there if she needed to, if it didn't work out.

With Damian, her chance came after a row that night. He'd bought the blue Citroën and was full of it, but after an hour of just driving around showing it off she'd said she'd had enough; then she'd been sourly unenthusiastic about anything he'd suggested doing. He'd lost his temper and told her he was fed up of her moodiness; she'd burst into tears. And then, like with her mum, there'd been hugs and explanations and she told him how sick she was of living at home with Jelly sleeping in her bedroom. . .

"Tell me about it. Little sod certainly puts the quellers on me when I'm round."

"And it's not just that. Since I left school Mum's made it her mission to fill up every hour of my day – she's loading all these jobs on me – I need to get a *paid* job."

"There was that one going in the Turk's Head. . ."

"He knows how old I am."

"So you're not going to college? I told you you wouldn't."

"I dunno. I do know I'm taking a year off."

"Yeah? Good for you, babe."

"And I want . . . I want to get away for a bit. Not from *you*, Day. From Mum, and Jelly and the Estate . . . and . . . I *hate* the way I've been acting to you, I know I've been a cow, I need to get away and sort myself out and. . ." She started crying again. Tears, she decided, were great camouflage.

Damian hugged her and told her ssshhh, it was all all right. "I want what you want, babe, what's best for you," he murmured. "You know that."

Over the next few days, until she went to Marcle Lees, she kept it all stoked. She broke it to Damian about the interview, feeding her plans to him bit by bit. She moaned on about how her mum was driving her crazy, how cramped it was in the flat with Jelly's stuff everywhere, how she'd go mad if she didn't get some space. She moaned to her mum about how possessive Damian was getting, how he was doing her head in, how she didn't want to split up but she needed a break to make sure they were right together.

Pretty soon, they both got sick of listening. Soon, both of them were actually encouraging her to get away for a bit, to sort herself out.

She didn't feel she was being badly manipulative, not really. She was doing what she needed to do to survive. She was driven by something completely alien to them and she knew if they could see what was going on inside her they'd take it as a huge criticism. She didn't really understand what was going on inside her herself, of course. Just enough to know that they'd be right – it was a huge criticism.

Chapter Five

The cab pulled sharply off the road, in front of a large sign that said *Morton's Keep* at the top and underneath *Opening Hours: Monday to* – but it was going too fast for Rayne to see. They drove down a long, earth-track drive, like the road to a farm, with ranks of dripping trees either side. Rayne looked out, marvelling. She hadn't seen real woods since her last school trip two years ago, when her mates had laughed at her for wanting to walk in them.

Then the road opened out; on the right the trees gave way to a wide lawn that needed cutting, with more woodland beyond that. They drew up in front of an ancient wall with a great archway in it. Behind the wall were two towers, three roofs, and five huge chimneys – the wall was too close, it looked as though the old buildings were trying to break out. It was familiar, somehow, as though she'd seen it all before, but she couldn't think where.

She got out of the cab and paid the driver, who reversed, gravel spurting from his wheels, and drove off. When his car had gone there was absolutely no noise at all. Was this, she thought, what people meant when they said the silence was deafening? As she stood there looking around, her ears throbbed with it.

She was standing in a curved forecourt, formed by the ancient wall to the right, a long, low building with columns in front in the middle, and a tall brick building to the left. The forecourt was like a bowl, a cauldron; it seemed to hum with energy.

She turned; behind her was a huge stone basin with two sea monsters, half fish, half horse, writhing out of a mass of vivid ivy. The pipes from their mouths showed it had once been a fountain, but now ivy, not water, flowed into the basin.

A bird's call broke the silence. Rayne walked over to the dark red door in the low building straight ahead of her. It had a worn stone shield, some kind of coat of arms, above it, and it looked important, as if it might be the main door. She took a deep breath, and knocked. A sinewy, elderly man opened it. "Yes?" he barked. He had a fork in one hand.

"I'm . . . um . . . Rayne Peters," she said. "I've come about the job in the tearoom. . ."

"That isn't here," he said. "It's Mrs Driver you need to see. Over at the Keep." And he jerked his head towards the ancient wall, and shut the door in her face.

"Bloody great," muttered Rayne, stomping over the gravel, "what does he mean over at the Keep? It's all the Keep, isn't it? That's all I need, a resident senile-dementia nutter. . ."

She reached the great archway. It was open, there was no gate, but she was full of reluctance to walk through it. She was filled with a sense that it was momentous to *cross through*.

21

But she did walk through, and then she was in a courtyard with high walls crowding all around at her, towers and chimneys lowering down at her, tiny crooked windows staring at her. The energy here was twice as strong as the forecourt, it blasted her as she walked unsteadily across the cobbled yard. In the centre was what looked like a wide stunted chimney coming out of the ground, with railings spiking out of it.

She made herself walk towards it, look over the railings. Dank, stagnant air came back at her as she peered into the pitchy dark. "A well," she breathed. "The well for the mansion house."

She looked up with a start. A church-like door across the courtyard was opening; a small, dumpy woman stood in the doorway. "Rayne Peters?" she called.

"Yes!" said Rayne, hurrying over.

"I'm Mrs Driver. Come through. I'm interviewing in the Tudor kitchen."

Obediently, Rayne followed Mrs Driver through the doorway and into a long hall. "These flagstones you're walking on," said Mrs Driver in a toneless voice, "are getting on for a thousand years old. They've seen so much history. The Black Prince himself walked across them."

Rayne wasn't sure who the Black Prince was, but he sounded off-putting. On the walls were suits of armour, old paintings, and two pikestaffs, crossed at the hilt. "Here we are," said Mrs Driver, opening another door and stepping down into a large room dominated by a massive stone fireplace and a long, battered refectory table. "Sit yourself down. Would you like some tea?"

Chapter Six

It was incongruous, weird, sitting in the ancient kitchen across from Mrs Driver at a table she'd announced that monks had once dined at, drinking tea from cheap mugs with pansies printed on them. Mrs Driver was around sixty years old, maybe more; she had wavy greying brown hair and a face you couldn't read. But the interview was pretty straightforward. She asked about work experience and Rayne told her about the waitressing she'd done in a local Greek restaurant. Then she'd taken her through a door at the far side of the kitchen, down some steps, and across another little courtyard, to look at the tearoom.

"It used to be the dairy," Mrs Driver explained, unlocking the door. "I love it, it's one of the nicest places here. Even in the heat we've had this summer it's been cool."

They went through a flagstoned vestibule that was painted white and filled with a green glow from the ivy-covered window. In the large main room, high arched windows cast light down on eight tables laid out in two rows of four. "As you can see, it's all very basic," Mrs Driver said, leading Rayne down the middle. "The last girl we had used to put jugs of flowers on the tables, to pretty it up a bit. When it's cold, you have to keep that going –" she pointed to a squat black stove against the far wall – "but we don't have to think about that yet. This is the kitchen, here."

They'd reached a partitioned area at the end. It reminded Rayne of a community hall kitchen, with its wide hatch, giant kettles and industrial-sized fridge. She looked up to find Mrs Driver staring at her. "Well, dear?" Mrs Driver said. "What do you think of Morton's Keep?"

"It's incredible!" Rayne blurted out. "I mean – it's the most amazing place, isn't it? Going across that courtyard . . . it's like you can *feel* all the years it's all been standing. . ."

Mrs Driver nodded, but she didn't smile. "Some people don't feel a thing. They walk across it as though it was a supermarket car park."

"When I arrived," Rayne went on, "I knocked on the red door, in the middle, and an old man answered. . ."

"Ben Avebury. He looks after the grounds and gardens."

"He was a bit grumpy, I think I interrupted him eating."

"Oh, he wouldn't like that."

"He talked about Morton's Keep as though it was only the bit behind the wall. . ."

"That's what it used to be. The other buildings are more recent. They're still several hundred years old, of course, but they never really. . ." She trailed off, then said, "So, are you interested in the job?"

"Oh, yes. I mean – yes, I think so."

"I'll be straight with you," said Mrs Driver, folding her arms. "We've had twelve applicants in the last two weeks,

24

most of them quite unsuitable. Three were single mothers with no idea how they were going to cope with their babies when they were on duty here, and others who just . . . well, right away I knew they were wrong. They wanted to come here because they were in a mess, they were running from something or someone . . . we can't deal with that sort."

I'm that sort, thought Rayne.

"But you . . . well, I'm not going to beat about the bush, you're the best I've seen and I'm going to offer you the job. They're not long hours – 10.30 till 4.30. No lunch break – you need to be on duty then, some of our visitors want a light lunch. We do salads, home-made soup, omelettes – can you make an omelette?"

"Yes," lied Rayne. She knew she could learn.

"Good. Well, every weekend off, that's a big plus for catering. And the pay is fifteen pounds the session."

"The session?"

"The day, dear. Fifteen pounds the day."

Rayne reeled, as she frantically did the maths. "But . . . the advert said basic rate. . . That's . . . that's not even three pounds an hour, is it? I mean – it's illegal!"

Mrs Driver's face sagged into resignation. "Not on paper, no. We charge for your room, you see . . . and basic keep. We deduct that from your wages."

Rayne looked down. This was a blow. She'd banked on earning over a hundred pounds a week – that's how she was going to justify taking the job. How could she turn round and tell Damian and her mum she was leaving them for less than three pounds an hour?

"Think of yourself as like an au pair," said Mrs Driver.

"You'll get the whole package, bed and board. And you'll eat well here – good, simple, local stuff. You look like you could do with a few square meals. I expect you'll take that as a compliment – girls seem to nowadays. Goodness knows why – they all look so pinched and parched and half-alive."

"I just – fifteen pounds a day – it's so *little*."

"We can't afford to pay more. The tearoom, you see – it barely makes a profit. Not if you account for my time, baking and so on. In the winter, if we break even, we're happy."

"So why . . . *have* one?" asked Rayne. "Why have a tearoom at all?"

"People who come here expect one. All the old houses do it – a cup of tea and a scone and a bit of a sit down at the end of the tour. If we closed the tearoom we'd attract even fewer people. And Mr Stuart, the owner – he's always hoping things will improve."

There was a silence. Mrs Driver looked out of the side window at a flowering bush flaring in the bright sun, a gloomy look on her face. Then she rallied and said, "There'll be a chance to make extra cash nearly every week, you know. Mr Stuart's full of these schemes – poetry readings, musical evenings in the library, grand dinners in the Old Stone Hall . . . we'll need waitresses then. Wear a nice dress, you'd be perfect. We'll pay the proper rate for that – and there'll be tips. And . . . oh, there's the Apple Fair here in September, in the barn – lots of help needed for that."

"But they'll . . . a lot of those things'll be at the weekend, won't they?"

"Yes, most of them. Friday night to Sunday."

"I promised to go home at the weekends."

Mrs Driver shrugged. "It's a long way to go."

Rayne felt she was on a tightrope, not knowing which way to jump, what to say, yes or no.

"I hope you'll take the job," said Mrs Driver. "I think you'll suit well here. And I think . . . I think the place'll suit you."

"What d'you mean?" Rayne muttered.

"Oh, just . . . you seem nervy. Like a battery hen, all nervous."

"Well thanks a *lot*! A *battery* hen?"

"Oh, don't take offence, dear. You *look* lovely. You just seem . . . like you could do with some freedom. Some open space to roam around in. And that's what you'll have here."

There was a long silence, then Mrs Driver sighed and said, "Why don't you take a day or two to think it over?"

"No, it's OK," said Rayne. "No, I – I'll do it. Thank you. Thank you so much. When can I move in?"

Chapter Seven

When Rayne looked back on how she got through the next few days – the days between returning to Cramphurst Estate and going back to Morton's Keep – she saw herself as an automaton, a robot programmed with the aim of *leaving* and doing everything necessary to that end. Faced with the reality of her actually going, Damian got deeply offended and her mum got really upset. So she lied, soothed and cajoled, made promises she had no intention of keeping. She lied about the money, said it was more than it was. She lied that she'd come home every weekend. She lied that she'd probably only stay till the end of September – who wanted to be in the country in the winter? She lied that she'd phone all the time, she'd be so bored she'd have to phone. As she looked into her mother's sullen, accusing face or Damian's sullen, angry face she felt like she was looking into the faces of mad jailers she'd tell anything to – so long as they let her go free.

As part of the *not really wanting to leave* plot she planned to get the last train to Marcle Lees on Sunday night, which meant leaving Cramphurst Estate around seven

28

o'clock in the evening. She wouldn't arrive at Morton's Keep until after nine-thirty. Mrs Driver, when she'd phoned to tell her this, had been decidedly critical, advising her to come earlier and give herself "time to get settled in". But Rayne, still in automaton mode, had replied smoothly that she'd be fine, she had a family farewell "do" to go to on Sunday, she couldn't possibly miss it – and Mrs Driver said she understood.

The family "do" was her mum opening a cheap bottle of wine at six o'clock and drinking most of it herself, leaving Rayne to spoon sloppy ready-made lasagne out of a tinfoil dish on to three plates and feed Jelly his. Her mum had talked endlessly about how hard it was going to be managing without her; Jelly had cried when she'd picked him up to kiss him goodbye and hit her on the face.

And now she and Damian stood at the bus stop at the edge of the Estate, waiting for the bus that would take her to the station. The weather had changed – the searing heat had given way to rain at last, and then wind, and now it was almost cold as they stood close at the bus stop. "*Sure* you don't want me to come with you, babe?" he murmured. "At least to the station?"

"No, come on, Day, we talked about this. I hate goodbyes. Let's just get it over with. It's not like I'm going for long."

"Long enough, babe . . . a whole *week*? How am I gonna do without you for a whole *week*?" She looked up at him and thought: "You're acting. And I'm acting. We say we love each other and it's crap. You want me because no one else has had me, that's all. And I don't even fancy you. I fancied who you were and the status I'd get going out with you but I actually don't fancy *you* at all."

It felt like a film, saying goodbye, a bad film. She let him pull her up close and smear his mouth across hers, jab his tongue into her mouth.

A police car roared past, siren wailing, then her bus swerved out of the stream of slowed-down traffic and bumped up against the kerb. Its doors grated open. "Bye, babe," she whispered. "No – let me go. Let me go or I'm really gonna start crying, honest I am."

She picked up the heavy case and he jabbed one more kiss on the side of her face and pushed her towards the bus steps. And she jumped on, practically vaulted on, and as she made her way to the back of the bus there was a roar of triumph inside her, a great crash of joy, because she'd done it, she'd got away.

She waved to Damian as he grew small and insignificant on the pavement, then she turned round and got her Itinerary out of her bag. She'd written it out the night before, a list of what stations to get off at, what connections to get, all the times, and the address and phone number of Morton's Keep . . . it was over the top, this Itinerary, she'd found her way there for the interview with just a few scribbled notes, but it was part of her believing that it was all real, that she really was leaving.

At Paddington Station she had nearly fifteen minutes to wait for the train. She bought a tall paper cup of latte and sat sipping it on the benches near the Paddington Bear stall with its furry toys and colouring books. Her breathing wasn't coming right. It was faster than normal, as though she was scared, but she was still filled with this joy, this triumph, that she'd got away.

As soon as the board displayed which platform her train was standing at, she went to it and found her seat. She stowed her case in the gap between her seat and the one in front of her, where she could see it. When the train started up and moved out of the station, she started to shake, physically shake with nerves and excitement. She tried to read, tried to sleep, but all she could do was look out of the window and see the miles stream away behind her, taking her away. She thought about the weird Hidden History website, wondered why the geeky girls had never emailed her back. She thought about the emptiness around Morton's Keep, the woods, the silence. She hardly thought about what she'd left behind at all.

She made the connecting train with no problems, and arrived at Marcle Lees Station at ten past nine. There were no cabs waiting so she called the number on the card the cabby had given her the last time she'd been there.

"Morton's Keep?" echoed the girl on the cab company switchboard, in disbelief. "At this time of night? You one of those ghost hunters or something?"

Rayne felt a flick of fear, and dismissed it. Morton's Keep was old, ancient, of course the switchboard girl would think of ghosts. "No," she said. "I'm the new waitress, for the tearoom."

"Ah. Well, I can't have a cab with you before . . . oooh, twenty minutes, OK? We've a rush on."

Rayne sat on the bench up against the station wall and waited. She thought of phoning Mrs Driver to tell her she'd be late, but the phone was probably in some office somewhere, and Mrs Driver would be in the Tudor kitchen, warming up the home-made soup she'd promised her . . . she'd only be half an hour or so late, it'd be fine.

A young man picked her up this time; he sat sullen and hunched over his wheel. He took his car to a grating halt right behind the ivy-choked fountain, as though he didn't want to get too near the buildings.

Rayne got out of the cab. It all looked very different at night. The tall building on the left and the long, low building in the centre had all but disappeared into darkness, but harsh spotlights shone on the ancient wall and more were trained on the two towers which bulged and glowed over the black stretches of roof. Hauling her case, Rayne hurried across the forecourt and propelled herself under the archway to the courtyard. Tiny blank windows on the high walls watched her; the two glowing towers looked like great squatting beasts against the black sky.

She went over to the church-like door. There was a lamp beside it, making a vague pool of light on the cobblestones. The knocker on the door was a brass hand, human-sized. She hadn't noticed it the last time – the door had been open, Mrs Driver standing in front of it. It was the hand of a strong man, severed at the wrist; its fingers shone where the brass had been polished by people picking it up to knock, but the rest was almost black. On the middle finger was a strange ring, a wide band with a curling clasp holding a jagged-looking brass stone, and this shone brightest of all. Uneasily, Rayne thought of a bronze statue she'd seen of the Madonna, where the left foot was luminous from people kissing it, worshipping it.

She didn't want to pick up the hand.

There was a sudden blast of wind, and the trees beyond the courtyard wall bucked and roared. Spooked, Rayne grabbed the knocker and let it fall down with a great bang. She waited, ears strained, to hear movement from the other side of the door, but heard nothing. "Come on, Mrs D, come on," she muttered. "You must've heard that." She was creeped out by the thought of knocking again, picking up the hand again, as if she'd be shaking hands with something malevolent, something that could harm her by its touch. Then footsteps, getting louder, sounded on the other side of the door, and there was the noise of a bolt being drawn and the door swung inwards on Mrs Driver, white-faced in the light from the doorway lamp.

"You're so *late*!" she exclaimed, anxiously. "I'd nearly given up on you! I was going to give you another fifteen minutes, then I was going to lock up and go to my room!"

What, and leave me standing out here if I came after that? thought Rayne, but she didn't say it. She said, "I'm really sorry. The trains were fine, just a bit slower than I thought . . . it was the cab that held me up. There wasn't one waiting, they were really busy. . ."

"It's getting on for ten o'*clock*. You said half-nine, latest. Anyway, you're here now. Soup? Like I promised you?"

"I'd love some," said Rayne. "If it's not too much trouble."

"Come on then," said Mrs Driver, drawing her in, bolting the door behind her, and setting off down the gloomy corridor that led to the Tudor kitchen. The suits of armour and the pikestaffs glimmered in the half-light.

"That's an unusual door knocker," said Rayne, to fill the silence. "Is it very old?"

"Yes . . . but not as old as the door. About two hundred and fifty years, we think. We've never had it changed."

That's an odd thing to say, thought Rayne, *why would you want it changed?* But she didn't say anything.

Chapter Eight

Mrs Driver told Rayne to sit down at the long monks' table, and disappeared through a doorway at the side of the room. Over by the fireplace, balanced on the back of a huge wooden chair, was a pile of bedding – a duvet in a fresh blue cover, pillows and sheets. Mrs Driver nodded at them as she came back in with a bowl of savoury-smelling soup and a plate of bread and butter. "I've not made your bed up yet," she said. "You have to decide where you're sleeping."

Rayne took the hint and ate fast. On the second mouthful, she discovered she was hungry.

Mrs Driver sat opposite Rayne. "Soon as you've finished that," she said, "we'll get you sorted, if you don't mind. Visitors don't start coming in till eleven or so, but I need to show you the ropes and so on first, so if you come here for breakfast around nine. . ." She seemed very on edge. She shot to her feet as soon as Rayne had put her spoon down, and picked up the bundle of bedding. Then she appeared to think better of it, and dumped it down again.

"Follow me, dear," she said. "I want to show you the two rooms you can choose from." They left the kitchen and walked further down the stone-flagged corridor, past more dark portraits and weaponry on the walls. "There's a room on the top floor here, or there's what we call the Old Sty, outside. I realize that doesn't sound very salubrious, a sty, but it's only called that because it was used to keep pigs in for a while in the nineteenth century. We've done it up since!"

At the end of the corridor hung a heavy dark-green curtain. They passed through it into a huge high-ceilinged hall with a massive dark-wood stairway leading up out of it – the scale of it took Rayne's breath away. The near wall was dominated by two carved baronial doors that looked like you could march an army through them. Opposite them was a great stone fireplace with two hefty plaster cherubs suspended over it, holding a fairground crown above a portrait of a woman. In the dim light from the single overhead bulb, all three had mad smiles.

"What do you think of the Great Hall, dear?" asked Mrs Driver.

"It's amazing," breathed Rayne, though she might more accurately have said terrifying. The hall bore down on her with all the years it had been standing, all the things that had happened in it, all the people, long dead, who had inhabited it. She felt as insubstantial as a moth flitting through it.

"It's much nicer in daylight," Mrs Driver went on. "There's a story from medieval days that the young lord of the manor, Lord Fulke, was wounded in one of the battles along the Welsh borders. His friend rode back with him laid across his horse, and he rode right through those doors and they bedded Lord Fulke down in front of the fire, there, to be tended. He fought death for three days and three nights but then he succumbed to his wounds, poor lad. You're supposed to still be able to see the bloodstains on the floor. It's only marks in the oak, of course, but it makes a good story to tell the visitors."

Rayne didn't want to dwell on young Lord Fulke, dying. There were two more doors on the far wall; she pointed to them and asked, "What's through there?"

"That one leads to the library, and this is the Old Stone Hall," said Mrs Driver. "The Old Stone Hall is aptly named – it's over a thousand years old. People were tried there, sentenced to death – the Black Prince dined there. I'll show you sometime – not now, not at night. Come along, dear."

And she started to climb the wide staircase. The banisters were massive, carved with strange beasts that had dragons' heads and the bodies of lions. Rayne, feeling thoroughly freaked, followed her close, heart thumping. She was filled with longing to be back in her tiny bedroom with Jelly and the noise of people all around her. What had she *done*, coming here? Saying she'd *stay* here?

They reached a landing halfway up, where a large oblong box was attached to the wall, screened by a dark-red curtain. Rayne thought of the curtain drawn across the end of her gran's coffin as it slid into the furnace. Mrs Driver turned the bend in the stairs, and started climbing the next flight. Something was beating along with Rayne's heart, in exact rhythm, in the huge silence of the hallway.

Tock, tock, tock.

"That's our famous clock," said Mrs Driver, as they stepped out on to a wide, imposing landing. "It's Dutch, early eighteenth century." Ahead to the left were three large closed doors – to the right, another corridor, lined by more closed doors and black windows and dark portraits of staring people who'd died hundreds of years ago. "It has only one hand. People weren't so fussed about minutes in those days. And a very loud chime! I'm grateful I'm down there, in the modernized quarters." She pointed to a door at the end of the corridor. Rayne had a strong compulsion to run past all the black windows and portraits, run to the door and escape through it into modern life again.

But she stayed where she was.

"Your room's up here, dear," said Mrs Driver, advancing on to the bottom step of the next flight up. These stairs were narrower, and they disappeared into blackness at the top. "There's a wonderful view from its window, all over the towers and rooftops and fields. . ."

Rayne thought that nothing, *nothing*, would make her go up there into that blackness. "Does anyone else sleep up there?" she asked, in a tight voice.

"Only when Mr Stuart has guests. You'd have it quite to yourself, bathroom and everything. Oh, don't worry, dear, you're just above me, and they're nice rooms up there, modernized again. Not like the bedrooms on this floor – they've been kept as they were since the seventeenth century, tapestry hangings, four-poster beds, the lot. . ."

Rayne looked at the three large closed doors, and took a step backwards to the stairs going down. "If you don't mind," she croaked, "I'll sleep in the Old Sty. I just liked the sound of it, when you talked about it . . . outdoors and everything."

Mrs Driver looked at her blankly. Then she said, "As you wish, dear. You're probably right."

Chapter Nine

They went swiftly down the great stairs, through the Great Hall, along the corridor and into the kitchen again. Rayne had the feeling that Mrs Driver was as glad to get back as she was.

Mrs Driver picked up the bedding from the chair by the fireplace, told Rayne to bring her case, and led her through the door in the corner and down the short flight of stone steps. "It's a shame the weather's changed," said Mrs Driver, as the trees thrashed overhead. "It's been that warm. . ."

They went across the little courtyard, and past the tearoom. "You'll be nice and near work," said Mrs Driver, "you can have a bit more of a lie-in." They went on into the dark, walking on grass now, past more old walls and looming outbuildings. Rayne was feeling almost sick with apprehension. "So this is my choice," she thought, "a bedroom in the attics of a horror-film mansion or an isolated hut out here?" Panic beat away in her, half-formed plans whirled in her mind. "I'll say I've changed my mind, I'll get a cab and book into a Holiday Inn for the night, then the next morning I'll go home, back to safety, back to the Estate. . ."

A lantern on a post at the top of a narrow flight of steps lit their way down into a shadowy walled garden. "Nearly there," whispered Mrs Driver. *Why was she whispering, who would hear her?* "This is the medieval garden. We still grow tomatoes and apples here."

The night pressed in on them as they made their way across the grass; Rayne could just make out the shape of trees and bushes and, running down the centre, beds laid out with tall plants. "Before the Old Sty was a sty," Mrs Driver whispered on, "it would be for the steward – so he could keep his eye on the farmland. And we think a religious person had a retreat here for a while. Here we are."

They'd stopped in front of a squat brick building, one storey high, with a low wooden door set into it. Mrs Driver drew a huge key from her pocket, unlocked the door, opened it, and flicked a switch on the wall. Then she went inside, Rayne following. The room smelt musty, and a bit damp, as though the summer hadn't touched it. "I aired it today," Mrs Driver said. "It'll freshen up more as you live in it."

It was like a monk's cell. The wall to the left was divided into two alcoves by a chimney breast with a small stove set into it. In the far alcove was a wide single bed; across the near alcove hung a heavy red curtain. Just inside the door, under the low window, was a square pine table and two wooden chairs.

Mrs Driver walked over to the bed and dumped the bedding down, then she came back and drew the curtain to reveal a rail and a chest of drawers. "Here's where you hang your stuff," she said, "and this . . ." She walked to a door set in the near wall and pulled it open. ". . . is the bathroom. It's shared with the room on the other side."

"The room on the other side. . .?" echoed Rayne.

"Yes, didn't I tell you? Mr Stuart had it split into two, with shared bathroom and . . ." She moved on, drew back another red curtain opposite the bed. ". . . kitchen. Well, you can hardly call it a kitchen. But there's a fridge and a sink, and a little cooker. . ."

Rayne peered into the tiny bathroom, looked at the little cupboard of a kitchen with its two curtains either side. Everything looked dreary in the light from the single naked bulb hanging overhead, dreary and a bit depressing. But it wasn't out of a horror film, not like the mansion house. It wasn't weighed down by history. She thought she could lock herself in here, and be safe. And *sleep*. She suddenly realized she was tired, bone tired. "This is great, Mrs Driver," she said, turning to her, making a broad smile. "This is perfect."

Relief played over Mrs Driver's face. "You're sure, dear? It'll be cold, in the winter. But the stove's a good one, and. . ."

"It's fine. Honestly. You get off. I've kept you up late enough as it is."

"Let me help you make up your bed, at least."

"No, honestly. You get back."

"All right, dear," said Mrs Driver. "Come straight to the kitchen when you get up. Tomorrow I'll give you some supplies, milk and tea and so on, you can be quite self-sufficient out here if you want to be, it's just a shame summer's nearly over, it's lovely in summer. . ." Rayne was backing her towards the door as she spoke, ushering her out. They said goodbye and Rayne shut the door on her, then she quickly made up her bed. The mattress was cold to the touch but it looked clean, and the under sheet was thick, it would take the chill off. She drew the short blue curtains at the window, lifted her case on to the table underneath it, pulled out her washbag and pyjamas, and hurried into the little bathroom.

The first thing she did was lock the door that led into the other room. It was quite neat, the way the bathroom had two doors, so whoever was using it could lock it against the other person.

She didn't let herself wonder why she was locking it when there was no one next door.

She peed, hurriedly cleaned her face and scrubbed her teeth, went back into the main room, stripped, dropping her clothes on the floor, scrambled into her pyjamas, fetched a glass of water from the kitchen and put it on the floor by her bed.

Then she went over to the light switch by the front door and turned out the light.

And pure black engulfed her, like she'd suddenly been blindfolded, like she'd been dropped into pitch. Fear gripped her – she knew she'd never be able to move, let alone find her way to the bed. She snapped the light back on again, ran over to the bed, and climbed in. Then she lay back on the frigid pillow and looked around. The room was desolate in the sallow overhead light from the naked bulb. The red curtains screening off the tiny kitchen were very close to her head. She thought of the curtains round the box on the landing halfway up the great staircase; she thought of her gran's coffin disappearing. The curtains stirred slightly, and she told herself *it's a draught, just a draught*, but she felt horror creep through her. She thought maybe she should draw them back, but that would just show a dark tunnel, on to more curtains, into the other room. . . She remembered locking the door in the bathroom that led into the other room. *Why had she done that?*

The curtains stirred again. *Just a draught, just a draught*, she told herself, a draught from the old chimney the stovepipe led into. She could feel it on her face. A pair of deer antlers was nailed on the wall above the stove; they cast a great reaching claw shadow on the wall. Her eyes swivelled as the curtains at the window moved. *Stop this*, she begged herself. *Shut your eyes, go to sleep.*

Sleep – she'd never sleep. Her heart was pounding.

And then she remembered that she hadn't locked the door to the outside.

Mrs Driver hadn't given her the key.

Chapter
Ten

She scrambled out of bed and as she hurried to the door, feet icy on the cold flagstones, she thought maybe Mrs Driver had locked it from the outside, locked her in. But no – she could open it. She let an inch of black night show round the edge of it, and slammed it shut again. There was a tiny bolt on the inside – she shot it home. But the wood around it was soft, crumbling with decay – one kick would burst it open.

She took hold of the table with her heavy case on top of it and dragged it in front of the door. Then she got back into bed.

She lay with the cold duvet pulled up to her eyes and scanned the room in terror. The table barricading the door, the red curtains stirring and trembling, the great reaching claw of the antlers – it was horrible. "If I turn out the light," she told herself, desperately, "if it's just black, I'll stop *watching* everything, and I'll get to sleep. . ."

Once more she slid out of bed and, on an impulse, went and drew back the curtains at the window. She hated doing it, because anyone, anything, could look in now . . . but she couldn't close herself in completely, she couldn't switch the light off and be buried in that black nothingness again.

Then she went to the light switch, turned it off, and stood there, using all her will power not to flip it back on again, making herself look into the blackness, trying to see the shape of her bed, the shape of the window. Her heart pounded harder and harder as she imagined something moving towards her. Dead people who'd lived here before – what had Mrs Driver said? – all the stewards, one after the other, keeping their eyes on the farmland, and the "religious person", a mad nun or something, gone crazy with loneliness. . .

And then as she peered desperately into the tarry black, she made out the faint oblong of the window. Dark, dark grey, just visible. She used it to navigate, turned her back on it and paced carefully, slowly, towards where she thought the bed was, hands out in front, groping for the end. As soon as she touched it she scrambled over it and under the duvet, and lay there, shaking. *Close your eyes,* she told herself, *let your heart slow down, and then you'll relax, you'll sleep. . .* But she kept staring, trying to see what might be there. The faint near-black oblong of the window was all she could see, but near her head she sensed the red curtains moving.

It's hopeless, she thought, desperately, *I'd be better off with that grisly light on again.* But she knew she was too scared to get out of the cold bed again. The air around her seemed malevolent, it seemed to shudder with some kind of presence. Her mouth was dry, but she couldn't reach out her hand to pick up her glass of water in case something touched her hand. She lay rigid, frozen. *Why had she come here?* She'd give anything, anything, to be back in her old room listening to the traffic and the sirens, watching the car lights on the ceiling, hearing the rows and the televisions and the thud of music. . .

Something was happening with her feet. They were lifting – *something was lifting her* – her legs were raising, *levitating* . . . she drew them up, drew herself into a tight ball. *It's just tension*, she told herself desperately, *you're so scared your legs have seized up*. She flexed her toes, rotated her feet, then lay still again. Trying not to listen so hard, trying to keep her eyes closed . . . the duvet was warming with the heat of her body. Eventually she drifted into a kind of doze.

And then, she had no idea how much later, she woke. Suddenly, sharply, but she had no idea why. She peered anxiously at the oblong of the window – it was no lighter. Then – she thought she'd die of fear. Something cried out, something not-human, it was ghostly, eerie, drawn-out . . . and then, while she was still shaking with fear, something inside her knew it was an owl, it must be, an owl hooting, and she thought – *how wonderful.*

She'd never heard a real owl before.

It hooted again, thrilling and terrifying in equal measure. Then again, fainter, as though it was flying away. It went through her mind that she'd liked to have seen it.

She dozed off again and slept on, uneasily, waking several times and staring over at the window, willing it to be lighter. *If I can just get through this night*, she thought,

I'll be OK, I can leave in the morning, leave and never come back. . .

The next time she woke, she knew exactly what had woken her.

She could still hear it.

Something was outside the door.

Chapter Eleven

It was a scratching, scuffling sound – she was sure she could hear breathing. *It was the steward come back to his cottage . . .* the bolt wouldn't hold, he'd kick his way in . . . *ghosts don't need to open doors.*

Breathing was all round her, blood thumping all round her. . . Then, a horrible scratching at the door, a scrabbling sound.

Then silence.

And inside her head, the word formed: *fox.*

That's all it had been. A fox.

The grey window seemed a tiny bit lighter. She huddled down under the warm duvet and gazed at the window as if her salvation depended on it. When dawn came, she'd be safe from ghosts. *As soon as it's light*, she told herself, *as soon as it's day, I can leave.*

She drifted off into another anxious half-sleep, and the next time she woke and looked at the window, she was sure it was lighter. It came in like hope. Yes, it was definitely lighter. She was going to be all right. The night was nearly over, and in the morning she could go home.

And then . . . the chirp of a bird, breaking experimentally through the silence. Then a whistling sound, then more chirping, and then the bird sound swelled, grew . . . *the dawn chorus*, she thought, and a deep relief filled her. Her gran used to talk about the dawn chorus, how sometimes when she was young she'd stayed out so late at night she'd hear it when she was on the way home . . . she said it was sad how you never heard it in the town, not any more. . .

And now Rayne was hearing it. The night was over. No ghosts had come, nothing had visited her. Just an owl and a fox. She was safe now. Surrounded by birdsong, she fell into the deep sleep of the saved.

When she next woke, low, early-autumn sun was streaming through the window on to her face, and the birds were still chirruping and singing. She seized the glass of water from the floor and downed it in one, laughing at how she'd been too scared before to reach out and pick it up . . . her watch said it was twenty to nine, she should be in the kitchen in twenty minutes, meeting Mrs Driver, but being punctual didn't matter now, did it, she was going to go home.

Home to Cramphurst Estate.

She went over to the door, shoved the table out of the way, shot back the flimsy bolt and looked outside. Shafts of sunlight came filtering down through the trees into the medieval garden, lighting up the wet plants and shrubs. Spiders' webs glittered like necklaces. A soft mist curled along the ground near the trees, playing along the dark edges.

Rayne stepped barefoot on to the grass.

The ground was cold and wet under her feet. The earth gave beneath her. The air smelt fresh. Everything around her was flourishing, healthy and rooted.

The garden was laid out in long, symmetrical beds with narrow grass paths in-between them. Curved shapes had been cut out of each bed corner, so that grass clover leaves were formed. It was very pleasing. Rayne walked slowly along the paths between the beds, toes flexing in pleasure, pyjamas getting soaked up to the ankles, and ended up by a wall at the end where three small apple trees grew, sheltered and laden with early fruit. She reached out and pulled an apple from its stalk and sniffed the fresh, fragrant smell of it before sinking in her teeth. Juice squirted in her mouth, and she realized that all the fruit she'd eaten in her life before had been stale.

Then she turned, and raced back to the Sty. She flew to the red curtains by the bed, yanked them back, and danced through the narrow kitchen into the other room. It was almost a mirror image of her room, bed, stove, everything. She ran back into her room, went into the bathroom, unlocked the far door and pushed it wide open. The only sound she could hear was the birds outside, and the sound of her feet on the floor. She danced through into the other room and came back through the kitchen and around again, loving the space, loving the emptiness. She wound round and round like she was casting a spell, making it safe, making it hers.

Then she stripped off her pyjamas, dropped them on the floor, pulled on underwear, T-shirt and jeans and left the Sty without washing, without even cleaning her teeth. She ran through the medieval garden and up the narrow stone steps towards the mansion house.

"I'm sorry I'm late!" she called out as she burst through the back door of the Tudor kitchen. "I slept badly, then I overslept. . ."

Mrs Driver came almost running from the little side room where the cooker and the sink were. "Oh, my dear, are you all right? I've just. . . Oh, I'm *so sorry*! I've just put my cardigan on, and there was the Sty key, still in my pocket. . ."

"Oh, yeah – that freaked me when I realized I couldn't lock the door!"

"I am so *sorry*! You slept all night with the door unlocked . . . you must've been *terrified*!"

"Well, I was a bit uneasy," Rayne admitted, thinking: *understatement of the year.* "Actually I pulled the table in front of the door – you know what it's like at night, you get jumpy. . ."

"Of course you do. Oh, you need to lock your door. I can't believe I was so stupid, walking off with the key in my pocket!"

Mrs Driver's shrill apologies unnerved Rayne. "I heard a fox, scratching about," she said. "That spooked me. But it's not as though it could open the door, is it? I was OK."

Mrs Driver held out the large black key. It was like something out of a fairy tale. "Here you are, dear. Keep it safe. It's the only one. It's so old, we couldn't get a locksmith to copy it. *Lock your door*, dear. Always lock your door at night. Now! Breakfast?"

Chapter Twelve

After a delicious breakfast of fresh coffee, fried tomatoes and egg and some bread-like things that Mrs Driver called "farls", Rayne arranged to meet up with her at the tearoom in about half an hour and headed back to the Sty to change. Mrs Driver had rather apologetically handed her a floppy black skirt and two white shirts that she said served as the uniform for the tearoom. "People expect a uniform of some sort," she said, "they think it's more hygienic. I think these are your size. Add your own bits of jewellery if you like – nothing too over the top if you don't mind."

Rayne didn't mind, not in the least. Being sent off to change gave her the chance to shower and clean her teeth and try to work out what the hell she was doing, acting like she was staying when she'd decided to go.

But as she ran through the misty garden and into the Sty, she was no nearer working it out. "It's OK now, in the sunshine," she told herself, "but you wait till night comes again, you'll be bricking it again, you ought to go back to Mrs D and tell her you're leaving. . ."

Instead, she shucked her clothes off and went into the

bathroom. The bath had a primitive shower over it. She showered with both doors open, light beaming in from both sides. She tried on her waitress's uniform in the other bedroom, and it was loose but all right with the shirt left out and one of her belts over the top. She left her legs bare, pulled on black pumps. There was no large mirror in the Sty, only a small one over the sink in the bathroom, so she couldn't see what the uniform looked like, but it felt OK.

She went to her bag to get her make-up and pulled out her mobile instead. Two texts were waiting, one from her mum and one from Damian, her mum telling her how worried she was that she hadn't been in touch, Damian demanding to know why she hadn't called him last night. . . Hastily, she tapped out: *sorry reception crap OK here but overslept. love U. will call later.* Then she sent it off first to Damian and then to her mum without altering a word.

She put on mascara and lipgloss and rolled her sleeves back and pushed three silver bangles on to her left arm. Then she stopped, just for a moment, listening. Silence, just the faint rustling of trees, and a bird calling. She left, locking the door behind her, and raced back to the tearoom.

"I've got the cheese scones in," announced Mrs Driver, wiping her plump hands on her flowery apron. "There's a party just gone into the Old Stone Hall – they'll be wanting their mid-morning cup of coffee and elevenses. Mrs Brooks should be here soon with half a dozen quiches for lunch so if you could make a bit of coleslaw and salad to go with it. . ."

She was shown the ropes, and it was all easy stuff. She only needed half her brain to make the coleslaw, make the coffee, smile at the middle-aged ladies and spindly old men who came in, take their orders and smilingly agree with them that they should treat themselves to a scone . . . and all the time the other half of her brain was chanting *decide, decide, decide* and she was acting as if she *had* decided, as if she was going to stay.

When lunch time was nearly through she went to the ladies' which led off the green-glowing entrance vestibule, and discovered a full-size mirror on the wall. She looked at her reflection as though she was looking at a stranger. She thought she looked good, even in her boring uniform. The belt and her bangles jazzed it all up nicely.

What are you going to do? she mouthed at herself. *Are you really prepared to sleep out there another night?*

She thought of her mum, and Damian. It had been a stroke of genius to tell them reception was crap. Now she could leave her phone turned off, and then when she turned it on and got their messages she'd make out she'd gone somewhere else to get a signal. . .

Are you really thinking of staying? You're mad.

When she went back to the tearoom, four tables needed clearing, and there were tips on three of them. She hadn't reckoned on getting tips, but from the elevenses lot she'd pocketed three pounds seventy. And now, here was another one pound fifty, and the old man she'd chatted to for a few minutes, listening to what he'd learnt about the Black Prince, had left her a fiver, tucked underneath his plate. She smiled to herself. These tips would make a real difference to her earnings. *Flirting with old men, ay?* she thought. *The way forward.*

"We need to make a batch of fruit scones for the afternoon visitors," said Mrs Driver. "Can I show you how, dear? Then if I can't be here, you can manage on your own. . ."

It wasn't till after five o'clock – after they'd shut up the tearoom and Mrs Driver had taken her back to the Tudor kitchen and loaded her up with provisions (milk, bread, tea, cheese, a packet of chocolate biscuits) and invited her to dinner and Rayne had said she'd be happy cooking for herself in the Sty and Mrs D had said "quite right dear, you need to settle in" – that Rayne had finally, definitely recognized that she was staying.

"At least for tonight," she told herself. "It'll be different tonight, and if it's not – I'll go tomorrow." She ignored the part of her mind that was absolutely terrified, that couldn't believe she was about to put herself through that fear again. She ignored it, she mastered it.

Then Mrs Driver had given her a raw lamb chop on a plate and told her to help herself to the tomatoes growing in the medieval garden, and Rayne had asked about lighting the stove just to air the place a bit and Mrs Driver had told her how to and they'd chatted about it being cold at nights now. Then Rayne had asked if it was all right to explore the grounds.

"Go anywhere you like, dear," said Mrs Driver. "Explore all you want. The grounds are beautiful, and you've got hours before dark . . ."

Dark. Rayne wished Mrs D hadn't said that word – *dark*. But she pushed it away as she hurried back to the Sty. She stowed the food in the tiny fridge and once more walked through into the far room, came back via the bathroom, circling like an animal, making the whole space hers, then she got changed into jeans and a T-shirt and left, locking the door behind her.

The sun had come out again and the wind had dropped – it was quite warm. She set off through the medieval garden and followed the path that went past the apples trees at the bottom. It led her to a small lake, gloomy and overhung with trees. In the centre was a tiny island with a white hutch-like construction on it. As she stared, three white geese erupted noisily from some nearby bushes and shrieked across the lake to the hutch. She thought of the fox, scratching at her door last night, thought that was why the island had been built. The geese glared at her indignantly. There was something desolate about them, the way they all huddled on the tiny, sour-looking island, safe but trapped.

She walked on, veering to the right now, following a stream that led from the lake into a wood. Sun shafted down through the branches like little spotlights, picking out twigs and making leaves vivid. It was very still and beautiful. She looked up and the sun dazzled her, and she remembered the time she and Damian had gone to the park and lain under a tree. She'd been near to tears because looking up at the leaves had been so beautiful but kids kept running by yelling and there was rubbish everywhere and the grass stank of dogshit. . .

This was why she'd been almost crying, she thought. Longing, for this.

She walked on, and the silence was so heady it was like wine, making her heavy, languid. There was no one to watch her, no one to judge her. She felt like her shape had gone, like her skin wasn't holding her in any more, she was just flowing through into the woods. She sat down on a fallen tree trunk. The wood was all around her, silent but for tiny rustling noises, glowing in patches where the sun got through. She was flowing into it, she was part of it, all her edges were blurred.

You could sit here for ages, she thought, you could just *sit*, on and on, lose all track of time. . . The thought scared her. She stood up again, and started walking faster along the path. "If I'm going to stay," she said to herself, "if I'm really going to stay on here, I'm going to have to meet some people a bit less than fifty years older than me. Maybe those website girls have emailed me by now – I could tell them I'm here now. They're probably complete nerds, all into history and that, but at least they're human. If I stay I've got to get *out* a bit at night, or I'll be chatting to old men for the buzz not the money. . ."

The woods thinned, and then she was stepping out on to wide lawns with great ornate wrought-iron gates maybe five metres high to her left, and to her right, the back of the mansion house. It gave her a strange feeling, because while she'd been in the woods, she'd somehow forgotten Morton's Keep.

All the windows were closed, except for one of the little ones at the top, right under the roof. She had a sudden strong feeling that she was trespassing on the lawn, that she was being watched by someone who didn't want her here. She turned round and went back into the woods again. She needed to get back anyway, well before it got dark.

Chapter Thirteen

On the way back, she collected thick twigs and dry wood that she could break and fit into the stove. Mrs Driver had explained how easy it was to keep alight, and told her to help herself to the huge pile of logs by the greenhouses. Rayne told herself she could find the greenhouses later – for now, there was all the wood she needed just lying around for the taking. She had a huge armful by the time she got back to the Sty.

She dumped the wood by the stove, then opened its glass door. Then she fetched some matches and newspaper from the kitchen and set about laying a fire, putting the driest twigs on top of the paper and setting it alight. Soon, the twigs were crackling energetically; she angled two small logs on top and after a few minutes, they too ignited. She gazed at the fire proudly. It was the first one she'd ever lit and to her it was magical, practically miraculous. She loved the aliveness of it and the warmth as she crouched on the chill flagstones. Soon the room was full of the wonderful smell of burning wood.

She went over to the table, opened her suitcase, and

started pulling out her clothes. She hung her skirts, dresses and trousers in the curtained alcove, and put her underwear and tops in the drawers – there was plenty of room. Then, smiling, she strung her belts and jewellery on the antlers over the stove. "That'll stop you looking so freaky at night," she said. "Later, I'll dry my knickers on you. . ." Then she went outside to find the tomatoes Mrs Driver had told her to pick. She was hungry.

It was the first time Rayne had picked a tomato from its stalk. The strange, sharp smell of it – it amazed her. She picked three fat, ripe ones, sliced them and sprinkled salt on them, and overcooked the lamb chop under the tiny grill. With a couple of slices of bread to mop up the juices, it was delicious. She ate at the table by the open window, gazing outside or into the fire, mind drifting in the silence. She found herself sighing, deeply, and realized it was with contentment. She'd never really felt contented before.

She was trying not to think about the night, but she knew it was waiting. Waiting like a beast crouching in the shadows. The room was growing darker as the sun went down.

Suddenly, her mobile went off. She'd meant to turn it off, but forgotten. She sprang up and picked it off the bed, saw *Damian* and answered it guiltily.

"Hey – Rayne! Why didn't you *call*?"

"I was just going to, Day. I've only just got away, seriously. She's working me like a slave."

"So jack it in. Tell her to stuff it."

"I might do. The tips are good."

"Yeah? How much d'you make?"

"Dunno," she lied. She'd made exactly twelve pounds seventy pence. "Fifteen quid, maybe twenty?"

"That's cool, babe. Hey – how come we can talk? You said there's no reception."

"Not where I'm sleeping there isn't. I'm outside, outside the library, she made me dust the books." *God*, why was she lying like this?

"It sounds like complete shit there, Rayne. Why don't you come home?"

"I dunno. I will, probably. It's just – you know. What we talked about."

"Needing a break from your mum. And the little monster."

"Yeah. And the Estate."

"*God*, it kicked off last night. The Mill End Massive came up, they had about twenty cars, big sounds *bla-aring* out. . ."

"Oh, Jesus."

"It was cool. We saw 'em off. Someone chucked a load of rubbish down off the third floor, the Bill came, there was a proper stand-off. . ."

All the time he was talking, she was thinking: Was I wrong? Do I miss him? Something in her was stirring at the sound of his voice, wanting his arms round her.

"So you back at the weekend, Rayne?"

"Babe, I can't," she said. "There's this big event, a wedding, they're paying me loads. . ." *Why did she say that?* There wasn't a wedding.

But she didn't go back on it. "I'll do the wedding," she went on, "then I can come home the weekend after. . ."

"Yeah, OK, then." He didn't sound that bothered. Maybe

he was already after someone else. Did she care? She had no idea.

"Do me a favour, Day?"

"Yeah, what?"

"I can't face talking to Mum tonight. She'll put all her shit on me, moaning on about how worn out she is . . . can you call her? Tell her I'm all right but I need to get well out away from the house to phone, and I'm really tired?"

"Yeah, OK. Tell you what, I'll go round."

"Oh, Day, would you? They'd love that." Her mum liked Damian, she practically flirted with him – told him how good it was for Jelly to have a role model. Role model, that was a joke. But Jelly liked him too – maybe they'd have a rough and tumble together in the rank-smelling corridor outside the flat and then Jelly'd sleep well and her mum would be pleased. . .

He was starting an automatic chant of *goodnight, love you, can't wait for next weekend, can't wait for you to come back again* . . . she echoed it all, blowing kisses into her mobile.

As she put it down on the table, the room was almost dark.

Chapter Fourteen

Rayne decided to get to bed right away. She told herself she was knackered, after all she'd had a lousy night last night, hardly any sleep, and then her first day at waitressing, everything new, it was bound to be tiring. To say nothing of all that walking and fresh air.

But she knew she was kidding herself. What mattered was to get to sleep before she got too scared. One of her gran's old phrases floated into her mind – *steal a march on the enemy*. It had never made sense at home, but here. . . *Stupid*, she told herself; what march, what *enemy*? She was just tired, that was all.

But she still undressed in a rush, leaving her clothes across the chair, brushing her teeth and washing her face fast, rubbing in moisturizer. She half-knew she was hurrying so she wouldn't have to turn the gloomy overhead light on, because it would make the room and the shadows like last night, when she'd been so terrified. But she wouldn't let the thought surface and become clear.

She locked the door and bolted it, shut the window but left the curtains open. Then she closed the glass doors of the stove, thinking that the fire might last longer that way, and got into bed.

There was no draught now, hardly any air at all. It was very still in the room, it smelt of wood smoke and it was too warm, but she didn't want to push the duvet down. She tried to remember what she knew about fires and updraughts and downdraughts – maybe the heat from the stove stopped air coming down the chimney. She stared over at it. The waning fire glowed through the dark – warm, red and comforting.

Soon, she was asleep.

She woke once in the night, she had no idea what time. Heart thudding, waiting for the fear to grow, she gazed over at the stove; the glow had gone, there was just the faintest glimmer in the ashes now. She could still smell the wood smoke, though. She looked over at the window, willing it to be growing lighter, telling herself it was turning grey with the dawn. And into the absolute silence came the hoot of an owl – it must have been the owl that woke her. Then another hoot came, louder, from a different direction, answering the first. Two owls – and they were calling to each other. She smiled into the blackness, huddled down under the duvet again, and was asleep within seconds.

The next time she woke it was past eight o'clock. The room shone with sunshine; the birds were singing and chattering. She jumped out of bed, ran over and threw the window open. Fresh, earthy, dewy smells streamed in. All she could see was trees and the sky – no buildings at all. As she showered and dressed, she couldn't stop smiling. *I've done it*, she told herself, *I faced it down, I conquered it, I'm a hero, and it's my place now . . . all mine, only mine.*

I'm going to stay.

Chapter Fifteen

The next few days, up to the weekend, went by very fast. More and more, Mrs Driver left Rayne in charge of the teashop. "You've a deft touch with the scones," the housekeeper said. *Deft.* Rayne liked the word, though she had to imagine what it meant.

She was managing fine. She liked the work. She liked having to concentrate on what was right in front of her: taking deliveries of bread and vegetables, making pots of tea, serving up soup, clearing away, washing up. It was busy and varied enough to stop her thinking. She picked early-autumn flowers to put on the tables; she charmed the elderly visitors and collected lots of tips.

Every evening, she walked for at least an hour in the woods and the grounds of the house, deeply contented, absorbed by the green life growing all around her. She kept away from the wide lawn overlooked by the back of the house, though. She came across Ben Avebury, the old gardener, a couple of times and he smiled and nodded at her but didn't speak. On the third evening, she discovered the greenhouses and the large pile of wood beside them.

One of the greenhouses had a great palm tree growing through it – it had shattered the glass roof and was growing straight through to the sun. She stood and looked at it for ages, loving it, but not knowing why, then she picked up an armful of logs and headed back.

It wasn't really cold enough for the stove but she lit it every night because she liked the flames, the smell of wood smoke, and the rich glow as she was going off to sleep. She slept deeply in the absolute blackness and silence, sometimes waking to hear owls or foxes. She cooked for herself with food Mrs Driver gave her; she had no television, no music. She texted Damian and her mum every other day, often sending the same text to each. She tried to avoid speaking to either of them.

It had only taken a few days for the texts from everyone else at home to stop coming. She was amazed how fast it happened, once she just stopped replying. Maybe they thought she'd lost her phone.

She was floating, coasting. She was free of other people's needs and wants and demands and expectations for the first time in her life. It was like she'd fallen through a crack somewhere and it was unimaginably good.

When Rayne reached the tearoom on Friday morning, the door to the vestibule was open. A girl with a swinging brown ponytail was just ahead of her, carrying a large tray. The light from the ivy-covered window turned her green as she walked past. Rayne followed her into the main room, and down through the tables, but she didn't look round; she was concentrating on carrying the tray.

Mrs Driver's head emerged from the large fridge. "Good morning, Becky!" she cried. "Put those quiches down here, dear, and meet Rayne!"

Becky laid the tray on the kitchen counter, and turned round. She was about Rayne's age and height but much curvier; she had big slate-blue eyes in a roundish face. She gave Rayne a quick, suspicious smile and a lovely dimple appeared in her left cheek.

"Hello," they said, both at the same time.

"Oh, I'm *so* glad you two have met up," said Mrs Driver, beaming. "Becky's mother makes these wonderful quiches for us, Rayne. She makes the *best* pastry. And she does a spot of cleaning, too, up at the house. I don't know what we'd do without her. And sometimes Becky helps out too, don't you, dear?"

"Sometimes," said Becky, looking at Rayne. "When Mum makes me."

"Oh, now, that's not the attitude!" said Mrs Driver. "Your mum works so hard, I'm sure you want to give her a hand now and then. And you like the events, you know you do!"

"Some of them," said Becky. "The summer ones are OK."

"Ah, well, yes, we all like the summer ones best," said Mrs Driver, then she turned away and began to unstack the dishwasher.

"Are you *living* here?" Becky blurted out.

"Yes," said Rayne.

"In the *house*?"

"No – outside. In the Old Sty."

"Oh my God, that's worse! Right by those *woods*—"

67

"It is a bit creepy at night. But I love the woods – I love all the space. Where I came from, there wasn't any space."

Becky rolled her eyes. "I wouldn't stay here if you paid me a thousand pounds. It's bad enough in the day, but at *night*—"

"Ghosts?"

"Millions of them. You should hear the stories in the town. Where d'you come from?"

"East London."

"You left *London* to come here?" Becky's large eyes grew larger. "God, I'd love to be in London. It's so quiet here, nothing's ever going on. . ."

"Well, that's what I wanted. Where I came from, it was blam, blam, blam all the time. Really crowded, endless traffic, noise, fights. . ."

"Sounds exciting."

"It wasn't," Rayne almost snapped. "Not day after day. It was doing my head in. I lived in a tiny flat with my mum and little brother. . ."

"I've got *three* little brothers," said Becky, self-righteously. "*God*, sorry – I just think you're mad, coming here. I'd love to be in London. I mean – what will you do in the evenings? Just stay in that old sty?"

"No. Not necessarily."

"Well *I* wouldn't go out. You'd have to come back – up that drive – in the dark. There's a story in Marcle Lees of a horseman who rides up the drive around midnight, into the courtyard—"

"Is he headless?"

"*What?*"

"Horsemen are usually headless."

"No. I don't think so. You laugh – people have heard the horse's hooves on the cobbles, seriously. And if you see him, he *gets off his horse* and kind of *comes at you* with his arms outstretched. . ."

"Becky," said Mrs Driver, loudly, "is your mother waiting outside in the car?"

"Yes. I better go."

"I thought I heard a car horn. You'd better hurry, dear. Don't keep her waiting."

Chapter Sixteen

Rayne decided she didn't think much of Becky, and she dismissed all her rubbish about ghosts. But even so, she found her words working on her throughout the day. Maybe she was right and Rayne was a bit mad, wanting to live like this, so isolated and uneventful, not wanting anything more than the trees and the silence. Maybe she was going weird like Mrs Chrysler on the Estate who never left her flat.

Even Mrs Driver, paying her week's wages in cash on Friday afternoon, seemed concerned. She apologized for there being no "do" at Morton's Keep that weekend, and asked her if she planned to go home. When Rayne said no, Mrs Driver mentioned that Becky often went off to the cinema on Saturday night with some friends, and she might not mind Rayne going too. . .

"It's OK," said Rayne, horrified at the thought of being foisted on to Becky, of Becky lecturing her again on how insane she was to leave London. "I'm fine. There's people I know in the next town I can call if I want to." *Why had she said that? More lies. And if Mrs D asked her which town, she was stuffed.* "I'm going home next weekend," she went on, hurriedly. "To see my boyfriend."

"Oh, that's nice, dear. Although it's a shame in a way – we've a big dinner on, Friday night, in the Old Stone Hall. . . I was hoping you could waitress. . ."

"Well, I can," said Rayne. "I can always go home Saturday. Or get him to come here. Nothing's fixed."

Then she hurried out, before Mrs Driver could ask her anything else.

It felt strange and a bit alarming to wake up on Saturday morning with absolutely nothing to do. She took her washing over to the mansion house to put through the machine in the utility room off the Tudor kitchen, as Mrs Driver had told her she could – she'd given her two keys to the back kitchen door, so she could come and go as she pleased. She wouldn't let herself walk in the woods – she spent an hour or so tidying up the Sty, brushing the floor and cleaning the kitchen and bathroom. Then she was faced with the rest of the day, and it wasn't even lunch time. She could feel panic circling her, trying to get in. It was OK just to drift in the evenings, when she was tired from work, but today she needed to *do* something.

She decided to go into Marcle Lees, to explore. She could find the library, and log on to see if there was an email from the geeky Hidden History girls. Mrs Driver had told her about the buses – there were two an hour; you turned left at the end of the drive and the bus stop was just down the road. She set off to get the twenty past twelve bus and ended up running for it because she'd forgotten quite how long and winding Morton's Keep's drive was. It hit her that it was the first time she'd left the grounds since she'd moved in.

The bus took about twenty minutes to set her down in the middle of Marcle Lees. She was amazed by the place – she'd thought it would be some kind of backwater, but it was buzzing. Narrow arcades with upmarket shops fanned out from a central square where a little market was in full swing. She wandered about, considering where to get lunch, spoilt for choice among the restaurants and cafés.

There were quite a few young people moving about in groups. They strode out, assured and glossy. They had to be from private schools, Rayne thought – boarding schools even. Compared to Cramphurst Estate, it was a different country.

She ate a tuna and salad sandwich in a coffee shop, then headed for the library, where she logged on. There was the usual junk mail, and a few messages from friends at home that she didn't answer, but nothing from the website girls. She googled Marcle Lees again. And amid the list of Musical Evenings and WI Meetings and Horticultural Shows, there it was – the *Hidden History of Marcle Lees*.

She brought it up on screen.

The homepage had changed, it was much more powerful now. The two girls no longer looked geeky. They were wearing long cloaks, and they were drifting through skeletal trees against a smoky, shifting, purple background. The new navigation buttons were a set of snarling griffons' heads that reminded Rayne of the fantastical carved creatures on the stairway in the Great Hall. Bemused, she clicked on *Pictures*.

And there was Morton's Keep. She recognized the photo from the first time she'd looked at the site, and it hit her that that was why the old wall and the towers had looked familiar when she'd arrived for her interview.

But the photo had been altered. The colours were bleak and stark now, the towers looked ominous, threatening, and a great stain like blood or a distorted hand reached out from behind them.

She clicked to the next photo. It was the back of Morton's Keep, the great gates and wide lawn she felt she was trespassing on; it had a sinister, brooding air. The next photo was through trees to the steps outside the kitchen; then came the medieval garden – and the Sty. It made her uneasy, looking at her new home on this strange website. She felt relieved when pictures of the local church came up, menacing-looking against a thundery sky, followed by gloomy shots of its interior.

Rayne went back to the homepage and clicked on the griffon that said *Our Philosophy*, and read:

History is nearly always written by the victorious. If a rebellion is brutally repressed, the brutality will be played down and the heroism of the victors played up. History is always distorted by the people who tell it. So much of it is hidden, censored, sanitized.

"Pretty obvious," thought Rayne, skipping through, and then her eyes landed on:

It's the hidden history of Marcle Lees that we're interested in, the events that generations of local people have played down and tried to forget. We are particularly interested in descendants of people who were forced to move away, perhaps even emigrate, because of the troubles in this place. If anyone can help us with this, please contact us.

"Weird," thought Rayne. "What are they after?" She scanned lower, and came across the final sentence in special gothic script:

We don't think any history should be forgotten. Beauty is Cruel, Cruelty is Beautiful.

Rayne let out a puff of breath. Maybe these girls weren't as geeky as she'd thought. Maybe she didn't want to know them. But they were the only contacts she had here. Before she could dither about it any longer she hit the *Contact Us* button and wrote:

I emailed you before about Marcle Lees but you didn't reply. Anyway, I'm here now – working at Morton's Keep. Do you two do anything else than study history?

It was a shot in the dark – maybe she'd get a reply, maybe she wouldn't. But almost instantaneously, one came back:

Yes, lots. Do you want to meet up?

Wow, she emailed back, stalling, *first no response, then a really fast one. How come?*

There was a long pause after that. Then, just as she was about to switch off and leave the library, a reply: *We didn't get your last email. Let's meet up. Where are you?*

Rayne paused for a minute, considering. Then she emailed back: *In the library.*

And the answer came back: *See you in Paulo's café in fifteen minutes. Turn left out of the library and keep going.*

Chapter
Seventeen

At first, she thought they weren't there. She was looking for two girls, but the only young people in the café were a very attractive group of three girls and two boys, sitting together on two sofas round a low table. One of the boys had just arrived; he was dark-haired, good-looking, and a pretty blonde girl was shifting up, making room for him beside her. Rayne scanned the café again, wondering whether to leave, or get a coffee and wait for ten minutes, when she noticed that two of the girls were looking at her. They both turned to the dark-haired boy, said something, looked at her again. . .

Slowly, she moved towards them. One of the girls called out, "Did you email us?"

She countered with: "Are you the *Hidden History* people?"

The girl smiled. "Yeah. I'm Amelia, this is Petra. And you're Rayne, right?"

She nodded.

"Hello, Rayne," said the dark-haired boy. He had a good voice. Very clear, sure – no pretension in it. "I'm Sinjun. And this is Flora. . ." He put his arm round the shoulders of the blonde girl sitting next to him. "And that's Marcus."

"Sinjun?" queried Rayne.

"That's how it's pronounced," said Flora. "It's really Saint John. Which is incredibly ironic, actually." St John smiled and hugged her to him, not taking his eyes off Rayne. Rayne felt a rush of attraction to him, and a simultaneous shot of envy of Flora. There was something so hot about him, and it wasn't just his good looks – something more, some surety.

"So," said Amelia, "what did you think of our website?"

"Um . . . to be honest, I only went on it because of the Marcle Lees link. I'm not really all that interested in history and old places and stuff."

"So whatever made you want a job at Morton's Keep then?"

Rayne shrugged. "To get a break from London?"

"Aaah," said Amelia and St John together, as if they understood. Then St John said, "Petra, are you going to get the coffee? What would you like, Rayne?"

"It's OK," mumbled Rayne, embarrassed, "I can get one—"

"Come on," St John said, grinning at her, "what would you like?"

"Oh, OK. A latte, please," she said. Petra lifted a small, battered-looking brown leather bag off the table and drifted elegantly off to the counter.

"Sit down," said Amelia, moving along the sofa to make space. "So . . . how are you finding Marcle Lees?"

"I don't know yet," said Rayne. "I mean . . . I've only just got here. I was . . . it was a real impulse to come. I was kind of doing a runner."

"Yeah? What from?"

There was something very seductive about the group. At first, Rayne felt quite intimidated, sitting with them. But they were relaxed, persuasive; they seemed really interested in what she had to say. Prompted by questions, Rayne described life on Cramphurst Estate, her feeling of being intensely trapped, both at home and with her boyfriend. And unlike Becky, they didn't seem to think she was mad to run away from it.

"I think you're so brave," purred Amelia. "Making that break, that jump. It takes nerve. Doesn't it, St John?"

"Definitely," he said. "I admire you."

Rayne felt herself redden. "I just hope it's going to work out," she muttered. "I mean – I hope I won't regret it, leaving all my friends behind—"

"You'll make new friends," said Marcus.

"Like us!" said Amelia, and everyone smiled, and then Petra came back with the coffees.

After that the conversation got more general but somehow, it always came back to Rayne. She felt she was being drawn in, accepted, encouraged to speak. It felt good, putting her life into words for these calm strangers. Somehow, it validated her – it validated what she'd done.

"So," said St John, staring at her over the rim of his white coffee mug, "d'you like it at Morton's Keep?"

Rayne shrugged. "Too early to say, really. It's the . . . contrast I like best. The lack of hassle, the space. . ."

"The grounds are beautiful."

"Yeah. The house itself is a bit weird though. I mean, it's amazing, but it's so old. It freaked me out when I first got there. What's your interest in it?"

Something passed through the group when she asked that. She had no idea what, or why she thought that something had shifted, but she knew something had.

"Our interest?" echoed St John.

"You know. It's all over the website."

The group seemed to relax again. "Oh, Amelia and Petra have got a thing about local history," drawled Marcus, "and Morton's Keep is easily the oldest place here. That's all."

"But what's all that stuff about cruelty being beautiful, and local people repressing the facts?"

"Morton's Keep has a pretty violent past, you know," said Amelia, intently, tucking her lovely auburn hair behind one ear. "My great-aunt used to say its walls ran with blood. And we just find it . . . interesting. You know – what people have tried to cover up over the years."

"They're *ghouls*," said Marcus, screwing up his face at Amelia. "*Loathsome* girls."

Everyone laughed, then Petra said, "So – are you sleeping in the mansion house?"

"No way," said Rayne. "I could've done – I could've slept up in the attics – but it was too scary by far. There's this . . . *box* thing, halfway up the stairs. . ."

Again, that shift in the group, like a current passing through them. "What d'you mean, box thing?" asked Amelia.

"On the landing. It's like a . . . it's a glass case, I suppose, on the wall. . ."

St John leaned towards her. "Did you see what's inside?"

"That's the thing, it had this creepy red velvet curtain drawn around it, like a. . ."

"Coffin," said Flora, briskly. "Nice. So where *are* you sleeping?"

"Outside. They call it the Old Sty."

"I know it," said St John. "Don't you find *that* scary? Right by the woods?"

"I did at first. But I love it now. The silence . . . and the owls. . ."

Abruptly Flora checked her watch and said, "We should go, St John."

Rayne felt a stab of panic. Were they just going to walk away, and that would be that? She wanted to see these people again. She wanted to be part of it.

But it was all right, St John was leaning towards her. "Are you busy on Wednesday night?" he asked.

"No – I don't think so," she said.

He fished in his pocket, drew out a small flyer, and held it out to her. It advertised a band called Straitlaid, and listed their venues for the next six weeks. "They're local," he said, "we sort of know them. Their music's bluesy, funky – really good, actually. Next Wednesday they're at the hall at the back of The King's Head – just off the market square. Why don't you come along?"

"Thank you," she said, taking the flyer from his long fingers, "I'd like to."

On the bus on the way back to Morton's Keep, Rayne took the flyer out of her pocket and read it, happily. "This," she gloated, "is one in the eye for Becky saying I'm mad to move here because nothing ever happens here. Those people were *great* and they really seemed to like me. *Stuff* Becky."

She put the flyer away safely, and looked out of the window. The road was old, winding, with high banks of dense woodland on either side. The sun was setting and the sky was streaked with light and dark. She found herself thinking about St John – about his eyes, how they'd open and look straight at her. He had very dark hair, and his eyes were the same colour, and both had this wonderful sheen. He had to be tall. His legs, spread out beside the low café table, had been so long.

She thought about how still he was, how self contained. Damian was never still, he was always jiggling his leg or nodding his head to some beat in his brain or jerking round to talk to someone else or swearing . . . but St John had been so *still*.

Why was that so attractive?

She smiled as she stared out of the window. It was really, really good to be feeling this for someone, this kick of longing. She hadn't felt this for Damian. Not in the same way.

Not that anything would come of it. St John was clearly with Flora, who was pretty and vivacious. . . "Although no prettier than me," she thought. "Just fair where I'm dark."

Stop it, stop it, focus on the whole group. They'd been great, hadn't they? Pretty cool, even Damian would have to admit that they were OK, if not his sort. It had felt good, sitting around talking with them . . . and they'd been friendly and interested in her, asking all those questions. . .

She smiled again, because she'd just had the weird thought that what they'd been doing had been interviewing her.

Chapter Eighteen

After that meeting and the invitation for Wednesday night, it was all right to be on her own for Saturday night and Sunday. It was like she'd ticked the *I'm not going to end up like Mrs Chrysler* box and now she could give herself up to the isolation and just *be*. She walked and slept and ate and lied to Damian on the phone about how much she was missing him. She lay on her bed and allowed her mind to go wherever it wanted. She felt like she was floating in a beautiful vacuum. She had a sense of her self – of who she was, quite separate from the roles she played – and it was a totally new experience for her.

At about three o'clock on Sunday afternoon, she was woken from a light doze by a bright shaft of sun through the window. She got up and stood in the doorway looking out. Everything looked green and growing, and she felt suddenly happy, almost joyful. She stepped outside and started to walk, no idea where she was going, and soon found herself in the woods again, heading for the grounds at the back of Morton's Keep. She decided to keep going. It was ridiculous to be put off by a vague sense that she was trespassing. It was the only area she hadn't fully explored yet.

She walked on to the wide lawn, and again, she had that creepy feeling that someone was watching her from the house, someone who didn't want her there. But she walked on. Mrs Driver had told her the house was empty for the weekend – there were no events and Mr Stuart, the owner, wasn't in residence. She was happy. It was OK.

The great gates to her left glinted in the low sun, casting long, spiky shadows in front of her. She kept walking, across the shadows that caged her as she crossed them. It was like swimming too far out in the sea, and she had an urge to turn round and get back to the woods, to safety. But she kept going.

A weathered red-brick wall marked the boundary of the lawn on the far side. It had a narrow archway in it with an old wooden door that was standing ajar. Rayne hurried towards it, slipped through, and found herself in a long, walled garden. Right in front of her, dominating the garden, was a squat, circular tower with a cone-shaped roof. As she looked, three white doves flew from one of five evenly-spaced holes in the side of the tower and flapped over her head. *A dovecote!* she thought. *A massive dovecote – how lovely!* But somehow, it didn't feel lovely. There was something sombre about the dovecote, even with the sun shining down on it.

The garden was divided up by stubby, waist-high box hedges, set out confusingly, like a maze, with stretches of overgrown grass in between. Rayne started walking towards the dovecote and found herself taken off at an angle and led into a grass square with a bench in it. She laughed, and set off again, and this time was led in exactly the opposite direction – then back on herself almost to the door in the wall.

It had stopped being funny. She glanced up at the side of the mansion that overlooked the garden – three windows were set high on its wall. *If someone's looking out on me*, she thought, *they'll think I'm a right idiot.* Part of her wanted to leave, but another part was determined not to be beaten, determined to reach the dovecote. She set off again. This time, she was led to the far end of the garden. She was just considering stepping over the hedges and blundering her way in the right direction when the grassy path opened out on to a strange little area. It was hexagonal in shape, and right in the middle three lozenge-shaped stones were laid out, half-overgrown by grass. They looked a bit like grave markers, except the stone in the middle was out of line with the other two. And in the middle of each one was something squat and round and black.

Rayne felt her skin crawl.

It could be fungus, but fungus doesn't grow on stone.

She made herself take a step closer, and trod on something hard. She jumped back, peered at the grass. She'd trodden on a fat black candle, burnt right down. Its wax had set in a shape like a deformed toadstool; stubby and evil-looking. She scanned the area. There were seven more candles, laid out in a ring round the three stones, all of them burnt right down.

Rayne felt so spooked she didn't hesitate. She turned to face the door in the wall and blundered her way through a gap in the hedge ahead of her, then scrambled over the next hedge and reached the door. Then she ran across the great stretch of hostile lawn and into the trees. Her good feeling had gone, gone completely.

Back at the Sty, Rayne lit the stove even though it was so warm she had to keep the window and the door wide open. Then she made herself spaghetti and grated cheese with yet another fresh tomato salad, and as she ate it she started to feel better. Whenever an image of eleven black candles, burning slowly to the ground, came into her mind, she'd shoo it out before the image could include anything else.

Like who'd lit the candles.

The sun was softly going down. It was a beautiful evening. She felt safe, at home, in the Sty now. She told herself the candles had been part of some kind of drama thing, some "event" that Morton's Keep was so keen to put on. She told herself she'd ask Mrs Driver about it tomorrow.

Chapter Nineteen

When Rayne turned up at the tearoom the next morning, Mrs Driver said, "We've just got the one tour this morning, a large one. They're coming down from Leicester by coach – they'll be here around ten. Why don't you get the scones done, then tag along with them? It'll give you a chance to see the rest of the house."

"Oh, I'd like to," said Rayne. "If that's all right."

"It'll be fine. No one'll mind one extra." Mrs Driver smiled, turned away and started taking teacups down one by one from a large cupboard on the wall.

"I went into that long walled garden yesterday," Rayne blurted out, "the one with the dovecote in it."

It seemed to her that the housekeeper's plump shoulders tensed up just a little, but she couldn't be sure.

"Are there a lot of doves living there?" she went on. "I only saw three."

"Oh, there's a few more than that," said Mrs Driver, turning to face her. "They breed, but not all that successfully. It's not a proper dovecote, you know. It used to be a tower in medieval times. It had a bit of a . . . horrible reputation.

When Morton's Keep was being done up three hundred years ago they lopped the top off it and gave it over to the birds. I suppose they hoped that that would. . ." Mrs Driver trailed off, then she said, "To my mind, it's still a depressing sort of place. No wonder the birds don't thrive."

"I found these candle stumps," Rayne said, in a rush, "*black* candle stumps – in the grass, in a kind of circle. . ."

Mrs Driver turned back to the cupboard, and started pulling teacups out again. "Near some flat stones?" she asked. Her voice sounded weirdly high.

"Yes. Three were on the stones, the rest were in the grass." She stopped. It had hit her that the three stones were laid out like an arrow, pointing at the dovecote. "Was it from an event or something?" she went on, in a rush. "I thought maybe there'd been a . . . I dunno, a *play* or something. . ."

"It must have been," said Mrs Driver, rattling the teacups down. "Some silly play or masque. I told you, Mr Stuart puts on all sorts of things here. Or . . . we get ghost hunters sometimes. They get up to some odd things. Yes, it was probably ghost hunters."

"So," asked Rayne, as breezily as she could, "Becky's right, Morton's Keep is haunted?"

"Oh, all places of this great age have ghost hunters," said Mrs Driver. "It's a lot of nonsense. I've never seen anything." She turned to face Rayne again. "You'd better get on with the scones if you want to join that tour. Just get them in the oven, and I'll see to them and get the kettles on and you come along when the tour's over and help serve."

*

Rayne joined the coach tour as it was entering the huge wooden doors into the Great Hall. Ms Barton, whom Mrs Driver had briefly introduced to Rayne during her first week, was leading it. Mrs Driver clearly considered Ms Barton to be highly intelligent and indispensable to the running of Morton's Keep. As well as doing the tours, she kept the mansion accounts and did lots of organizing and ordering.

"Good job she's clever," thought Rayne. "She needs something going for her."

She was somewhere in her thirties, tall and awkward-looking. Her hair was cut in an unflattering bob, and she wore no make-up and sensible shoes.

She nodded at Rayne, waved her to the back of the group, and started her talk.

"This is the oldest part of the great mansion we call Morton's Keep," she said. Her voice was dry, a bit like a bark. "A remote backwater in many ways, but in and out of this remote backwater have swept the broad tides of history. . ." After more of this and a whole string of facts about the battles along the Welsh borders and the Fulke family, Rayne stopped paying attention. Mrs Driver was right, the Great Hall was less terrifying in daylight. The hefty cherubs over the fireplace looked less hideous; the sun glinting through the low windows cheered the wood panelling and the dark staircase. But it still wasn't a comfortable place to be. She glanced up the stairs to the half-landing. She could just see the lower half of the strange coffin-shaped case, and this time, unlike that terrifying first night here, the curtains were drawn back. She remembered

St John leaning towards her, bringing his face close to hers, asking her if she'd seen what was in it.

"So if you'd like to follow me now into the Old Stone Hall. . ." Ms Barton said, and the group shuffled forward. Despite the crowd in front of her, and the warmth of the September day, and Ms Barton's voice droning loudly on, as Rayne stepped over the stone threshold she had a sense of stepping alone into a great, silent vault. The hall seemed to hum with ancient power, and it was cold, the type of cold that couldn't be banished no matter how hot the day or how big a fire you lit. Windows were set high on its walls to the left, too high to see out of. At the far end was a great stone table with a long crack in it, and five antique chairs ranged round it – the only pieces of furniture in the room. On the right was a massive fireplace, its mantelpiece supported by worn, weirdly-shaped columns of stone. Rayne looked closer and saw that the columns were goat-legged men, and the spheres they were standing on were severed heads.

"The table there is over a thousand years old," Ms Barton lectured on. "That crack was bomb damage during World War Two. You can see where the ceiling has been patched up above it."

Several of the old men brightened at the mention of the war. "Any other damage to the place?" asked one.

"The top of one of the towers was knocked off," said Ms Barton, with a little smile. "But apart from that, nothing. To Morton's Keep, the two World Wars were just another few years of violent history. Now. Turn and look behind you."

Everyone turned round. A balcony was strung from

one side of the room to the other, just above head-height. "Anyone know what that is?" she asked.

"A minstrel's gallery?" piped up one of the women.

"Nothing so pleasant, I'm afraid. It was the dock the prisoners stood in. Rebels and raiders, usually, from along the Welsh border, with the usual smattering of thieves and murderers. The lord of the manor would pronounce sentence from that great table, and if they'd been found guilty, they were taken straight out and hanged in the courtyard. The fireplace you see there is a later edition, despite its ancient appearance. It was put in only three hundred years ago."

"It looks almost pagan," said someone.

"It does, doesn't it," agreed Ms Barton, and paced towards the exit.

Like sheep being loaded into a truck, the group slowly mounted the wide staircase. Rayne strained to hear what Ms Barton was saying about the contents of the case on the half-landing. "And here we see a few artefacts of significance to the house . . . nothing of real worth or value. The most notable is a comb that Anne Boleyn was supposed to have worn on her way to execution, picked up on the scaffolding by a nephew of the then-lord of Morton's Keep. . ."

"Why the curtains?" asked a stern-looking woman with cropped grey hair.

"Sunlight," said Ms Barton, smoothly. "We protect the old artefacts from the light as much as we can."

"There's not much sun on these stairs," muttered an old man to Rayne's left.

And why, thought Rayne, keep them drawn at *night*?

She stopped alongside the case and stared in. Arranged in rows was a fusty, rather depressing collection of brass medals and solemn jewellery, old china, two daggers . . . and Anne Boleyn's comb. It was thin, delicate and bone white; it would have shown the blood. At the back were some long, soft-leather gloves, elaborately embroidered with weird-looking flowers that looked a bit like faces. . . Rayne peered closer. They *were* faces. Faces contorted with torment and terror. What kind of sick mind had embroidered *those*, she thought; someone who thought torment could look pretty, someone who could make something beautiful out of. . .

She remembered the *Hidden History* website.

"Come along," called Ms Barton. "Let's all move on to the Spanish room."

Beauty is Cruel. Cruelty is Beautiful.

Chapter Twenty

The Spanish room was so called because on its walls was four-hundred-year-old tooled leather from Cordoba in Spain. Ms Barton called it "exquisitely beautiful" but to Rayne it was sinister and repulsive. It had rotted and hung down in strips in some places; in others it had swelled and buckled, and all in all it seemed to Rayne like a huge, diseased lizard.

The dark portraits on the walls sneered down at her as though she had no right to be there; the four-poster bed loomed like a great sarcophagus in the corner, draped with shroud-like hangings. "Wouldn't want to be in *here* on my own at night!" exclaimed a plump woman just in front of Rayne.

"Well, it *is* supposed to be haunted," said Ms Barton, almost gleefully. "All the old rooms are, of course. Morton's Keep gets a great deal of revenue from ghost hunters. They're wonderful, they want no food, drink or beds, just freedom to stalk the mansion at dead of night. . ."

"And do they find any ghosts?" demanded the woman.

"Oh, certainly they do. Well – their instruments do.

They grade the ghosts, depending on how powerful the vibrations are."

"Have *you* ever seen one? A ghost?"

"That would be telling!" trilled Ms Barton. "Shall we move on?"

The next room was apparently haunted by Abigail, the unfortunate daughter of an eighteenth-century lord of Morton's Keep. She'd been shut up in the room for over thirty years, growing more and more insane, for the crime of falling in love with a peasant boy. Ms Barton pointed out where she'd scratched a pitiful little poem in the glass:

Love leads us ill, Love leads us to our doom.
I seek the path of Virtue, safe in this room.

Higher up, on the outside of the glass, was scratched the first three letters of her name . . . Abi. It was supposed to have been the peasant boy who had climbed up to scratch this, before having his head blown off by the irate lord's close-range pistol.

"No wonder she went bonkers," thought Rayne, as they trudged on to the third bedroom. "Seeing that." She was beginning to feel she'd had enough, that she'd like to escape back to the tearoom, but she didn't know how to do that without looking rude.

Ms Barton had saved the best till last – the Red Queen's bedroom. It was named for Mary Tudor, Bloody Mary. The tyrannical queen had slept there twice, and it was supposed to be the most haunted, not only from vicious emanations from the prodigious burner of Protestants herself, but from the spirit of a Catholic priest. He'd been hacked to bits there by Roundhead soldiers, and at midnight he was said to run to and fro in panic. *As you would*, thought Rayne.

The atmosphere in this room was hateful. The portraits round the walls looked evil, sinister. There was a large family portrait in which all seven of the graded-in-height children had the same disturbing, moon-blank face. Rayne stood near the door, longing to escape.

"And you say," demanded the plump lady, "that these rooms are actually *used*? Slept in?"

"Certainly they are!" said Ms Barton. "Why, I made up that bed myself only last week, for a trustee of the Morton's Keep Fund! Now . . . please note the *altar* over there, which for many years. . ."

As she spoke, Rayne was edging out of the door. She was feeling really claustrophobic; she was desperate to get outside again, get some air into her lungs. She ran down the main stairs, and as she crossed over the half-landing, she shivered.

Someone had drawn the dark-red curtains over the glass case again.

The next couple of days, with their regular routine, passed quickly. Even calling Damian and her mum had become a routine that she didn't much think about or worry over any more. She was half-hoping Becky would turn up so she could tell her about meeting St John and his friends, but Becky didn't put in an appearance.

And then it was Wednesday evening and she was getting ready to go to the King's Head pub. She felt almost ridiculously excited. It was her first night out since she'd got to Morton's Keep, over ten days ago now – and it was the first time she'd enjoyed getting dressed up for maybe months before that. Damian put so much pressure on her to look the way he liked that it took all the pleasure out of it. She showered, and smoothed body lotion into her skin. Then she made her eyes up dramatically, loving the way her lashes thickened and the way the eyeshadow emphasized the greeny brown of her eyes. "You," she said to her reflection, "you're not bad-looking. You'll pass."

It was a warm evening. She'd been going to wear jeans and a thin top, but on an impulse she got out one of her summer dresses. Damian hadn't been too keen on it, he said it was too old for her – the truth was it wasn't revealing enough for his taste or his need for status from a girlfriend. But Rayne loved it. It was bronze-coloured, very simple – it made her dark skin glow. She put on a silvery necklace and her bangles, and some stylish sandals with low heels she could walk in. She couldn't check her full-length reflection, but she knew she looked good.

As she locked the Sty door behind her, it hit her that she'd be coming back here in the dark. She remembered Becky's spectral horseman and for a few seconds she was flooded with panic. Then she remembered the torch that Mrs Driver had given her on her third night here. She went back inside and got it, stowing it in her bag, and as she left, she turned the gloomy overhead light on.

She took the bus to the market square and found the hall at the back of The King's Head easily. It was twenty to nine – the flyer St John had given her said the band started at nine, so she figured this was a good time to turn up. She paid the small entrance fee and bought a Coke, then stood in the open doorway feeling exposed, reluctant to go in, scanning the hall for St John and the others. There were no tables or chairs, just a small stage at the end. The lighting was dim; people were standing in groups around the walls, balancing their drinks on the narrow shelf that ran round the room at elbow height.

Then she spotted St John right at the front, to the left of the stage. Her stomach tightened with excitement. Flora was very close to him, one hand up on his arm; Amelia, Petra and Marcus were in front of him, listening to him, laughing – they were all focused on him.

Rayne felt her breath coming, ragged and anxious. She didn't think she could walk up to them and interrupt – she didn't have the courage. They looked like such a tight, glamorous group. She took a sip of her drink, and looked around again, making out she was searching for someone; then a couple walked by her holding hands, and she followed them into the room, sheltering in their slipstream. When they veered off to the right, she stood still. And then St John looked up, and spotted her.

"Rayne!" he called, and he opened his arms as though he expected her to run into them.

She smiled, moving towards him, and he detached himself from the group and came right towards her and, deadly confident, put both hands on her shoulders and smiled down into her face.

"You came!" he said. "I'm really glad you came! I said

to Flora, we should've got your mobile number, to make sure."

Rayne, thrilled, a bit overwhelmed, said, "It was no problem to get here. D'you know what time it ends? Only I checked, and the last bus goes at eleven, so I gotta. . ."

"Oh, sod the last bus. I'll give you a lift. Seriously, it's no problem."

"Really? That'd be great. Last buses at home were awful, always full of people throwing up. . ."

"*Much* the same here," he laughed, drawing her over to the rest of the group. Everyone smiled and said hello, but Flora had a kind of iced look, and her smile didn't reach her eyes. Suddenly brave, Rayne stared straight at her. "She thinks I'm competition," she thought. "Well, maybe I am."

Then, amid enthusiastic clapping, Straitlaid walked out on to the stage, all self-consciously casual. St John and the others moved to the centre of the hall; Rayne found herself standing next to him. Flora was on his other side, hanging on to his arm possessively. *She's feeling nervous*, Rayne thought, and smiled.

The band tuned up for a few minutes – then they were off. It wasn't music like Rayne was used to – Damian would say it was bloody awful. But she started to enjoy it – it was original, sophisticated. People weren't exactly dancing, but some were moving their heads and arms to the beat and swaying in time, eyes fixed on the musicians on the stage.

After a while St John leaned down towards her, brought his mouth to her ear, and asked, "Well? What do you think?"

She loved his face so near hers. "They're good!" she

mouthed, and he smiled, and drew back, but he was standing even closer to her now.

The interval came. Flora and Marcus went off to the bar for drinks; she was carrying the same small, battered brown-leather bag that they'd had in the café. Rayne wanted to ask St John about it, wanted to find out if they were such a tight group that they ran some kind of kitty, but she thought it might sound as if she was angling to join them, so she didn't.

He started the conversation. He turned towards her, asking, "Have you seen round the mansion house yet?"

"Yeah. I tagged on to this tour of old fogies from Leicester. I saw the Old Stone Hall, and these awful horror-film bedrooms rammed full of ghosts that people actually still *sleep* in. . ."

"Did you see inside the case? The one you told me about?"

"Yeah – the one halfway up the stairs? The curtains were drawn back, but when I went downstairs again they. . ."

"What was inside it?" He'd got very close to her now; his mouth was inches away from hers. She thought about stepping back, but she didn't want to. "Why are you so interested?" she said, smiling.

"I just am," he grinned. "Was there a dagger?"

"Yes, with a carved handle. And these *horrible* gloves. . ."

"Gloves? What were they like?"

"They were sick. They looked like flowers at first, then as you got closer, you saw they were these twisted-up agonized faces. . ."

He was so close, he was almost touching her now. "What colour were they?" he asked.

Rayne frowned, trying to remember. "Yellow," she said. "Yellowish brown."

St John exhaled, a long, low breath, and turned away again, just as Flora appeared at his elbow with a tray of drinks.

Flora looked stonily at Rayne. Not angrily, Rayne thought . . . not even jealous. Just . . . cold.

Stone cold.

Chapter
Twenty-one

St John stayed next to Rayne for the second half of the gig, with Flora on his other side. The three of them were huddled up close. Once, to test him, Rayne moved away a little, and he shifted sideways to be close to her again, pulling Flora with him. "If I was her," Rayne thought, "I'd be really pissed off by now."

She was feeling more and more turned on to him, sure he was feeling the same. It was crackling between them, this interest, this excitement.

The band did two encores, and by the time the group meandered out of the fug of the hall and into the fresh, quiet night air it was eleven-thirty. Flora pushed her hand through St John's arm as they walked along.

"You did mean it about that lift, didn't you?" Rayne said to him. "Only I'm stuffed if you didn't, the last bus has gone."

"Sure I did," said St John.

"Where's your car?"

"It's a bike. There." And he gestured at a black and silver motorbike, shackled to a lamp post at the entrance to the pub.

Rayne was stunned. "But—"

"It's OK, it's safe, I've got a spare helmet."

"Doesn't anyone. . ." She glanced at Flora, whose face hadn't moved. "I thought you had a car. Doesn't anyone else need a lift?"

"Nope. They can walk. They don't live far. It's only you and me who live so far out from the centre." He grinned at her, then he twisted round and kissed Flora once, on the mouth, and looked at her intently. Something passed between them but Rayne couldn't tell what. Then he hugged everyone else, saying goodnight. "OK," he said, turning to Rayne. "Let's go."

The rest of the group stood and watched as he led her towards his bike. She didn't look back, but she could feel their eyes on her as he handed her the spare helmet and helped her tighten it under her chin. "You done this before?" he asked.

"Once or twice," she said, all casual. Although it had been a much smaller bike she'd ridden on.

"OK. Lean with me as we go." He got on, and she got on behind him. "Hold on," he said, and kicked the bike into life. She put her arms round his waist. Then they were off, swerving out of the pub car park. He picked up speed and soon Marcle Lees was behind them and they were on pitch-black roads with fields and woods on either side. The only light was from the beam of their headlight. No cars passed them; none came up behind them. They were roaring through blackness and Rayne loved it, loved being this close to him, racing through the night. She held on to him tighter, pressed her face into his shoulder. Then, just as she thought she should look out for the entrance to Morton's Keep, he swerved off the road and into its drive. "Well spotted!" she called, but her words were snatched back, lost behind her.

He juddered to a halt on the forecourt, and turned off the engine. Silence descended. The two spotlit towers glowed behind the ancient stone wall.

"OK?" he asked, twisting round. She nodded, and he got off the bike and she scrambled off after him, pulling off her helmet, laughing, exhilarated.

"That was amazing," she breathed. "God, my legs have gone. . ."

He reached out, got hold of her elbow. "You're not gonna collapse on me, are you?"

"No," she laughed. "God, that was *amazing*—"

"I thought you said you'd been on a bike before?"

"I have. Just – it wasn't such a big one. And you went really fast."

"Well, you got the hang of it. I was turning corners before I knew it, the way you were leaning into them."

"*God*, I'd love to ride it myself," she said fervently.

He didn't answer, just unbuckled his helmet and laid it on the bike seat. There was something deliberate, intent, about the way he did it, the way he freed his face. Rayne couldn't meet his eyes. She was overcome by . . . what? Panic? Exhilaration? He turned to her and put his hand on her arm, then he leaned in close and she didn't pull away, and he kissed her.

It was so unlike the way Damian kissed. Damian jabbed his tongue into her mouth; gnawed at her like she was food; breathed into her face. This was slow, sure, subtle; it waited for her.

She responded, and the kiss went on. Then it was too much, it was overpowering, and she pushed him back. "What would Flora think about this?" she said, making her voice amused.

"She wouldn't like it," he said. "What would your boyfriend think?"

"Damian," she said. "He's miles away." St John laughed, and moved in again, his mouth warm. Rayne kissed him back. *The rules are different out here*, she thought. *I'm free. I can do what I want.*

This time he pulled back first. The glow from the two towers lit his face from the side, made his jaw and cheekbones sharp. "The thing is," he said, "Flora and I split up over a month ago. But we're staying friends. And it's hard. She watches me."

"*Watches* you?" repeated Rayne, tamping down on the glee she'd felt when he said they'd split up. "There's a bit more than that going on, isn't there? She's obviously dead keen on you still . . . and – *Christ*, you're all over each other. . ."

"I'm weaning her off me," he grinned. "Gradually."

"God. *Arrogant*, or what?"

"Well, it's hard. When you're both in this group of friends. . ."

"You're a real tight group, aren't you?"

He smiled. "We like each other."

"And you're the leader."

"What?"

"Oh, come off it. Don't tell me you don't know it. They all . . . *defer* to you. It's like you're the centre. You love it."

He laughed down at her, didn't answer. Then he said, "Someone's watching us."

She spun round, chilled, as much by his calmness as anything. "Where?" she said, scanning the buildings in front of her.

Then she saw the dark shape in the window, just beside the red door.

Chapter
Twenty-two

"It must be Ben Avebury," she whispered. "The gardener. He lives there, in that middle building."

"He doesn't care about us seeing him, does he?" murmured St John. "Nosy old sod."

The shape wasn't moving, just standing there, square in the middle of the window. Rayne felt scared just looking at it. "Maybe he thinks we can't see him," she said, "'cos he hasn't got a light on."

St John lifted his middle finger and raised it at the window with slow deliberation.

"Don't!" cried Rayne, grabbing his arm.

"Why not? He shouldn't be perving on us. Watching us kiss." He laughed. "*Stopping* us kiss." He put his hand on her neck, bent towards her again.

"Don't," she said. "He's really creeping me out. He must've seen you give him the finger, but he's still *standing* there. . ."

"If it's him. Maybe it's a Morton's Keep ghost."

"Shut up."

"What's he like?"

"I don't really know him. I mean – he never talks or anything. Look – I'm gonna go, and you'd better. He's not going to move till we do."

"Give me your number," said St John, pulling a little black and silver phone out of his pocket. "We'll see each other again, won't we?"

The fear she'd felt from the shape at the window disappeared under pleasure. "If you want to," she said. "If you've *really* finished with Flora."

"God, you city types," he laughed. "So hidebound. So convention-bound. Have *you* finished with Damian?"

"Yes. He doesn't know it yet, but I must've done. I've started lying to him all the time – you can't be with someone you lie to, can you?"

St John smirked. "If you say so, Moral One. Come on – what's your number?"

"You can have it," she said, "if you give me yours." And she delved in her bag for her phone.

They exchanged numbers, then he said: "I'll call. Soon." Then he kissed her on the side of her mouth, got on his bike, and roared off.

Ben Avebury – if it *was* Ben Avebury – was still in the window, looking at her. As she stowed her phone away in her bag, her fingers touched the torch she'd brought with her. She pulled it out and switched it on. Then she trained it full on the window. The sudden sight of mouth and nose and eyes, the sudden forming of a face, staring at her – it freaked her out completely. She turned, and ran.

"It was Ben," she told herself as she sped past the steps to the Tudor kitchen, past the tearoom, "of course it was

Ben." But she'd snatched her torch away too fast, it could have been a woman at the window, it could have been anyone, any age. There was no moon and the night was pitchy black apart from the thin bright beam from her torch. She kept it trained shakily on the path ahead of her through the trees. Darkness bulged on either side of her, stirred and rustled all around her – suddenly, she heard a violent scuffle, and three tiny, agonized shrieks. *Something's made a kill*, she thought, and hurried on, heart pounding. The lamp at the top of the steps down into the medieval garden wasn't switched on, and as she trained the torch beam down and took each step with care she had the thought that anyone, anything could be creeping up on her out of the night and she wouldn't see. . . *Damian would have seen her home safe. Damian was more of a gentleman than St John, despite his snobby name.*

Breathing fast, terrified, she ran through the garden, between the long beds with their tall, waving plants. The darkness seemed to seethe around her, full of life and death. She reached the door of the Old Sty and pushed the key into the lock, desperate to look over her shoulder but making herself focus on unlocking the door. Then she burst inside, slammed the door shut, and locked it behind her.

The light was on; the room was around her, familiar and safe. She started laughing at how scared she'd been.

Two beeps from her bag told her she had a text. She pulled out her phone. It was from St John, and it said: *Sleep well.*

She smiled, and turned her phone off.

Chapter
Twenty-three

When Rayne turned up at the tearoom the next day, Becky was coming out of it, carrying her large tray. "I saw you there last night!" she squawked. "At The King's Head! I couldn't *believe* it when I saw you there with St John Arlington!"

Rayne laughed, taken aback. "I didn't see you," she said.

"We were at the back, we got there late. We saw St John and Flora and that lot; all my mates were wondering who the new recruit was. They couldn't believe it when I said you were working here!"

"Why didn't you come over to say hello?"

"Are you *joking*?" Becky let go of one side of the tray and dropped it down so it rested on the floor. "None of us can stand them . . . they're weird, that lot."

"Yeah? I thought they were great. Really interesting. Different."

"Oh, they're that all right." Animosity was crackling between them. "How d'you meet them?"

"Why d'you think they're weird?" countered Rayne.

Becky shrugged. "They just *are*. That whole group is.

They're dead cliquey, and so *up* themselves – they think they're better than everyone else. Seriously, they never even *talk* to anyone else."

Rayne smiled to herself. They'd talked to *her*.

"I used to know Amelia really well," Becky went on, "she was OK till she got in with that lot, now she's all superior and full of how good she's looking and she can't be bothered with me. Well, I can't be bothered with her, either. Did you like the band?"

"Yeah, they were good."

"At least it was something to do. It's so dead here, there's never anything on."

Mrs Driver appeared in the doorway. "Oh, hello, Rayne dear," she said.

"Rayne dear," sniggered Becky. "*Reindeer.*"

"Don't be silly, Becky. Rayne – I hope you're still all right for tomorrow night? Mr Stuart's grand dinner in the Old Stone Hall?"

"Sure," said Rayne. "I've told my boyfriend I won't be back." She liked mentioning *her boyfriend* in front of Becky. But she hadn't told him anything of the sort. Damian fully expected to see her back at Cramphurst Estate by eight o'clock Friday – he'd texted her there was a party on. But he seemed so far away from her now – he seemed unreal. She knew she had to finish with him, but she couldn't face it, not yet. Maybe she'd just tell him she was feeling ill, and go back on Saturday morning. . .

"We've got sixteen guests coming," Mrs Driver went on, "it's going to be quite a do. We'll need both of you to be on your top form."

"Oh," said Rayne, turning to Becky, "are you waitressing too?"

"Ye-*ah*," said Becky, a touch indignantly. "I've done it loads of times before. Well – three times or so at least."

"What happens at these dinners?"

"Not a lot. Mr Stuart sits at the head and Ms Barton sits at the other end and he tells stories about his childhood here and Ms Barton fills everyone in about the history. . ."

"It all gets quite atmospheric," added Mrs Driver. "Or so I'm told. I've never actually *experienced* one, just dashed in and out with the food."

"Is that what people come for?" asked Rayne. "The atmosphere?"

"That," said Mrs Driver, "and to eat at the Black Prince's table . . . and to meet other well-to-do people from the area . . . it gives everyone a sense of a shared past, I suppose. And they come for the wine and the food, too, of course. This wonderful pair of ladies from the town always do it – their specialty is authentic historical cooking, although I think they mix the centuries up a bit. I know they're doing pheasant tomorrow, there's over a dozen hanging out the back."

Rayne pulled a face.

"I know," said Becky. "It's gross."

"You'll make quite a nice bit extra, dear," Mrs Driver went on. "We charge an arm and a leg for the meal, so I can afford to pay you both a decent rate."

"And we get tips," said Becky. "We split those."

"Now, Becky – you're coming at seven, aren't you?" asked Mrs Driver.

Becky nodded.

"Rayne, can you start earlier – say six o'clock?"

"Sure. No problem."

"The guests arrive at seven-thirty but first we need to light the fire, lay the table, get the candles sorted out. . ."

"What do I wear?"

"Don't wear heels," said Becky. "You'll go arse over tit on the stone floor, it's dead uneven."

"Whatever you like, dear," said Mrs Driver. "As long as it's . . . you know . . . in keeping."

"Great," said Rayne, "I'm looking forward to it."

At five past six that Friday, Rayne, carrying a pile of snowy, starched napkins, pulled back the heavy green curtains that led from the kitchen corridor into the Great Hall. She was wearing a long, swishy black skirt, low-heeled boots and a rust-coloured top, and she'd made her eyes up dramatically. A quick check in the full-length mirror in the tearoom ladies' told her she looked gorgeous and slightly sinister, which she felt was perfect for the grand dinner. Mrs Driver had exclaimed in approval when she'd seen her.

The fact that St John had just texted her added to her attractiveness. She was crackling, glowing.

She'd heard nothing from him all yesterday, and she hadn't contacted him. But she kept thinking about him. She'd dwelt on his dark brown eyes and the way he looked at her; his long legs and elegant profile. She'd dwelt on the amazing way he kissed. There was a quiet power about him that she found both intriguing and exciting.

He'd asked if she wanted to meet up tomorrow. She'd replied yes – where? He'd said he'd pick her up on the bike at eight, and they'd go to an old country pub he knew, and eat. It sounded wonderful.

Rayne crossed the Great Hall, smiling to herself, and noticed that the third door, the one tucked in beside the fireplace, was open. She knew it led to the library, and she was suddenly curious to see it – she'd missed that bit of the tour. She went over and peered round the door. A narrow, curving corridor with arrow-slit windows led away from it. She started down it, telling herself she'd just have a quick look, rounded a corner – and froze.

A tall man in a faded tweed jacket was standing there in the light from one of the narrow windows, staring intently at an old wood-framed painting. He turned, beaming, and said, "Are you the new girl?"

"I . . . I think so," she breathed. "Rayne Peters."

He extended a slender, sandy-coloured hand, and, nervously, clutching the napkins to her middle, she stuck out hers. He took it and lifted it up and down a couple of times. "Harry Stuart," he announced. "I've been hearing wonderful things about you from Mrs Driver." Then he turned back to the portrait and said, "Just been having a few words with Sir Philip Musgrave. He likes to come to the little concerts we hold in the library, you know."

Rayne felt the back of her neck prickle. She shifted her gaze uneasily from Mr Stuart to the man in the portrait.

"Several people say they've seen him, sitting at the back," Mr Stuart went on. "A string quartet is his favourite, he's not so keen on singing. . ."

Sir Philip Musgrave was dressed in seventeenth-century clothes and he looked thin, ill even, but the portrait was eerily luminous. His red-rimmed eyes looked alert and knowing.

"Have *you* ever seen him?" she asked.

"No. But then I've never seen any of the damn ghosts that are supposed to haunt this place. Once, when I was a child. . ."

"Yes?" she prompted. They were both staring at the portrait as they spoke.

"I heard something. Dancing. Like twenty pairs of feet, all in unison, tapping out a rhythm . . . but the strange thing is. . ."

Rayne turned to look at him. "Yes?"

"Oh, I was a fey boy, a fanciful boy – who wouldn't be, brought up in this godforsaken old place. But I can still remember the feeling. It was . . . *horror*. Not because I thought they were ghosts, I was always looking for ghosts. I'd've liked a ghost for a pal, I was so damn lonely out of term time. It was just – a *terrible* feeling that came over me, absolute dread."

"Are you sure it was *dancing* you heard?"

"Absolutely sure. Rum, wasn't it? Dancing's supposed to be happy. My mother said I had flu brewing and put me to bed. She was probably right. So! Have you seen the library?"

"Not yet. Actually—" Rayne was suddenly overcome by not wanting to go any further down the narrow stone corridor. "I'd better go back. I'd better go and get the table laid."

"Ah. You're helping serve tonight, are you?"

"Yes."

"Good girl. I hope it's not too tedious for you. It's awful hokum, really, but it pays the bills. And I like to think the Old Stone Hall's still used . . . as it used to be, you know."

Rayne smiled. "Not totally as it used to be, I hope."

"What? Oh – the death trials! No, ha ha. Not totally, no. Well, goodbye, Rayne. See you tonight. And look in on the library any time you want, won't you? There's some good books in there."

Rayne, still smiling awkwardly, backed away, and went straight to the Old Stone Hall.

The chill that had beset her when she'd stepped into the hall that first time, on the tour, settled round her shoulders like a cold cat. There was such ancient heaviness in there, the air was thick and clotted with it – she felt like a wisp of smoke drifting through. She glanced behind her at the wooden gallery, imagined all the brave young rebels who'd stood there just minutes before having their necks broken by a rope in the yard. . .

"What kind of weirdo wants to *eat* in here," she thought, and headed resolutely for the great stone table. Extra chairs had been positioned round it; someone had placed trays of exquisite glasses and bundles of cutlery on top. Earlier, Mrs Driver had run through with her how to serve and the strict order that the cutlery was to be laid out. She'd mentioned that they never used a tablecloth because part of the thrill was to eat straight on top of the stone.

Rayne set to work, laying out the knives, forks, spoons and glasses for the five courses they were to have. A dull silver candelabra made of coiled serpents holding candles in their mouths was the centrepiece; she'd suggested flowers, too, but Mrs Driver said, rather sharply, that they were never used.

When she'd finished arranging everything she stood back to admire it. "Posh or *what*?" she breathed. It was stunning. And despite the harshness of the stone table, it had a decadent feel – it looked like the setting for a vampire feast.

The light was almost gone from the hall.

"I've got the kindling, and a few logs."

Rayne looked up, startled. Ben Avebury had come silently through the door, carrying a huge wickerwork basket, full of logs and twigs, on his sinewy shoulder. It hit her that it was the first time she'd heard him speak since the day of her interview – he had a pleasant-sounding voice, soft and deep. "We want to start the fire sharpish," he said. "It takes well over an hour for this place to heat up."

"I can't imagine it ever getting warm," she answered.

"Well, it never gets cosy, put it that way. But a good log fire takes the chill off. I'll get it going for you, if you like."

"I can light a fire," she replied, walking over towards the massive fireplace.

"I'm sure you can." Ben tipped out kindling into the grate. "But you don't want to mess your outfit up." He pulled out a box of matches from his back pocket, struck one, and applied it to the thin, dry twigs. When they sparked into life he laid three logs on top. Rayne watched as the flames licked upwards, sparking light on to the two weird goat-men who held up the great mantelpiece. "That's gorgeous," she murmured.

"Like fire, do you?" he said, and turned to look at her for the first time. She met his gaze uneasily – he had piercing blue eyes, despite his age. There was something frightening about them. For a moment she thought he was going to say something about Wednesday night, when he'd watched her from the window – maybe come out with an excuse about wanting to check she'd got back safe.

But he didn't. He just said, "I'll get some more logs in. Enough for the evening," and stamped off.

Chapter
Twenty-four

It was eight-thirty. Mr Stuart, looking dignified in a dinner jacket, and Ms Barton, looking uncomfortable in an ugly green evening dress and dangling earrings, had welcomed all the guests. They'd been plied with champagne and canapés, seated round the massive table, and fed chestnut-and-mushroom soup. Now Rayne, Becky and Mrs Driver were carrying through little dishes of grilled scallops, six to a tray. It was all going perfectly to plan. "They love you, dear," Mrs Driver whispered to Rayne as they hurried back down the long corridor to the kitchen. "You look so lovely, and you *move* so well! Have you studied dancing?"

Rayne smiled and shook her head, pleased by the compliment. One of the sports teachers at her old school had told her she was graceful; no one else, she thought, had ever noticed.

Certainly not Damian. She was still simmering from the row they'd had. After she'd finished getting the Old Stone Hall ready, she'd texted him: *babe feeling so ill b home 2moro*. Even though she knew she wouldn't be home tomorrow, because she was going out with St John. She kept thinking of getting on his bike again, driving to the old pub, sitting close in a secluded corner. . . On Saturday, she planned to tell Damian she was still ill.

Damian, though, had phoned her straight back. "What about the *party?*" he'd snarled. "I don't wanna go on my own. I wanna go with you on my arm."

"On your *arm?*" she'd snapped. "What am I, a falcon?"

"*What?* Where d'you get that from?"

"I – I dunno—"

"You been at that old place too long. It's making you weird. Now look – you *promised*—"

"I did not. Day, I'm *ill*. Don't you care about that?"

"What's wrong with you?"

"I've got a really bad headache. I've taken aspirin, they won't shift it."

"For Christ's sake, it's only a headache. It'll be better by the time you get here."

"It's a really long journey – I don't wanna do it, not tonight."

"If it's too far for you to come you shouldn't be bloody working there!"

"*Don't you tell me what I should or shouldn't*—" Her phone went dead. He'd cut her off. She was filled with a kind of angry exultation that *he'd* been the one that had stopped their conversation. It made it easier.

And now her anger was buoying her up, adding to her excitement. She'd finish with him, finish the ridiculous double life she was leading, stop all her lying, cut her old ties, float free here . . . have something absolutely different with St John.

117

She could do anything she chose, anything she wanted. She was free.

The windows in the Old Stone Hall were black now, apart from the wavering candles reflected in them. As well as the great serpentine candelabra in the centre of the table, there were smaller candles placed all along it, one to each person, and four huge standing candelabras in the corners of the room. The only light in the room was from these, and the great roaring fire. There was no artificial light at all.

Rayne was working hard, serving, clearing, adding logs to the fire, and all the time she worked she was amazed by the sheer luxury of the event. She felt she was pulling off some kind of a trick, being there in the hall – someone would find her out, find out this wasn't her world – they'd laugh at her. But it didn't happen.

The guests were on the pheasant, their third course; they were also on their fourth or fifth glass of wine. People who'd been content to listen to Mr Stuart and Ms Barton began to ask questions; voices grew louder. A red-faced man to Ms Barton's left grinned at her and said, "All right, so we've heard all about the Black Prince and the trials in here – all good stuff. But what about more recent history?"

"Well . . ." began Ms Barton. "Morton's Keep dwindled in political importance over the last few centuries, it—"

"Oh come on. You know what I'm talking about. What about those *dinners* they'd have here . . . the parties? You know . . . the ones that caused a big scandal at the time?"

"Yes," said a woman wearing large gold earrings. She had a deep, confident voice. "I heard Morton's Keep had its very own little hellfire club. Much naughtiness and goings-on, hmm?"

Mr Stuart was staring fixedly at the plate in front of him. Then he cleared his throat and said, "Something of that sort went on, we believe. In the late eighteenth century Morton's Keep became a sort of centre for certain . . . er, wild parties. There's no *written* evidence, of course. Only evidence based on rumour."

"Rumour, good old rumour," boomed the red-faced man. "What did rumour say?"

"Oh, well – there were tales of the usual debauchery," said Mr Stuart, looking acutely uncomfortable. "You know. Wine, women and . . . er, song. . ."

"Oh, surely more than *that*!"

"I'd heard there were *abductions*," said the confident woman. "But not from round here, or there'd have been trouble. They crossed the border and got girls from Wales. . ."

"And I'd heard," said a thin man at the end of the table who'd barely spoken up till now, "that all rumours, no matter how vile, were mild compared to what actually went on. The lord of the manor here was at the centre of it, the core . . . I forget his name, do you know it, Mr Stuart?"

"No," said Mr Stuart, shortly. "Morton's Keep changed hands rather frequently in the eighteenth century. I have no idea who you're talking about."

"It went on for years, here. They made a cult of cruelty and amorality."

"Oh, all salacious supposition. Honestly!" spluttered Mr Stuart.

There was a sudden flurry of eating; plates were emptied, knives and forks were laid down. None of the diners wanted to be accused of grubby, tabloid-type interest in the nasty side of life. A blonde woman at the far end said, "Well, I don't listen to rumour. What about all that nonsense a few years back about the local fire-festival people being a cover for devil worship?"

Rayne thought of the eleven black candle stubs half-hidden by grass. She drew nearer to the table with her bottle of red wine, and started refilling glasses.

"Absolute nonsense and mischief-making," the blonde woman went on. "People with not enough to do making up silly stories."

The confident woman was laughing. "Oh, yes – I remember all the fuss there was about that. Stories of rituals in the woods and so on. Well, they are a slightly *strange* lot, that fire group, but I'm sure they're harmless. A little country town like ours breeds all kinds of stories. . ."

"It's all this modern emphasis on paganism," said the red-faced man. "What used to be a lively bit of local tradition turns into some sort of dark ritual. . ."

"Surely you know," said Ms Barton, a touch acidly, "that what you call *a lively bit of local tradition* almost always has its roots in paganism? All around the country old rituals are carried out that once used to have powerful pagan significance for those involved. . ."

"Oh, going back hundreds and hundreds of years, maybe," he said, comfortably. "But it's just a bit of fun now."

"I disagree. I think people take part in it for more than

fun – I think the past still resonates for them, they have a deep, perhaps buried belief in the old meanings of the rituals. . ."

"You've lost me, I'm afraid, dear." He beamed across at Ms Barton, who huffed, and slammed her fork down.

"Well, I think we can clear our local fire group of any nefarious doings," said Mr Stuart, hastily. "As a matter of fact, they're pitching up at our Apple Fair next month. They'll be Morris dancing."

"There – you see?" cried the blonde woman, triumphantly. "You can't be a Morris dancer and be up to no good – it's too silly for words!"

"Actually," began Ms Barton, "Morris dancing too has its roots in paganism—"

But she was silenced by a look from Mr Stuart, who then signalled to Rayne and Becky to start clearing the plates, even though a couple of diners hadn't finally put down their knives and forks yet.

The girls hurried to the kitchen with their heavy piles of plates. "What d'you make of all their chat then, ay?" asked Becky. There was a sly edge to her voice.

"Creepy. Trying to get my head round it. . ."

"I wouldn't bother. Too freaky. Trust me, the *stories* about this place . . . there's been loads of murders here, you know. Absolutely *loads*."

"Er – centuries ago? There were murders everywhere, centuries ago."

"But not like here."

"Becky, do me a favour and shut up?"

Becky laughed, and they reached the kitchen. Mrs

Driver and the two wonderful lady cooks had an air of triumph and relief about them, as they lined up perfect little blackberry-topped tarts on trays. "Aren't they a picture?" cooed Mrs Driver. "We've saved a couple for you two. For when it's over."

"Wonderful," said Rayne. "I'm starving."

"Oh, well, there'll be lots of leftovers! How's it going in there?"

"Good. They're all talking about local history."

Mrs Driver's face seemed to close down a little. "It's part of the appeal, I suppose," she said. Then she handed Rayne a tray, and another to Becky, and they both set off for the Old Stone Hall again.

The blackberry tarts had been devoured; the grand meal was coming to a close. Rayne was left alone in attendance as a sumptuous cheese board – "all local cheeses!" as Mr Stuart proudly announced – was handed round, and port was poured. The candles had burnt right down – some of them were guttering, soon to go out. The fire was dying. Rayne put another log on top, thinking it would be the last, and turned back to the table to hear the thin man saying, "I've remembered the name."

"What name?" asked Mr Stuart, coldly.

"The name of the lord of the manor who was at the centre of all the scandal and rumours. It was Lingwall. Sir Simeon Lingwall."

There was a strange shift in the hall. Rayne, staring, saw that no one was smiling; one of the women darted a nervous glance at the black windows.

Mr Stuart cleared his throat. "It rings a vague bell, that name," he said, "but I'm not familiar with it. As I said, this old place has changed hands so many times. . ."

"They still live here, don't they, the Lingwall family?" said the blonde woman. "I've heard they never left the area."

"Well, I've never heard of that name," said the red-faced man, "and I've lived here seventeen years. . ."

"The name might have died out, through only the women surviving," said the confident woman. "That often happens."

Mr Stuart got abruptly to his feet, port glass in hand. "May I propose a toast," he said, "to a wonderful evening and wonderful guests. Keeping the old traditions of Morton's Keep alive. We do hope you'll join us again for another of these superb meals. Menus can be checked on our website, or by calling the mansion house. Now, on your way out, I do hope you'll pick up a leaflet about our Apple Fair and join us on that merry occasion. . ."

People were taking the hint, draining their glasses, dropping their napkins back on the table. "He hasn't offered them coffee and chocolates," Rayne thought, anxiously. "It's all laid out in the kitchen . . . the cooks'll be livid. . ." She tried to catch his attention, but he wouldn't meet her eye.

It hit her that he wouldn't meet anyone's eye.

Chapter
Twenty-five

Rayne had the most wonderful lie-in the next morning. She woke at eight as usual, listened to the birds singing for a little while, then went back to sleep. She woke again around nine, made herself a cup of tea, and took it back to bed. Then she dozed off and on until she got out of bed around eleven and made herself some toast with a sliced apple.

What a weird night it had been. All that stuff about Morton's Keep's wicked past, and the devil-worshipping fire group, and . . . what was his name? Sir Simeon Lingwall. With a grimace she remembered the way the room had shifted when his name had been spoken – but then the whole night had been an exercise in stoking up creepiness. Mr Stuart probably hoped everyone would sign up for one of his ghost-hunting sessions afterwards. It had been worth it, though. She'd pocketed almost thirty pounds in tips. People had dropped notes and coins on the table as they left – the red-faced man had leeringly pressed ten pounds into her hand. She'd collected it all up and taken it through to the kitchen and Becky had divided it up greedily and scrupulously between them.

She wasn't quite sure what to make of Becky. Working alongside each other, they'd started getting on better – but then at the end of the night Becky had had trouble ordering a cab and Mrs Driver had suggested she stayed in the other room in the Sty and she'd practically *screamed*, just at the idea of it.

She was a bit flaky, that was clear. St John and his friends were more her sort.

She smiled to herself. She'd have fun telling them about the night. Maybe it would give Amelia and Petra something for their *Hidden History* website.

She planned to spend the day just walking, just ... *being*. It was becoming addictive, this simple wasting of time. And the weird thing was it felt like *waste* was the last thing it was about.

The weather was fine. She packed a sandwich, a couple of chocolate biscuits and a bottle of water into a tiny backpack, and started out. When she got to the mansion boundaries she found a little public footpath running away from Marcle Lees, and set off on that.

The knowledge that she was meeting St John later freed her to enjoy the space and solitude. She walked for hours, through the open countryside and alongside woods, passing dog walkers and ramblers, stopping when she felt like it for a break. When she'd eaten her food and begun to feel hungry again, she turned back. It dawned on her that she'd be knackered for the evening, that she'd been daft to walk so far. Then, in the distance, across some fields towards the right, she saw what was unmistakably the two towers of Morton's Keep. The footpath she was on would take her the long way back – it would be much quicker to cut straight across the fields.

She studied the field she'd have to cross. It was full of corn stubble, nothing else, no sheep or cows. A wide wooden gate was just ahead of her, chained shut with a padlock. She looked around to check she was alone, and clambered over the bars.

She crossed three fields without trouble, climbing over a gate each time, seeing no one, always keeping the two towers in sight. Then she crossed into a muddy meadow of patchy green grass. It sloped upwards, and it had some kind of barn in the middle of it. The towers looked very close now. She hurried across the grass . . .

. . . and out of the barn walked an enormous beast. A Shire horse, a carthorse, its broad back easily eight feet high, its great head much higher. . .

Another had followed it out of the barn. Then another. Three carthorses, all heading slowly, deliberately for her.

She felt like she'd turned liquid with fear, like she could just run into the grass and soak away in terror. The horses lumbered on towards her. She was a tiny doll in their path.

They were unreal, alien, too huge to exist. She couldn't run, couldn't move. They came right up close – and parted, swerved gently by her, two on one side, one on the other, great fringed feet the size of dustbin lids. Making the ground move beneath her. They lowered their massive heads like they were greeting her, and she thought: "They're checking to see if I've got food."

She started walking slowly towards the towers, and the

great horses came with her. One plodded right behind her – two more to her side. An escort of giants. The air around her was charged, transformed, by their presence.

After a moment or so, she knew she had absolutely nothing to fear from them. After a moment or so, she was laughing out loud, exulting.

Chapter Twenty-six

When she got back to the Sty, still high from the Shire horses, there were still nearly four hours to go till St John arrived to take her out. She ate a peanut butter sandwich, then decided to do her washing, even though she didn't really have enough to fill a machine. And while she was waiting for it to finish, she thought, she'd go to the mansion library. Mr Stuart had invited her to, hadn't he? She could see if there were any books worth reading – maybe there'd be some on the history of the place, and she could check out old Simeon Lingwall and his debauched parties.

She collected her dirty clothes together, shoved them in a bag. Then she got the keys from the cutlery drawer and went over to the Tudor kitchen. No one was around; the silence seemed heavy and ominous to her, so different to the lovely silence of the woods. It was modern and ordinary in the utility room, but even so, as she loaded the washing machine, she kept wanting to look over her shoulder.

She left the kitchen, walked resolutely down the stone-flagged corridor towards the Great Hall, and went through the heavy green curtains. She could hear the tick, ticking of the one-handed Dutch clock on the upper landing as she crossed to the library door; the plaster cherubs over the fireplace smirked down at her. She turned the handle and stepped into the corridor.

The late low sun was coming in through the arrow-slit windows; as she went along she passed through bands of light, bands of darkness. The portrait of Sir Philip Musgrave, who liked to sit in on the concerts, was all lit up by a shaft of sun; it hit her that maybe when his ghost walked, the picture frame would be empty. Spooked, she hurried past, eyes on the ground, and reached the second library door.

She wasn't prepared for how beautiful the room was. It was large and perfectly proportioned, with grand latticed windows. Bookshelves lined the walls, floor to ceiling, interspersed with strips of dark oak panelling. On every strip there was an ornate, diamond-shaped mirror with candle holders and cascades of teardrop-shaped candelabra glass. Rayne thought they were gorgeous; they'd look even more beautiful alight. Two long sofas were drawn up either side of the fireplace; a large piano stood in the corner, by the door. The scale of it was immense and yet it was human-sized, too. You could *be* in here.

Rayne started to look at the book titles. Sets of Shakespeare; sets of Dickens. Autobigraphies; novels by Thomas Hardy and Jane Austen, all leather bound. Then she came across some books about military history and tucked beside them, a small battered book called *Morton's Keep – The Story of a Herefordshire Manor*. She picked it up and went over to a low couch underneath the window. There was still just enough light to read by. On an impulse, she reached out to the old-fashioned bronze bolt on the casement window, unscrewed it, and opened the window a little. Delicious evening air came in, blowing away the musty smell of the library. She sat down on the couch, and opened the book.

It was all very much what she knew already about the place and its turbulent history – the trials and hangings, young Lord Fulke dying in front of the fire, the priest being hacked down by soldiers. It mentioned ghosts quite a bit; Rayne felt it had one eye firmly on the tourist market. Then she remembered the notorious Simeon Lingwall. She turned to the extensive index at the back of the book. Simeon Lingwall wasn't listed.

She looked up. The library door was opening slowly. She watched, heart thumping – and breathed in relief as Mrs Driver came round the door.

"Oh, it's you, dear!" the housekeeper exclaimed. "I was doing my evening check on everything, and I saw that the door to library corridor was open. . ." She seemed nervous. She had one hand up on her chest, as though to calm her breathing.

"It's OK me being in here, isn't it?" asked Rayne. "Mr Stuart said I could look at the books. . ." Instinctively, she kept her hand over the title of the book on her lap.

"Of course it is, dear. Just – it's better to keep those windows closed. The ones on the ground floor, we always keep them shut. Because of the insurance, you know."

"But surely when I'm in here it's all right?"

"As long as you remember to lock it after you leave, dear. A few months back, one of the lower windows was

130

left open and . . . and the insurance was very difficult about it."

"Stuff was stolen?"

"Damaged. There was damage done." Mrs Driver seemed agitated just at the memory.

"What was it," Rayne persisted, "vandals?"

"Yes. Vandals."

"But they didn't steal anything?"

"No. Just remember to lock it, all right?" Rayne nodded, and Mrs Driver left. And a thought floated into Rayne's mind, clear as a whisper: *She isn't telling you the truth.*

Then she remembered how upset Mrs Driver had been after her first night here, because she'd forgotten to give her the key to the Sty. What had she said? She could almost hear her say it now, it had spooked her so. "*Lock your door,* dear. Always lock your door at night."

Rayne looked up at the casement window. The panes of glass were dimming as the light faded; the library was growing gloomy, shrouded in shadows. She checked her watch. It was ten to seven – she had to collect her laundry, get herself ready to go out with St John.

She stood up, drew the window closed, and locked it. Then she put the book back on the shelf and left the library, shutting the door loudly behind her.

Chapter
Twenty-seven

The pub that St John took her to was called The Green Lady. It was a beautiful old unspoilt tavern whose ceiling was so low in parts that St John's head brushed against it. They found a table for two wedged behind an ancient oak support-beam and the bar, and sat facing each other.

There was a candle on the table, in a little glass jar; it glinted on their drinks. Rayne looked across at St John, all clenched up with excitement. He looked even better than she remembered. But she wasn't intimidated by this, quite the opposite – she felt confident, reckless. She was going to have *fun*, she told herself. That's all.

"Reckon this is better than your London pubs, then?" he asked, smiling. His teeth, Rayne thought, were almost perfect. White and even and strong.

"It's different, definitely. Why the Green Lady? I've heard of loads of Green Man pubs, but never the Green Lady. . ."

He shrugged. "No idea."

"Maybe she's the Green Man's missus." She looked around her. "Anything like this would've been tarted up ages ago, in London. I like it. I like the way there's young people, and old people, and posh people, and people just in their work clothes, all mixed up together."

"That's because of the food here. It's local stuff, all cooked on the premises. Good enough to tempt the *posh* people, as you call them – they feel smug they've discovered it."

"Do you feel smug?"

"Very," he grinned.

"It's certainly off the beaten track."

It had taken them twenty minutes to get there. The last five had practically been along a farm track. Rayne's jeans, bought just before she left home, had got a bit mud-splattered, but she didn't care. She felt fantastic; she felt she looked fantastic.

They were leaning towards each other across the table, hands almost touching. St John picked up her arm by the wrist, looking at it, and said, "You've still got your summer tan."

"Are you *joking*?"

"What?"

"That's the colour of my skin. I'm mixed race. Can't you tell?"

"Oh – right. Sorry." He let go of her arm.

"What you sorry about? You think it's an insult?"

"No, of course not. I think – I think you look gorgeous."

"Hm. What are you, pure-bred Anglo-Saxon?"

"Yes, actually. Borderline aristocratic."

"Hm. That explains the name."

"My family – it's really old. We've lived round here for centuries."

133

"And you think that gives you some kind of advantage, do you?"

There was a pause, then he said, "In a way, yes."

It was so exactly not what she'd been expecting him to say that she found it exciting. Challenging.

"In *what* way, Mr Pure-Bred?" she demanded.

"Just – there's so much change and intermixing and moving about now, I think it's good to know where your roots are. I think you can get a lot out of – staying put."

"So you don't want to travel?"

"Sure, I do travel. I go abroad all the time. But I know what it is I'm coming back to, and I like that. That's all." Then he laughed, and said, "Stop looking so indignant. God, let's change the subject. What have you been up to since I saw you?"

She laughed back at him, and told him about the lavish Morton's Keep dinner, the formal way she had to serve, the candles and the wine and the food. As she spoke he leant closer across the table, listening, asking the odd question . . . it was very flattering. Damian had never focused on her like this. "All the guests, though," she said, "they wanted all the gruesome history of the place. It creeped me out. I'm starting to think—"

"What?" he asked. On the table, his hand was touching hers.

"I dunno. There's something weird about the house. I bet there *are* ghosts. Or something. This girl Becky, she was there last night serving with me – she comes to the tearoom sometimes to deliver quiches her mum makes—"

"Oh, God. Becky Brooks?"

134

"Yeah, that's her! She said she knew you lot."

"I bet she did. Slagging us off, was she?"

"A bit. She said you were this cliquey little group and you all thought you were better than everyone else."

St John smiled. "Well – I suppose we're pretty selective about who we spend our time with, but what's wrong with that? I know why she's pissed off with us, though. She tried to pull Marcus once and *naturally*, he wasn't interested."

"She didn't mention that."

"She wouldn't."

"She said she knew Amelia quite well."

"Hm. Amelia might disagree."

There was a pause. St John was looking steadily at her, still smiling. They both knew the real communication between them had nothing to do with words. She met his gaze for as long as she could, then she picked up her glass and said, "*Anyway*, Becky's always going on about how creepy the house is, how there's all these awful stories about it. I thought she was just winding me up, but last night, she couldn't get a cab home – and she was really scared at the thought of having to spend the night in the Sty with me. I mean – *genuinely* scared."

"Rayne – Becky's an ignorant little tart. Why would you waste even five seconds worrying about what she says?"

"OK. Maybe. But what about the people at the dinner . . . wanting to hear all the grisly stories?"

"Because people like a scare, that's all! It titillates them! Come on, Rayne, you're too intelligent to let that kind of stuff get to you." He sat back, took a sip of the dark-red

135

wine he'd ordered. "Morton's Keep is a fine old house. You're lucky to be living there."

"You think?"

"Yes! It's special. I'd love to see round it again. I haven't been there since . . . God, I must've been ten or something."

"Go on one of their tours. They're easy enough to book."

"Yeah, but they cost money. And you have to listen to a load of drivel." He leaned towards her again. "Can't you show me round?"

"Sure," she shrugged. "If you want to see it."

"Would you have to clear it with anyone first?"

"No. I've got the keys to the kitchen."

He grinned, got to his feet, and pulled a couple of menu cards from the bar. "Let's eat," he said.

They both ordered sausages with "leeky mashed potato". The sausages were delicious, like no sausages Rayne had ever tasted before, and the leeks were vibrant with flavour. "See what I mean?" said St John. "Real food."

As the evening went on, Rayne's pleasure and excitement increased. She felt she was feasting on the look of him; his face, his throat and shoulders, his hands. They were getting on brilliantly – really connecting. He made his glass of wine last, interspersed with icy water. He told her he wanted to get her home safe on his bike along the dark country roads. "And you can start the tour," he added, meaningfully, "by showing me your Sty. Yeah?"

She looked across at him, blood racing. "Maybe," she said.

Then the pub door opened and a whole crowd of men came in, at least a dozen of them, all different ages. "Oh, *Christ*," groaned St John. "I didn't think *they* came here."

"Who are they?" asked Rayne.

People all over the pub were greeting the men like celebrities; the landlord started pulling pint after pint and lining them up on the bar.

"It's the local *fire festival group*," sneered St John. "They'll have been having one of their meetings, getting ready for the marches."

"Marches?"

"It's big in autumn here. They parade up and down with flaming torches, light bonfires, let off fireworks—"

"Sounds like fun."

"If you're *ten* it is! But they take it so seriously. They're absolute wankers."

"Fire festival . . . someone was talking about them last night."

"Yeah? What did they say?"

"That they're weirdos. Something about . . . devil worship in the woods?"

He laughed. "That would be about right."

"You are *joking*? They don't really do that stuff, do they?"

"Well, there're some woods near here – we passed them on the way, actually. They're called Fleet Woods and they have a weird reputation. For witches, and pagan rituals and the like . . . it goes back centuries. Not many people like to walk in them, especially after dark. And the fire festival folk have been spotted going into them many times. . ."

"What," scoffed Rayne, "sacrificing to the devil?"

"Something like that."

"Oh, come on. You can't—" She broke off. One of the men had moved away from the group, and was standing right next to their table.

He was young, not much older than St John. He was broad-shouldered, well-muscled on his chest and his arms. He would have been good-looking if he wasn't scowling. "What you doing here?" he growled.

"I'm having a meal," said St John, "with a friend. Do you mind?"

The boy turned to Rayne and said, "You've got strange tastes."

St John got to his feet. "Why don't you just clear off, Ethan," he said. "I didn't know you lot would be here tonight."

"Well, now you do know," said the boy. "Saturday nights from now on." There was a silence. Something passed between them, something intensely hostile. Then Ethan turned away, barging St John in the shoulder as he did so. St John sat down, pretending it hadn't happened.

But it had.

"Who the *hell* was *that*?" hissed Rayne.

"Ethan Sands," he muttered.

"How d'you know him? Do you go to school with him?"

"Are you *joking*? I go to the Abbey. He goes to the comprehensive dump in the next town. This is a small place. You get to know *everyone*."

Rayne looked over at the bar, where the fire festival crew were gathered. "There's quite a few young guys in the group. What on earth attracts them?"

"Oh, they love it. Getting to rampage through the town with torches, getting to set fires everywhere . . . 'legalized arson', my father calls it. And the devil worship in the woods, of course."

Something slotted into place in Rayne's mind. "I think I've been warned about them," she said.

St John leaned towards her. "Who by?"

"The housekeeper, Mrs Driver. Oh, nothing direct. It's like she's not exactly sure what's going on herself. But she forgot to give me the key to the Sty the first night I was there, and nearly freaked about it the next day. She went on and on about locking my door at night. And earlier today – I was in the library – she went into one about locking the windows because there'd been *vandals* breaking in. . ."

"Yeah, that sounds like them," said St John. "Oh, don't look so scared. They probably just set off a brace of bangers in the fireplace. She say anything about people building fires in the woods?"

"No," said Rayne. She was thinking about the eleven black candles burnt down to stubs in the gloomy garden by the dovecote. She didn't want to mention them.

They finished their drinks and left – St John seemed eager to get away. As they walked out he gave the fire festival men – especially Ethan Sands – a very wide berth.

St John kicked the pub door shut behind them, and took hold of Rayne's hand. They walked across the car park to where they'd left the motorbike. "How's Flora?" Rayne asked.

"She's fine. I mean – I haven't spoken to her for a few days."

"So she doesn't know you're seeing me tonight?"

He shrugged, then he put his arm round her shoulder, and pulled her to him. "I thought it would be cruel to tell her."

"Not beautiful as well then?"

"What?" He was laughing down at her, their mouths were close.

"*Beauty is Cruel, Cruelty is Beautiful* . . . God, don't you know what's on Amelia and Petra's wacko website?"

"Oh, God – all their stuff. No, I don't."

"I thought of them, last night. When the guests were plugging poor old Mr Stuart for details of the *hidden history* of Morton's Keep."

"Really? What kind of things?"

"They reckoned it had been the scene of wild parties and debauchery . . . one man was hinting at a sick cult thing going on. Someone else said they abducted girls. It was all to do with . . . Sir Somebody Lingwall. Sir *Simeon* Lingwall, that was his name."

St John put both arms round her, bent down and kissed her. And this kiss was as good as the first two times . . . better even, more direct. Underneath his jacket, she could feel his heart pounding. It added to her excitement – her heart started thumping harder too. "Let's get back, ay?" he murmured. "Let's get back to your *Sty*."

When they got back to her room, Rayne was tense, expecting the kind of pressuring tussle she'd got used to with Damian. After all, it was obligatory for a guy to try it on, wasn't it – he'd look soft if he didn't.

But St John was different. She went into the tiny kitchen and made them coffee and when she got back he was stretched like a big cat along the bottom of her bed. She sat up at the head against her pillow, facing him, waiting for him to start edging towards her. But he didn't.

The space between them seemed to shake with tension, but he didn't move.

As they drank the coffee they talked a little more, then he stood up and said he should go. She stood up too and went with him to the door, confused, beginning to feel hurt. Then he put his arms round her and kissed her as though he was obsessed with her, kissed her in a way that made Damian look like an amateur. Then he said goodbye and left.

She stood listening to the roar of his bike leaving, wanting to be with him again.

Chapter
Twenty-eight

Rayne woke late on Sunday morning with every nerve ending in her body sparking. She'd had a night full of dreams of St John, full of yearning and some kind of fear. Her room seemed like a box to her, a cage. She scrambled out of bed, pulled jeans and a T-shirt and trainers on. Then she grabbed her bag and went outside, driven simply by the need to move.

It was a strange day outside. The sun was out but there were flint-grey clouds gathering.

As she hurried down through the medieval garden and along the path at the bottom, thunder was rumbling in front of her. She went past the lake, turned away from the house, and was soon on a little track beside fields. She had no idea where she was going, she just needed to walk, keep her legs moving to ground the energy coursing through her. She walked faster, trying not to think about St John, the way he'd lain like a big cat across the bottom of her bed, not moving.

Giving her space to look at him.

She tried not to think about the way he'd kissed her.

She climbed over a stile, and started crossing a field towards the woods just beyond. There was a thin whiplash of lightning, and thunder crashed, right overhead – and then the storm broke. Huge raindrops pelted down on her, soaking her, splattering the soil, mixing it to mud. She raced for the trees as the wind got up and started throwing the rain against her.

The drama of it all was staggering. She'd longed for the silence of the country – it hadn't crossed her mind that it could be full of noise too. The great tree ahead of her was roaring like a motorway, each leaf sending out sound in the wind. But she loved this noise. She stood under the tree and looked up. It was thrashing, whirling, purely alive. The sky behind it was almost black with storm clouds, but the sun had come out and it lit up other trees on the horizon with a strange, strong light. They stood out theatrically against the dark sky.

It was thrilling; she lost herself in it.

And then a voice out of nowhere shouted, "You shouldn't be standing under a tree. Not in a storm."

She spun round. She'd thought she was completely alone. It was the boy from the pub, Ethan Sands, St John's enemy. He was looking at her, unsmiling.

"Where the hell did you come from?" she demanded.

He shrugged, moving closer, so they wouldn't have to shout against the storm. "That's my field you walked across. This is my dad's farm."

"Oh. Sorry."

He shrugged again. "You got right of way. The woods are open to anyone. Where are you heading?"

"Just . . . walking."

"You're the new one, aren't you. At Morton's Keep."

"Yes. News gets around here, doesn't it."

Another blast of storm-wind shook the tree. "Get out from under there!" he ordered.

"What, and get even more soaked?"

Another flash of lightning; a crack of thunder. "*See?*" he shouted, above the roar of the tree. "This tree is the highest in this line – if it gets struck. . ."

She hurried out from under it, into the open, and they stood facing each other in the pelting rain. She was shivering.

"You want to get yourself dry," he said. "The pub's just along that road – five minutes or so."

"Which pub?"

"Don't you know where you are? The Green Lady." He grinned suddenly, and not very nicely. "Where you were last night with your *boyfriend*."

"*What?* God, I've walked for miles. . ."

"You have, if you've come from Morton's Keep. You want to get yourself to the pub, get dried off, and get a cab back. Anyway. I'm off home."

Then he turned, and went into the woods.

"Wait!" she called. "Are these woods—"

"Fleet Woods," he yelled, over his shoulder. And disappeared into them.

Rayne found The Green Lady easily, just as Ethan Sands said she would. On a rain-lashed board just inside its car park, it was advertising Sunday lunch for £8.95. Rayne, reading it, realized how hungry she was – she'd had no breakfast, she was starving. She ducked under the shelter of a small tree by the roadside and pulled out her mobile. It told her it was five to twelve – nearly lunch time.

It also told her she had three missed calls and a text from Damian, from last night, asking her how she was, wanting to make up, probably. And two missed calls and a voicemail from her mum. She felt a stab of guilt. She hadn't given them a thought. But she couldn't deal with it now. She texted Damian *Bit better xxx* and her mum *Call soon promise xx* then headed towards the pub door. She was soaking, dripping – she'd just have to brazen it out.

A group of five walkers with big boots and backpacks appeared at the end of the pub pathway. Rayne let them go past, then tagged on after them, hoping that the wet commotion they'd make going into the bar would mean no one would notice the water streaming off her clothes.

The landlord was bluff and welcoming. He waved them all towards the inglenook fireplace where a fire was just getting going – he even provided a pile of towels that looked threadbare but clean, and Rayne took one. The walkers were so absorbed in working out how many miles they'd done that they hardly noticed her.

She decamped to the ladies', dried her hair off a bit with the automatic dryer, brushed it through and slicked some lipgloss on. Staring at her reflection in the mirror over the sink, she thought that no one would guess at all the stuff going on inside her. She was just a girl who'd got caught in a storm.

Back in the bar, she ordered a double tomato juice and

roast beef, and sat at a tiny table in a corner by the crackling fire. If she craned her neck a little she could see the table that they'd sat at last night.

It only took a few minutes for the flashbacks to start.

She could see St John's face, smiling, subtle, intriguing, sitting across the table from her. She could feel her chest against his back as she rode on the bike. Her mouth felt the single incredible kiss they'd had, just before he'd left.

She drank some of the tomato juice and the taste delighted her. She felt so aware, so alive – more alive than she'd ever felt before. Then suddenly she saw Ethan's face, shouting at her to get out from under the tree. She saw him disappearing into Fleet Woods, where the devil worship went on.

And then St John's face rose up again, coming towards hers, and she was flooded with wanting to be with him.

She came out of her reverie to see someone staring at her. A woman of about seventy, maybe more, was sitting at the end of the bar, twisting round to look at her. She had untidy white-grey hair caught up in a tortoiseshell clip and a sweet, slightly vacant face. "You're warmer now," the woman said. "You're hot."

This was so absurdly on target that Rayne felt herself blushing red. "Yes," she said, "it's a lovely fire."

"You're wet," said the woman.

"Yes, I got soaking wet," said Rayne. The old girl was obviously a bit simple, she thought. Sitting there on her own with a lemonade in front of her.

Suddenly, the woman leant urgently towards her. "*Such*

a storm. It's the balance, see. It's got to be kept in balance. If *they* get more, *she* gets more too."

"All right, Patience?" asked the landlord, walking between them with a plate of roast beef. He put it down on the little table in front of Rayne, jerked his head towards the woman and pulled a face that said: *Don't mind her. Daft, but harmless.*

"I'm all right," said Patience, "are you? *Such* a storm. Fire, flood, fury."

"That's right," said the landlord, smiling at Rayne. "Well, flood and fury anyway. Now, you enjoy your meal, love, all right? Patience won't bother you." And he went back to stand behind the bar.

Rayne could feel Patience's eyes on her as she picked up her knife and fork, but the old woman didn't say anything else. The food was delicious, it calmed her as she ate, sent new energy into her. Steam rose off her clothes as the fire warmed her. She thought about St John again, and smiled to herself.

When she'd cleaned her plate, she sat warming herself for a while longer, then rummaged in her bag for the taxi-firm card she'd got when she'd first come to Marcle Lees. She called them on her mobile and they promised to be at The Green Lady within ten minutes. The storm outside had lifted a little – sun was gleaming through the wet windowpanes, lighting up the pub. Patience seemed oblivious to her now; she was gazing at the fire, rocking herself slightly, chanting a little song or something to herself.

Rayne checked the time, and stood up to go and wait

in the porch for the cab. As she walked past Patience, she could just hear what she was singing: "*Fire, flood, fury. She is fire, flood, fury.*"

In the cab, Rayne relaxed further. She planned to get back, take a shower, maybe sleep for a while. . . The cab turned into Morton's Keep, sped down the drive and drew up on the forecourt by the ivy-choked fountain, gravel spurting from its wheels.

Then it parked beside Damian's little blue Citroën.

Chapter Twenty-nine

Rayne's first impulse was to tell the driver to turn around and get her out of there, fast. But that would have been ridiculous. Damian was here, here now – she had to face him.

She had absolutely no idea what she'd say to him, but she knew she had to finish with him. Each minute ahead of her – it was unknown territory, terrifying and thrilling. She was like a fox, living on its instincts, minute to minute, and she had to trust to each minute to tell her what to do.

She got out of the taxi, and paid. One of the trees at the edge of the forecourt had been uprooted in the storm; she skirted round its trunk and branches and walked through the ancient archway. It was still raining a little, but the wind had dropped. She crossed the courtyard to the main door. The severed-hand door knocker with its shining brass ring glowed in the wavering sunlight, water dripping from its fingertips. She didn't want to touch it. She turned back, deciding to walk round to the tearoom to see if Damian was wandering about. And then the door opened, and Mrs Driver came out, looking anxious. Close behind her was Damian.

"Rayne!" he said, and stopped. His face looked blank. He didn't come towards her, didn't kiss her. "You feeling better, then?" he said, his voice tight with anger.

"Rayne, dear," said Mrs Driver, breathlessly, "this young man says he's your boyfriend. . ."

"That's right," she said. "Damian."

"He's driven down . . . he was worried you were ill . . . I . . . I think I may have. . ."

"It's OK, Mrs Driver. Thanks for letting him in. Day, shall we. . .?" And she jerked her head towards the archway.

As she walked round the house towards the Sty, she could sense him behind her, fuming, ready to explode. She only glanced back once, as they walked through the dripping medieval garden. His bright, stylish jacket looked ridiculously out of place – *he* looked out of place.

She unlocked the door and he followed her inside. "Coffee?" she said. "Tea?"

"Coffee," he snapped. She knew he was waiting to yell at her, waiting for the right moment.

When she got back to the main room, a mug in either hand, he was sitting on the bed. She wondered if he knew about St John being there, lying across it – if some sixth sense had told him. She was sure she'd know, if it was her.

"So," Damian said, face bunched and ugly, "*bit better, kiss, kiss, kiss*?"

"You got my text, then," she said.

"Yes, I got your stupid text. *Finally*. But I set out for here hours before I got it. Christ, Rayne, don't you realize how *worried* we were? I phoned your mum – she said she'd

150

called you last night, too, but you hadn't got back to her – she was going on about you having a brain tumour—"

Rayne let out a shriek of laughter, she couldn't stop herself. "A *brain* tumour?"

"It's not *bloody* funny, Rayne. You say you've got a really bad headache – you don't call us back. *And* she said it would explain why you'd been acting strange for ages now." He paused, glared at her full of disgust. "She was really wound up about it, in a real state. In the end I said I'd drive down. I thought there was something really wrong, too. I didn't expect to see you swanning back here in a sodding *cab*. Been out for a nice lunch, have you? Sunday lunch?"

Her heart hammered as he railed at her, but there was a space inside her too, a space between his anger and her scared reaction to it. And in this space, maybe there was what she was really feeling, but she couldn't work out what that was, not yet.

"You could've called Morton's Keep," she muttered. "If you were so worried. Talked to Mrs Driver."

"What, so your *fat little lies* wouldn't get shown up?" he exploded. "Only they still would, wouldn't they? *She* didn't know anything about you being *ill*. *She* said you'd seemed fine, Friday night, *serving at dinner*, and she couldn't be sure, but she thought you were out last night too, and then the penny seemed to drop for the poor old cow, and she realized you'd *lied through your teeth to me*, and she got all flustered and said she'd show me to the *Sty* – that what it's called, is it, this place? Pretty *good name* for your place, isn't it?"

She looked at him, wondering why she didn't feel more guilty, more sorry for him. He sprang off the bed and

151

came towards her. She stepped back. The thought of him touching her – she was revolted by it.

"What the *hell* is going on?" he yelled. "Why are you *being* like this? What's got into you?"

She took a deep breath. "Look," she said, "I don't know. All I know is – I had to get away from the Estate. I was going mad. I needed a break. I . . . I don't know."

"And you needed a break from me. So much so you *lied* to me about coming back—"

"Yes. I couldn't come back. I . . . I wanted to stay. I couldn't come back."

He gave a low whistle. "You're losing it, babe. Have you looked at yourself recently? You're losing it. Up here." He rapped at his head. "What d'you like so much about this place, ay? It's weird, if you ask me. Like some creepy old castle, all overgrown. . ."

"It's not the house. I don't even like it all that much – you're right, it's creepy. I just like . . . being here. On my own. I like the . . . I like the woods. And the silence."

"*Jesus.* So you're turning into a hippie or something, are you. A sodding hippie hermit."

"Don't, Damian. Look – I shouldn't've lied to you. Just – I didn't know what to say. I just – I need to do this right now. Be on my own, like this. I need you and Mum to understand that, to let me—"

"Oh, no, babe." He took a step back, folded his arms, looked at her almost with loathing. "You're not keeping *me* hanging on, waiting for you to sort your head out. You've lied to me, you've treated me like shit. You've worried your mum, she doesn't know what's going on either. You've got

152

some serious making up to do. You're not keeping me on as some kind of reserve. It's yes or no, you want me or you don't. You come back with me now – or it's all over. You stay – and I never want to see you again."

To her horror, she heard herself laughing. He threw out his arms in rage and for a moment she thought he was going to hit her. But instead he grated out, "Which is it gonna be?"

She turned, heart pounding, fled into the kitchen, ran water into a glass and drank it down. He appeared at the narrow doorway. "Come on, Rayne," he said. "This isn't healthy. You're sick. Come back with me now – pack your things, and we'll go."

"I can't," she choked out.

"*What?*"

"It would kill me. It would kill me to come back."

There was a silence like a bomb blast, then he turned and walked out.

She heard the old wooden door slam.

She didn't move.

Chapter
Thirty

After a few moments, Rayne crept out of the kitchen and went over to the door and locked it. Then she pulled her phone from out of her bag, and spelt out, *I really need 2 c u. ASAP.* Then she sent it to St John, lay back on the bed, and waited.

After ten, maybe fifteen minutes, she heard the roar of a bike on the road below Morton's Keep. She knew it was St John. He hadn't bothered to reply to her, just got on his bike and come. Maybe he'd passed Damian in his car. She thought of getting up, going to the top of the drive to meet him, but she didn't move, she just lay there. "He knows where the Sty is," she thought. Then she heard birds calling in alarm to each other, and footsteps in the garden, then there was a knock on the door.

She got up and unlocked it, and let him come in.

He came straight through and put his arms round her. "Rayne," he said, into her hair, "what's happened?"

"Damian's been here. My boyfriend."

"Your ex-boyfriend."

"My ex-boyfriend. Oh, God. It was such a big deal when we

started going out, it was like I'd made it, like it was happening, like what was supposed to happen . . . was happening. . ."

He didn't say anything, just held her. In the stillness she felt full of wanting him. "He thought I was going mad," she muttered, "lying to him and everything, and wanting to be *here*. He wanted me to go back with him. I told him it would kill me. Then he left." St John stroked her back, lulled her to talk. "It *would* kill me, as well," she murmured. "I couldn't do it. It was . . . *God*, it was. . ."

"What?" he asked, still stroking with long, smooth strokes. "What was it you wanted to get away from?"

"I've told you. The noise and the fights and that horrible crowded flat. . ."

"Poor baby. Poor Rayne." He'd got her ear between two fingers, he was pulling on it gently.

"I'm scared," she went on. "He'll tell Mum, she'll be against me – maybe he's right, maybe I am going mad. I feel as if I've just – kicked away all my old supports. Smashed them up. I'm on my own now, I've got no one to turn to. . ."

"You've got me," he murmured.

And he smiled, over her head, into the room that was already growing dark.

"Could we . . . could we go out somewhere?" she asked, after a few moments. "Could we go to The Green Lady again, get a drink?"

"Rayne, I can't. My godmother's round for lunch – they were all on the cheese and port as I left – I have to get back to say goodbye."

Rayne was silent. Godmothers, cheese, port . . . it all sounded so grand, so out of her league. They walked out of the door together into the gloom of the ancient garden. "Thank you for coming round," she murmured.

"Of course I came. I came right away."

"I know you did."

"I left my bike here," he said, and veered off into a gap between some large bushes. The bike was pushed half inside a laurel bush. "I thought I'd better not park in front of the house. I saw the gap as I was coming up the drive and thought I could hide the bike. Whoever was watching us last week – they might come poking around."

Rayne shrugged. "I'm sure that was just Ben, the gardener, being a perv. I can have visitors whenever I want. You don't have to hide."

"Oh well," he said. Then he stooped and kissed her.

The fifth kiss, she thought. All his kisses were events, somehow, vivid to her. This one was gentle, loving; it said *trust me*. "When am I going to see you again?" she asked.

"Soon. Tuesday, maybe? I've got this big essay to get through, but I've got free periods Tuesday afternoon . . . I'll text you. . ." He got hold of his motorbike and steered it through the bushes on to the drive, Rayne following. Then he got on and kicked it into life and roared away, waving with one hand.

Essay, thought Rayne, as she watched him disappear. *Free periods*. How stupidly young and *normal* – it didn't fit with everything that was happening. She felt restless, on edge. She turned to go back through the gap in the bushes. It had vanished. The foliage had sprung back into place after the bike had gone through – the gap was only visible from the medieval garden. She frowned. How had St John seen it from the drive?

Shrugging, she pushed her way through into the garden again. It was dusk, the light had nearly gone. She didn't want to go back to her room. She prowled restlessly past the lake and alongside the little stream that fed it towards the wood, walking, walking so her thoughts wouldn't start up again.

As she entered the wood, three crows flew down towards her and hung in front of her, cawing and beating their wings. She stopped and flapped her hands at them; they flew up a few feet and hovered there, cawing. They looked like black crucifixes hanging over her. Or vampires, waiting to strike. "What d'you want?" she said, loudly. "My soul?" One by one the birds settled on branches nearby but she had the feeling if she walked past them they'd fly at her again. She stared into the woods – they looked dark and dismal. Then she turned back.

"This place," she told herself, walking fast, "is getting to you. Go home, light a fire, cook some pasta, think about St John and the amazing way he kisses. . . You're *free* now – no more lies to Damian. And tomorrow you can call Mum and try to explain."

She headed towards the greenhouses, to pick up a couple of logs. But as she got there she saw Ben Avebury standing in front of them, puffing on a pipe. Her instinct was to veer away but it was too late, he'd seen her. "Just getting some wood," she called. "For my stove."

"Ah yes," he said. "You like fire."

"Well, it's cooler at night now."

"It is. So." He puffed ruminatively. "How did you get on at that great dinner on Friday?"

"It was OK. Bit weird." She edged past him, to the woodpile. The palm tree that had broken through the greenhouse roof nodded above her, waving its huge green fronds. "They all seemed to be obsessed with the history of this place," she went on, chattily, nervously. "Trying to wring all the grisly details out of Mr Stuart. He should write a book on it, he'd make a fortune."

"There is a little book as it happens, on Morton's Keep history, on sale at the entrance."

"*The Story of a Herefordshire Manor* – I know, I've seen it in the library. But it hasn't got what they want."

There was a pause, then Ben said, "Sometimes a house has two histories. One that's less well known. One that people have an interest in keeping less well known."

Rayne stooped to pick up a couple of logs. She was beginning to feel creeped out. And then Ben Avebury said, "You've seen that boy again, haven't you?"

"What boy?" she snapped.

"The one who brought you home, Wednesday night. I saw you together. And I saw him hide his bike in the bushes back there. You want to be careful of his sort. Mr Stuart – he won't want him round here."

"My private life's my business," she said, sharply. "And if Mr Stuart doesn't want him here, *he* can tell me." *You creepy old pervert*, she added silently, and stamped off.

A noise – she couldn't remember afterwards what noise – made her turn round.

And for a vivid moment, the palm tree waving above the greenhouse was a woman, a giant woman staring straight at her. Her green hair flowed, her green arms flailed in warning, in fury. . . She was so real, so alive and threatening that Rayne slammed her eyes shut, terrified, and when she opened them again the palm tree was back, growing out through the cracked panes of glass.

Chapter Thirty-one

It was just as well it was Monday the next day. Rayne craved a return to normality, to routine. The calm atmosphere of the tearoom, its good smells, the kindly, matronly women, the mildly flirtatious old men, even the fussy old ladies demanding more hot water for their tea – they were all soothing, supporting to her.

Mrs Driver had met her with an anxious, "Everything all right, dear?"

"Oh, yes, Mrs Driver. I'm sorry about yesterday."

"That's all right. These things happen. That was your boyfriend, was it?"

"Well – my ex, now."

"Oh well. That's life, isn't it. He seemed so upset, so *angry*. . ."

"He was."

"I'm sorry if I put my foot in it, dear. He was so worried about you, I just wanted to assure him you were all right, and then I suddenly realized he might have been checking up on you." She gave a little mirthless laugh. "It's been so long since I . . . you know. . ."

"Played games? Lied to boys?"

"Oh, well, dear. That's life, isn't it. Now, are you really *sure* you're all right?"

Rayne took in such a deep breath it made her stand up straighter. "Yes, Mrs Driver. Honestly."

Monday was unusually busy, and Rayne buried herself in her work. Flashes of drama would come back to her – Damian shouting at her, St John pulling her towards him, Ethan Sands in the storm, and that freaky hallucination she'd had, by the greenhouses. . . *Jesus*, she thought, don't dwell on *that*. Forget it.

When work was finished she phoned her mum and told her that she and Damian had split up. Her mum said she already knew – she'd bumped into Damian on the Estate and, all choked up, he'd told her. "He kept saying how funny you were, how much you'd changed since he first met you," she said, accusingly.

"Maybe I have," Rayne said. "Maybe it's a good change."

"You sound so cold. Aren't you upset about it?"

"Of course I am, Mum. But – come on, we hadn't been together that long."

"Yes, but you were so happy when you started going out with him. Over the moon."

"Probably not for the right reasons."

"What? What are you talking about?"

"Oh, never mind."

There was a silence, then her mum asked, "Are you happy there?"

"Yes," Rayne answered, and she realized it was true. "I am. It feels . . . *right*. It's what I want for now, anyway."

"Well, Jelly misses you. *I* miss you. When are you coming back to see us?"

And then the thought slotted in, beautiful and simple. "Not for a bit, Mum. I'd bump into Damian and it's too much right now, it'd be too upsetting. . . You can come and see me here, the two of you. There's an empty room, right next to mine – you could stay the night."

She knew it wouldn't happen. Her mum would never get it organized, she wasn't up to it. They said goodbye to each other, and a feeling of relief and potential flooded into her. She was finally free from her past, free from the Estate, at least for now.

That night she slept like the dead, remembering no dreams.

When Rayne arrived at the tearoom on Tuesday morning, Becky was already there in the kitchen, unstacking the huge dishwasher. "Mrs D phoned me last night," she said, "asked me to help out. There's two coach trips coming, we have to clear the first lot out fast to make room for the second."

"Shouldn't you be at school or something?" asked Rayne.

Becky bridled. "I'm at *college*. And Tuesdays I only have one lesson, and it's rubbish, so I'm missing it. I need the money!"

"Well, it's good you're here," said Rayne, appeasing, and started measuring out flour and butter to make scones.

Becky came up alongside her and began laying out cups and saucers beside the coffee machine. "Mrs Driver told me what happened," she said, in a sympathetic voice. "She said you might be a bit wobbly."

It was Rayne's turn to bridle. "She told you about Damian?"

"Only so's I wouldn't put my foot in it with you, and upset you. Anyone'll tell you I'm not known for my *tact*." Rayne smiled, and Becky went on, "So, are you OK? I was, like – *destroyed*, when my boyfriend dumped me. I couldn't even say his name without bursting into tears."

"Well, this was more like me dumping him. I mean, I got this job here partly 'cos I wanted to get away from him."

"*Really?* Why didn't you tell me that before?"

Rayne shrugged.

"Mrs D said he was very good-looking," Becky went on. "And *black*. And he had his own car. That is so cool."

"He is, I suppose. But he wasn't what I wanted."

They talked on about life and love as they got the teashop ready, and when the first coachload came through the doors (loudly announcing their need for good, strong coffee) and they had to stop, Rayne thought how surprisingly good it had been to mull it all over with Becky. Maybe she'd misjudged her.

They worked flat out from then on, and when there was a lull after the two lunch sittings they each grabbed a large plate of quiche and salad and went to sit outside on an old wooden bench up against the dairy wall. In front of them, broken twigs and branches littered the grass, but the afternoon was warm and sunny, a real contrast to Sunday's storm. Becky said three trees had been felled on the estate – Ben Avebury had already started sawing them up for firewood. Everyone was talking about how strange the weather was being. Ms Barton put it down to global warming but Mrs Driver said that England had always had tempestuous weather.

As their eating slowed, Rayne said, "You know Friday's dinner, all the chat about Morton's Keep's nasty past?"

"Yes?" said Becky, guardedly.

"Well, have you ever heard of Sir Simeon Lingwall? Who used to live here? I can't find anything about him in the library, but they were all talking about him."

"*Oh my God*, were they?" Becky rolled her eyes theatrically. "He must be the one who used to eat people."

"*What?*"

"He had loads of grand parties and people would come to them but not all of them would come out again so they reckoned the missing guests were on the menu for the next one."

"Oh, *right*! Like the new guests wouldn't notice they were eating an arm or a toe or something."

"*Gross!*" spluttered Becky, then she said, "Seriously, this place has the *worst* reputation. We moved here three years ago and my mum needed a job and she got a *huge* load of shit for coming to work here. People going on about the house being steeped in blood and a curse on it and stuff."

"Well, I reckon Mr Stuart stokes all that up to get more ghost hunters in."

"Maybe. Have you ever . . . seen anything? *Felt* anything?"

Rayne considered for a moment. "Nothing . . . definite. But the vibes in the house . . . they're awful, aren't they? I mean – they're *powerful*. What about your mum?"

"She's fine. She doesn't believe in all that stuff. And anyway I got her an iPod last Christmas, and she cleans with that in. If she saw a ghost I reckon she'd just suck it up into the hoover. But that's in the day – I can't *believe* you sleep here, I'd sooner *die*!"

"But I don't sleep in the house!"

"No, you're in a pigsty in the big outdoors – I don't know which is worse!"

Rayne put her empty plate down on the ground. "What's wrong with the big outdoors?"

Becky turned to look at her. "Oh, nothing. Just it would spook me, being all alone. Right next to all those trees."

"I've heard rumours about Fleet Woods."

"Oh, right, I've heard them too. Giant green witches and scary rituals going on. . ."

"Something to do with the fire festival group?"

"Oh, that's rubbish. I *love* their festivals. Some of those fire boys are *fit*!"

They were interrupted by Rayne's mobile bleeping the arrival of a text. It was from St John and it said *pick u up at 4?* Just the sight of his name on her phone thrilled her.

Becky was watching, agog to know if it was from Damian. Rayne grinned at her and said, "Cover for me if I get off a bit early?"

"Are you meeting your ex?"

"No. St John."

"Oh, *God*. . ."

"Becky, stop *judging*, OK?"

"You wanna be careful. You're on the rebound."

"Oh *please!* Will you cover for me?"

"Yes. Sure."

"Thanks. I mean it."

And she texted back: *I'll b ready.*

Chapter Thirty-two

At four o'clock she walked down the drive to meet St John – he'd sent another text asking her to. He smiled at her, handed her the spare helmet and motioned her to get on the bike behind him. Then they set off.

She pressed herself against his back, inhaling the scent of him, and shouted, "Where are we going?"

"You'll see," he yelled back, and revved the bike along faster.

The drive took fifteen minutes or so, along wonderful country lanes. Trees, just turning bronze, flamed along the roadside. St John pulled off into a rough little lay-by, and stopped the bike. He turned to her, smiling. "We're here," he said.

"Where? The middle of nowhere?"

"Yup. No one here but us."

He got off the bike, and pulled a plastic carrier bag out of the pannier at the back. Rayne could see the neck of a bottle of apple juice sticking out of it. "Thought we'd have an autumn picnic," he said.

"Lovely. What you got in there?"

"Crusty bread. Brie. Little Scotch-eggy things. When I do a picnic, I do a picnic."

She laughed, and put her arms round him. "Come on," he said, freeing himself from her hug, taking her hand, and they set off down a little path between slender trees growing densely together.

They walked on in silence, and as they got further into the wood the trees got older, taller, and the filtering sunlight more sparse. "Don't worry," he said. "There's a clearing up here. We'll be right in the sun." Then he turned to her and grinned and said, "You don't realize where we are, do you?"

Something in his voice made her nervous. "OK, so where are we?" she asked.

"Fleet Woods."

"*What?* The creepy ones you were telling me about?"

"That's right."

"But – this is weird. We didn't come from the right direction."

"Yeah we did."

"Really? I know my sense of direction is pretty crap, but . . . I ended up here on Sunday too. It's like – everywhere I come from, I end up in Fleet Woods."

"They're huge, you know. They cover quite a bit of ground."

They walked on down the path. A great tree had fallen across it, bringing down two smaller trees, and as they clambered over the trunks Rayne thought about telling St John about the last time she'd been in Fleet Woods, meeting Ethan Sands in the storm, but she decided not to.

"So," she said, looking all around, "this is where they come to worship the devil, is it?"

"So the rumour goes."

"Freaky. What d'you want to come here for?"

"People avoid this place," he said, letting go of her hand and putting his arm round her, drawing her close, "and that's good because I really want to be alone with you. Look – there's the clearing I was telling you about. Up there."

Rayne walked towards it, feeling half excited and half scared. *I'm in charge*, she thought.

"Aaaaah," breathed St John. "They've been here before us. Look."

At the far side of the clearing were two flat boulders, one laid on top of the other. Moss grew over them; they had the air of having been there for a long, long time. On the top one, something black was piled.

"What is it?" she whispered, pointing.

"The remains of a fire," he said. "Those stones – it's like their altar." He gave a mock-horror laugh that bounced off the nearby trees. "I bet they sacrificed something there."

Rayne took a step forward, and looked down at the stones. There were two charred pine cones at the edge, but no sign – she realized she was searching – of any bones.

"Look," St John said. "Look up at the tree."

She glanced up. A weird kind of mobile was hanging there, made of twine and twigs, pine cones and seed pods and bird feathers. It was revolving slowly in the slight breeze. St John reached out and batted it. "*Don't!*" she gasped, as it whirled crazily round.

"Why not?" he scoffed. "Think we'll get cursed?"

"Well *I* dunno – what is it? What—" She broke off in horror as he seized hold of the twine and yanked it off its branch, scattering feathers and twigs. Then he whipped it down across the altar of boulders, spraying black ash into the air, and flung it away, into the undergrowth.

And turned to her, grinning.

"*Oh my God,*" she breathed.

"Am I?" he said. "Want some juice?"

The grass in the centre of the clearing was soft and short, cushioned by moss. It was still a bit damp from the storm, but St John put his leather jacket down and they sat very close together on that. They laid out the little picnic on the flattened carrier bag, and drank straight from the apple juice bottle. Large wood ants carried away the crumbs of bread as they broke it to eat.

He kissed her as she was still swallowing, and pulled her close to him. "I don't understand why you want to come *here*," Rayne said. She was finding it very hard to take her eyes off the stone altar. "Where they do their weird stuff."

"I don't give a monkey's about them and their stupid little rituals."

"*Obviously.*"

"Rayne, nothing's going to happen. What, you think I'll be *doomed*, because I *desecrated* their crap?"

"Well, no, but—"

"It's a lovely clearing. Why should those idiots be the only ones to use it?" Then he lay back, pulling her with him, so that they lay side by side.

"You sure no one's going to come here?" she murmured.

"I promise you," he said, "only that mad cult comes here. And if they turn up, we'll give them something to dance round, yeah? They can dance round *us*." He laughed, and leaned towards her, his face hard. For a second, it chilled her, then she put her arm round his neck. "I feel. . ." she whispered.

"What?"

"Decadent. Like I've done something wrong. "

"Good." His hand was on her throat. "That's *good*."

Then – suddenly – breaking the web of sensation between them – an extraordinary noise. Not loud, but full of power – like something huge a long way off, like metal falling, great sheets of metal crashing down. They stared wide-eyed at each other but, before they could speak, it came again, louder this time, and this time she knew the sound was animate, made by something that had life. She froze, like her blood had stopped flowing.

It came again, primal, savage – a dinosaur's roar, a monster's bellow – unreal, ridiculous. She told herself it was ridiculous. But her blood still didn't move.

"What the *hell* was that?" she breathed, at last.

St John was gazing at her, smiling. "You'll find out in a minute," he said softly.

Chapter
Thirty-three

She stared at him, horrified. His smile didn't move. Then, suddenly active, she shoved him back, rolled away from him. "What the *hell*?" she cried, scrambling to her feet. "What the *hell* was that?"

He didn't answer, just lay there, smiling.

"Look, St John, you are scaring the *shit* out of me—"

He got slowly to his feet. "Oh, come on, Rayne, what're you thinking? That it's the curse of the fire folk come upon us?"

"I don't know what to think."

"Or the devil roaring?"

"I don't know *what* to think, if you know what it is, why don't you just tell me, why—"

The roar came again, louder yet. Deep, ancient, rumbling, coming from the depths of the wood. "It's OK," he said. "It's OK." He took hold of her hand.

"*Is* it to do with the fire people?" she gasped. She didn't know what to do – should she trust him, should she run, should she get away? But she let him keep hold of her hand.

"Come on," he said. "Let's go and meet it."

Rayne couldn't act. She allowed herself to be led across the clearing and into the woods at the other side. The roar came again, the loudest yet, and this time there was an answering echo from deeper in the woods. "OK, let's stop," said St John, quietly. "Stop here. I think I can see it."

"Oh, God, *what*?" she wailed. "Why don't you just *tell* me. . ."

He nudged her sharply, and pointed.

Beyond thick undergrowth, a rough-shaped bush was moving. High up, higher than head height. It turned – the bush was bracken and white sticks, moving, coming closer—

It came out through the trees.

It was a stag, a strong, beautiful, terrifying stag, bracken and twigs all caught up in its antlers like a diadem, a crown.

Rayne's legs were liquid. She was filled with the impulse to drop to her knees in front of it.

The stag was looking straight at her. It was magical, supernatural, as though it had formed out of the stuff of the wood. The huge, branching antlers on the great solemn head were white-tipped where the bone showed through the brown. The great eyes were on her, steadily.

Another roar came, from a distance, and the stag turned, stretched its neck, opened its mouth wide and bellowed back.

The noise went on and on, Rayne could feel it vibrating inside her. It was thrilling.

"Ever heard of the rutting season?" whispered St John.

"*What?*"

"Autumn's mating season for deer. The males strut about, challenging each other. The strongest ones get the biggest harems. They bellow at each other and if one doesn't give way and run off, they fight. . ."

"God, yes," murmured Rayne. "I've seen it on the TV. They crash antlers together."

"That's why he's got all that greenery on his antlers. He's been thrashing about to strengthen his neck muscles."

The stag turned back from his challenge and regarded them again. "He's *magnificent*," breathed Rayne.

"Yeah, well, we should probably get out of here," said St John. His voice had lifted in pitch, it was starting to sound nervous. "If he doesn't go after that other stag, he might come at us."

"No, he won't," said Rayne. "Oh, he's beautiful." She was feeling incredibly stirred. She thought the stag was noble, powerful, free. Its great spreading antlers could kill, or protect.

The stag took a step to its left. Now it was lined up perfectly with St John. It looked at him steadily, as though it was weighing him up, then it lowered its great head.

"I mean it, Rayne," St John hissed. "We're going." And he grabbed her hand and ran, pulling her along behind him.

"You were *scared*!" she crowed, as they crashed back through the trees into the clearing. "You were scared of a *deer*!"

"Too right I was. I've seen them fight."

"God, I'd love to see that. Are there loads of deer in these woods?"

"Quite a few. They wander out occasionally, get on to

people's farms. . . Come on, let's go." He stooped down, picked up the bottle of juice from the ground.

"Are you kidding?" she exclaimed. She put her arms round him. "Don't you remember what we were doing before we were interrupted?"

"Yeah. But it was a bit of a turn-off, wasn't it."

"*I* don't think so." Something deep down inside her was awake, aroused. She pulled him to her, tried to kiss him, but he pushed her off.

"Sorry," he said, and he sounded detached, cold. "I want to go."

His rejection – it was humiliating. Like a slap in the face. Silently, she helped pack the remains of the picnic away in the carrier bag, and followed him back along the path out of the woods.

Chapter
Thirty-four

They were silent all the way back to where they'd left the bike, and on the ride back to Morton's Keep. St John turned the bike off into the bushes again, into the gap that you could only see from the other side. Rayne got off, and handed him her helmet. He couldn't like her that much, she thought, not if he could push her off like that – *God*, it was crushing to want someone more than they seemed to want you. Damian had never rejected her like that, not once. Not that she'd ever made the first move with him, not like that.

"Are you going to offer me a cup of tea?" asked St John.

She thought of telling him to *sod off* if all he wanted was *tea*, but she didn't. She nodded, sulkily, and he followed her towards the Sty.

She made the tea and they sat at the table in the window to drink it, not meeting each other's eyes. It felt all wrong being in the Sty – it was stale, hopeless. The unsaid things between them were like great rocks, all of them impassable. She watched his mouth as he drank, longing to kiss him. If he kissed her it would make everything all right again. Then suddenly he looked up at her and said, "You promised to show me round the house."

"What?"

"You said you had the keys. You said you could show me round."

She stared at him; she didn't know how to answer. At least he didn't want to get away from her. Maybe it wasn't such a bad idea, going to the house. There were no guests staying there – Mrs Driver would have told her if there were. And Mrs Driver herself would be tucked away in the modern quarters by this time, tucked away for the night.

"OK," she shrugged. "If that's what you want, let's go."

As they went up the steps to the back door of the Tudor kitchen, he put his hand on her back, like he was urging her on. The touch went through her like a pulse. They stepped inside and she locked the door behind them.

"So," he said, looking around, "this is where the great feasts were prepared, yeah? The stuffed swan and the wild boar and the flagons of mead. . ." He paced round the ancient refectory table, snuffing the air as though he could smell it now. "God, it must've been fantastic. *God.*"

"If you were eating it, maybe," Rayne said. She felt nervous, somehow, as though they shouldn't be there. "Not if you had to do all the work cooking it. Look, St John – I don't think we should hang about here too long."

"Why not? The old girl trusts you with the keys, doesn't she?"

"I know, but. . ." She trailed off. Into her head came a memory of Ben Avebury saying, "You want to be careful of his sort. Mr Stuart – he won't want him round here." And then something else happening, something terrifying, but she couldn't remember what. . . "Which bit of the house d'you want to see?" she asked.

He turned to her, his face blazing. "Upstairs," he said. Then he came towards her, put his hands on her shoulders, and kissed her on the mouth.

They held hands as they walked along the corridor and went through the heavy green curtains into the Great Hall, Rayne smiling with relief and triumph because of the kiss.

"Oh, wow," said St John, looking around at everything. "This is serious."

"D'you want to see the Old Stone Hall?" she asked. "That's meant to be the oldest bit, it's the bit everyone makes the most fuss over—"

"No," he said, pulling her towards the great staircase. "I told you, I want to go upstairs."

On the half-landing the red velvet curtains were drawn as usual in front of the glass case. Without letting go of Rayne's hand, St John reached out and drew them back, first one side, then the other, then stared into it. Rayne gazed at his face. His expression – it was greedy, hunting for something. The only sound was the old Dutch clock, keeping the hours above them. "What's so interesting?" she breathed. Her eyes were on his mouth, wanting it to come closer.

"Nothing," he murmured. "Come on." And they went up the next flight of stairs.

"God, I *really* don't like this place," muttered Rayne. "Especially now it's getting dark. OK – so that's the

Spanish room, that's Abigail's room, that's the Red Queen's room. . ."

"Abigail's room," said St John, walking towards it.

"Well, the Red Queen's is meant to be the most haunted, that's the one that—"

She broke off as he turned the handle to Abigail's room, and stepped inside. She hurried after him. He was waiting just inside the door; as soon as she'd gone through, he pushed it shut behind her.

He smiled at her, but his eyes were already scanning the room. He headed for the left of the huge fireplace, where there was another door. It looked like a cupboard door, except it had no door handle, just a lock with no key in it. He pushed at it; it stayed closed. Then he rapped on it, and the hollow sound brought another smile to his face.

"What are you up to?" she asked, nervously.

"Nothing," he said. "Just – I've heard there are secret passageways in this place."

"Bound to be, I suppose. Look – now you've seen it – can we get out of here?"

He came over to her and put his arms round her. "Aw, Rayne, don't you like this room?"

"No. It's like someone's in here with us, watching us."

"It's Abigail," he grinned. "Poor creature. Just think of her, trapped up here, slowly going mad for love of her yokel lover . . . d'you think that secret passageway was how he got in?"

"No. He got shot, scratching her name on the outside of the window."

"So he did. But maybe he used to get in before that,

that's why they took the handle away . . . I bet they used to do it, here. On that four-poster bed. Look at it." He turned her, so she faced it. "Think what's gone on on it. Deaths . . . and births . . . and horrible nasty sex. . ."

"Rape. Yes. Now can we *go*, please?"

The kiss he gave her was exquisite, the best yet. It was as though he was tracking her, exploring her. "Come on," he murmured. "*Come* on." His hands moved over her, he was pulling at her clothes. He kissed her again. His touch drove away the fearful atmosphere in the room. She kissed him back, and his hand moved to the fastener on her jeans, pulling it open, and for a few seconds she was going to do it, she was so driven she thought she'd shuck off her jeans and they'd do it, half on, half off the end of the ancient bed. . .

She looked up as he steered her backwards towards it, half-lifted her on to it. The hangings were like shrouds, like coffin cloth all rotted. "*No*," she said, horrified. "Let go. *Stop* it. I need to get out of here."

"No you don't," he said, kissing her neck, "you need to stay."

Again, that feeling she'd just give in, she'd just *go* with it. Then she pushed him back, yanked herself away from him, scrambled off the bed. "I mean it," she hissed. "I mean it."

"OK, *OK*," he said. He let go of her, and followed her out of the room.

Chapter
Thirty-five

On the way back to the Sty, St John apologized to Rayne. "Although really it's your fault," he said. "You really get to me."

Rayne was shaken, and trying to cover it up, trying to keep things normal. "It's OK," she lied. "It's just – I told you the house was freaking me out more and more." She glanced up at him. His face in profile was like beautiful stone.

"You don't want to listen to stupid gossip about the house," he said, dismissively.

"Maybe there's more to it than gossip," she retorted. "A . . . a while back I was in that garden where the old dovecote is? I saw these black candle stubs in the grass, in a ring . . . some were on top of some flat stones. . ."

"Yeah? How many candles?"

"Eleven. Who d'you think did it?"

"No idea. The fire festival lot, probably. Why d'you let it *bother* you?"

His scorn stung her. "OK, then, so why are *you* so

bothered about the house? Wanting to see round it, wanting to make out on the four-poster bed. . ."

"Oh, calm down. It's just – it gives me a kick, that's all. It's different." He stopped walking, and turned towards her. "Hey, let's stop fighting, OK? Come on. Let's go back to your room." Then he put his arm round her, and pulled her close, but she felt too chilled to respond.

"Listen – I don't feel too good—" she muttered.

"Oh, Rayne. I've upset you, haven't I? Being an idiot."

"It's OK. Listen – I'll call you, OK?" Then she pulled away from him and ran back to the Sty.

Inside, she prowled around restlessly, trying to make sense of what had happened. To just jump from kissing, amazing and mind-blowing kissing it was true, but just *kissing*, to . . . she didn't want to think about it. About how she'd nearly *gone* with it.

And now, where were they? Were they still going out together, or what? A jealous image of Flora rose in her mind. She walked through the tiny kitchen, into the empty room on the far side, came back again . . . then she came to a stop in front of the antlers, nailed above the stove. She'd hung two necklaces on them, and a bra to dry. They looked wrong now – cheap. An image of the stag in the wood came into her mind, the way it had lowered its head at them. She reached up and unhooked the bra and the chains and took them down. These antlers weren't anything like as large or magnificent as the antlers on the stag, but they still deserved respect.

*

Becky turned up to help in the teashop again the next day, just in time for lunch. Another large coach party had booked in and Mrs Driver was having the day in bed, feeling, as she put it, "a bit below par".

The girls worked hard, serving soup and rolls and quiche and salad, and as soon as there was a lull Becky hissed, "*So?* How did it *go*? Are you an *item*?"

"Yes," said Rayne. "No. I don't know. He's a bit—"

"Of a snob."

"I wasn't going to say that."

"Well he *is*!"

"I was *going* to say – I dunno. He goes hot and cold. And I think he's still tied up with his ex-girlfriend."

"She's still mad about him, isn't she? I saw them in town the other day. . ."

"What?" said Rayne, her voice sharp with suspicion. "What were they doing?"

"Oh, they were in the usual group. Walking along the high street like they owned it."

"Was he holding her hand?"

"No. They were arguing about something. They were arguing and the other three were just . . . listening. They're weird, Rayne. They're . . . *incestuous*. It's not funny. Why d'you like him so much? I mean – I know he's good-looking but he's such a *freak*. . ."

"He doesn't kiss like a freak. He kisses like . . . God, I don't know. It's a whole *performance*."

Becky let out a high-pitched giggle. "And you're thinking, if the kissing's that good. . ?"

"Absolutely. I can't tell you. He's amazing."

There was a pause, and what had happened in Abigail's room filled Rayne's mind. "Becky," she said, "you know the ghost hunters who come here. . ."

"Oh my God, they're not having more, are they? Well, I'm not helping out this time. No way. I nearly cacked myself, last time."

"They made you *help*? What did you have to do?"

"They were out in that creepy tower, you know, the dovecote. They were supposed to be trying to make contact with someone who'd been murdered there."

"Who?"

"I didn't want to know. I had to take them out sandwiches and hot drinks."

"What, at night?"

"Mr Stuart was with me or I wouldn't've gone. He offered me double pay to make the sarnies. Mrs Driver doesn't like ghost hunters, she won't do it. Jesus. I was shaking so much most of the coffee ended up on the tray. But the ghost hunters couldn't've cared less about the coffee. They were going on about other voices coming through, *clamouring* to be heard . . . this woman kept saying that word, *clamouring*. I remember it 'cos I had to ask Mr Stuart what it meant. . ."

"And what did the other voices say?"

"You think I stuck around to find out? The look on those ghost hunters' faces, it was gross, all excited and scared and kind of *insane* – I just ran."

"What did Mr Stuart say?"

"He just laughed it off. Said if they were bonkers enough to pay him loads of money to camp out in a damp dovecote all night, who was he to argue. Usually ghost hunters don't want refreshments. But if they come again and they want them, I'm not doing it. No way."

Five women came through the teashop door, telling each other they'd earned a nice cake with their tea. As Rayne filled one of the huge kettles she said, "Becky, have you ever heard of anything else they made contact with? The ghost hunters? Like – in Abigail's room?"

"The mad girl's room? No. Mum hates that room, though. She says if there's one room she hates cleaning, it's that."

Chapter Thirty-six

That evening an unknown number came up on Rayne's phone. She answered it and a voice said, "Rayne? It's Amelia, St John's friend? I hope you don't mind, he gave me your number – he's really upset, Rayne. He thinks he's blown it with you."

There was a tick of silence, then Rayne said, "Why doesn't he call then?"

"'Cos he was afraid you'd just dump him. Listen – there's some things you need to know about him and Flora."

"They're still together, right? He never really finished with her."

"*No* – the opposite! Listen – we can't talk about this on the phone. Petra and me are going to go out to eat tomorrow night – this gorgeous little bistro we know, it's such good value, we love it. Why don't you come along?"

Rayne was surprised how excited she felt as she got dressed up to go and meet Petra and Amelia. How pleased she was that she was included. She took care how she dressed, and she made her eyes up dramatically, a bit like the way they and Flora did.

She saw them before they saw her. They were sitting side by side in a little booth halfway down the bistro, and as she watched, Amelia laughed and laid her face briefly on Petra's shoulder. There was something so elegant about them.

She walked forward, and they saw her and waved, smiling. She slid in the booth opposite them.

"The thing is," Amelia said, as soon as their orders were taken, "you are just the *perfect thing* to have happened to St John. Seriously. He's been in this relationship with Flora for over two years and he's outgrown her but she won't let go—"

"He told me he'd finished with her."

"He has. Well he *tried* to. But she won't accept it."

"Well, maybe he should stop seeing her for a time."

"I agree with you," said Petra. She reached her hand across the table and it touched Rayne's. "But we're in this really tight group, the five of us."

"It's amazing, the group," said Amelia. "We love each other. When you're together, you don't want anyone else."

"Although – we'd love it if *you* joined in."

"As St John's girlfriend. We'd love that."

Rayne blushed, flattered.

"But what do we do about Flora?" Amelia went on. "We're at the same school, in the sixth form together. Who gets left out?"

"St John should," said Rayne. "He finished with her – he should be the one to go."

"I agree with you," said Petra, again. "But the thing is—"

"Basically, he means more to us than Flora does," said

Amelia. "He's like – he's *central*. It would be awful if he wasn't there."

"Unthinkable," added Petra.

Rayne sat back, shaking her head. "God, I don't know. That's the trouble with tight groups of friends. And you're *really* tight, aren't you? You've got this *kitty*, haven't you, this bag of money you buy drinks and stuff from—"

"Oh, that," laughed Petra, "that was from when we all went on holiday at the start of the summer, to Thailand. We had a wicked time but it was obvious St John was getting sick of Flora then – she's so possessive, she'd go mad if he even *looked* at anyone else. . ."

"He tried to finish with her when we got back," Amelia added, "and she got so upset he backed down and they've come to this agreement that they're having a sort of break—"

"In other words not sleeping together—"

"Although she *tries* to, all the time. . ."

"And she gets hysterical if he's cold to her."

"So he's letting her down gently."

"That's what he said to me," said Rayne. "He called it . . ." her mind went back to the night they'd first kissed, the night Ben Avebury had stared out at them from his window . . . "*weaning her off him.* God, it all sounds horribly messy. To be honest I think I should steer clear. . ."

"Oh, *please* don't," said Petra, and this time she actually got hold of Rayne's hand, and stroked it. "He really likes you. And you like him, don't you?"

"You know what?" said Amelia, excitedly. "Flora needs to see that you and St John are an item now. It's kill or cure."

"As long as the *kill* isn't me being stabbed by her," said Rayne, and both the girls laughed, cosily.

Then Amelia went on, "There's a party on this Saturday. Quite a big one. One of the guys from our class, Jamie, it's his eighteenth. It's at his house, his parents are clearing off at ten and leaving us to it. . . Are you free then?

"Yes," Rayne said.

"Well – in that case it's settled! We're all going, OK? Flora, and St John, and Marcus – and *us three*. It'll work out, Rayne. Once you're part of it all, it'll work out. It's going to be *amazing*."

St John called Rayne the next night and she invited him round for supper. At first, they were polite with each other; he washed salad and grated cheese while she made a sauce from onion and fresh tomato, and put the pasta on to boil. Then, as they sat down to eat at the table in the window, he said, "Amelia and Petra confessed."

"That I went out with them? What did they say?"

"They love you, Rayne. They think you're *great*."

"Really?" She was taken off guard, flattered. "Why?"

"Oh, loads of things. Your honesty, your straightforwardness. Plus they think you're gorgeous. And really good for me."

She looked down, smiling.

"They told me about the party," he went on. "I think it's a good idea. Rayne – I'm pretty screwed up at the moment. I'm so sorry about what happened – you know, in the house. Thank you for seeing me again."

They talked. They talked about possessive relationships and their hopes for the future and what had been wrong with their pasts. After the meal they lay across the bed together, not touching, and continued to talk. It seemed to Rayne that there was something circling round the edges, something at odds with it all, but she was so pleased with how they were getting on and the pull of energy between them that she pushed it out of her mind. And then, as dusk was settling in the room, their talking slowed, and they both fell asleep.

Rayne woke to find the room dark and St John gone. At first, she assumed he was in the bathroom, then the long silence told her that he wasn't.

She had no idea what time it was. She checked her phone – it was nearly eight o'clock. She'd slept for over an hour.

She got off the bed. The outside door was standing ajar. She pulled it open, and stared out. The ancient garden was full of the night noise that passed for silence – rustlings, creakings, the *tok tok* of large falling leaves. But there was no sign of St John.

She stood there, uncertain, upset. Why had he run off, why had he just left without a word to her? Then she saw him, coming through the trees. His smile looked ecstatic, weird, in the thin light from the new moon that shone down on him.

"Hey!" he called softly. "I didn't want to wake you!"

"Why did you go out? Where have you been?" she asked. He reached her, and put his arms round her, and his smile was human again, and his eyes shone with pleasure, he was crackling with it.

"I just wanted to walk," he murmured. "I felt so happy I wanted to walk." Then he put his arms round her, and kissed her.

Chapter
Thirty-seven

"Autumn's really here now, isn't it, dear?" said Mrs Driver, as they cleared up the tearoom at the end of that Friday's shift. "The nights are drawing in."

She was right; it was so gloomy they'd had to turn the overhead lights on to see what they were doing. Rayne had often heard her gran say *the nights are drawing in*, but there was something so dreary, almost frightening, about the way Mrs Driver said it, as though the nights were pressing in like ghosts, like zombies coming for you. . .

"Winter's on its way," the housekeeper went on, sadly. "By the time February comes, here, we're longing for summer . . . simply longing for it. It's the light, you see. Morton's Keep needs the sun coming in through its windows, or it's just so *dark*."

Rayne didn't answer, just carried on wiping the tables. Then Mrs Driver seemed to rally her spirits a bit, and said, "Mind you, it's the Apple Fair soon. That's always lovely, all the apples and quinces laid out in rows, piled high . . . the smell in the old barn's delicious. It's the Saturday after next, dear – I do hope you'll be here to help out."

"Definitely," said Rayne. "I'm not going back home, not for a while."

"Aren't you, dear? Well, it's probably for the best. After what . . . you know . . . *happened*. I'm so glad you're here for the Fair. Mr Stuart's determined to make it even bigger and better than last year's – he's got a lot of publicity for it, locally – there'll be stalls, local crafts and cheeses and so on, and we're having cream teas and a hog roast, and he's arranged musicians, and even Morris dancers. . ."

"Sounds great," said Rayne, meaning the opposite. Although the hog roast sounded good. "What will you want me to do?"

"Oh, there'll be lots to do. Help set it all out, help with the cream teas . . . just see what needs doing. We trust you, dear!"

"There's nothing on tomorrow, is there?" said Rayne. "Only I want to go out Saturday night. . ."

"Oh, no. If there was, I'd have given you more warning than this." She turned away, concentrated on shutting the cleaning-cupboard door and switching off the kitchen lights. "No, nothing we need help for," she went on, "just some of those silly ghost hunters turning up. Four of them, apparently, this time."

On Saturday morning, Rayne woke and lay on in bed, luxuriating in laziness, then she got showered and dressed and set off to go shopping in Marcle Lees. With all the free food and the generous tips, her money situation was pretty good, and she could spend it now she wasn't going back home anytime soon, because there was no need to save it for train fares.

She wanted to buy something fabulous to wear to the party that night. Flora might be very pretty but she, Rayne, had more style and drama and tonight she aimed to demonstrate this. Emphatically. She wasn't feeling kind.

It was after four when she'd finally finished shopping. She'd gone to a remade shop and bought a wonderful skirt – then spent ages finding the right top to go with it. Then she'd gone hunting for shoes, decided there was nothing better than the black suede ones she already had and, on an impulse, gone into a sharp-looking hairdressers and had her out-of-shape hair cut. Then she'd bought a new mascara and nail varnish.

She felt light-heartedly terrific on the bus on the way back, and as she rode along she decided to stop *angsting* over everything and just . . . see what happened. She couldn't wait to start getting dolled up for the night. It was ages since she'd been to a party. She missed the glamour of it.

"You look absolutely . . . you look *gorgeous*."

Rayne stood in the open door to the Sty, basking in St John's admiration. "Thank you! Isn't the skirt brilliant?"

"Brilliant. Unusual. And the shoes. And the *legs*. You look *gorgeous*. Give me a kiss."

"You keep off!" she laughed, holding him at arm's length. "I spent ages doing my make-up."

"I love it. I love the eyes. Hey – let's not go. Let's stay here."

"You are *joking*. I'm not wasting these clothes."

"OK," he laughed. "Just one beer, then. Let me have you all to myself for one beer. And I promise to keep a good two feet away from you the whole time."

He put his arm round her and steered her into the room.

The house that the party was held at was easily the largest and most expensive that Rayne had ever set foot in – apart from Morton's Keep, of course. But she didn't feel inhibited. She knew she was different – her accent, her colour, the way she was dressed – and she revelled in it. She felt so confident as St John took her hand and they walked in to meet everyone. Amelia and Petra were sitting together in a gigantic armchair, looking leggy and beautiful, and ignoring everyone. But as soon as they saw Rayne and St John, they scrambled gracefully from the armchair's plush depths and rushed over to kiss them. Then Marcus came over, too, with his arm round Flora, as though he was protecting her. Or propelling her over, Rayne couldn't decide. "You made it!" said Marcus. "Great to see you!"

"You look *wonderful*, Rayne," gushed Petra, and Amelia reached out and stroked her arm.

Rayne didn't dare look at Flora. The hurt coming off her – she could practically feel it, like waves of heat. She glanced up at St John. He was smiling like a sphinx.

"Let's get a drink, shall we?" he said, calmly, and steered Rayne off towards the end of the huge room where a bar was set up.

*

It wasn't a particularly good party. The food was excellent and the bar never stopped flowing with free drink, but the music was dull. And the forcible addition of Rayne into the group just didn't work. Not like Amelia and Petra had hoped it would. Rayne knew that Flora hated her. She could see it in her eyes – they were dead, like flint. When St John put his arms round her, Flora rushed out of the room. Petra went after her and Amelia turned to St John, shrugging, hands upturned, miming *what can we do?*

St John murmured that he was getting more drinks, and left Rayne and Amelia alone.

"I feel *awful* about this," erupted Rayne. "Maybe it wasn't such a good plan. It feels so . . . *cruel.*"

"It absolutely *isn't,*" said Amelia, soothingly. "Or if it is, it's like my gran used to say – *cruel to be kind.*" She was standing very close to Rayne, looking intently into her face, like a lover. "She has to know, Rayne. She has to accept it's over."

"I know. But it's one thing to talk about making her face it, and another to – *God.* If I was her – I'd have nothing to do with him. Seriously. Why can't she accept it, why doesn't she just . . . *stay away?*"

"I know, I agree – me too, I'd clear off bigtime. It's like rubbing salt in the wound, seeing you with St John. I told her – I *said* you were going to be here. But she wants to be with *us.*"

"You really think she'll get the message tonight?"

Amelia nodded. "Cruel to be kind," she murmured.

*

As the music slowed Rayne and St John danced close, then as they kissed she whispered, "Maybe we should've stayed at the Sty, after all."

"Not been much fun, has it?"

"Not with Medusa watching us. I think I want to go, St John. Back to my place."

"Rayne – I can't give you a lift back. I've had too much to drink."

"It's all right, I'll get a taxi."

She was waiting for him to suggest he came with her, but what he said was, "OK. I'm gonna crash here."

She stopped moving against him. Hurt was pulsing away in her, and the need for him to fix it, to make things right again.

"I've kind of promised Jamie I'd help clear up in the morning," he went on.

"And I was kind of hoping you'd come back with me," she said, in a rush.

He looked down at her, smiling. "Oh, Rayne. *Look*, I think you're right – this evening has been a real downer. Let's just call it a night, ay?"

Chapter
Thirty-eight

In the taxi on her own, on the way back to Morton's Keep, Rayne battled with humiliation and hurt. And something else. A nasty feeling that he'd been *handling* her invaded her. All of it, all of it – it didn't add up, she didn't know why, it just didn't. The gushing way Marcus had kissed her goodbye and Amelia and Petra had cooed over her, making her promise they'd all get together soon – it was weird, *phoney*. And Flora had still been there at the party, she was sure of it – she hadn't seen her go. Flora was probably hiding upstairs in a bedroom somewhere, waiting for St John, waiting to confront him. And when she did . . . what would happen?

The taxi pulled into Morton's Keep's dark drive, then drew up on the forecourt alongside a battered white van with strange purple symbols painted on the side. Rayne looked at it nervously. It could only belong to the ghost hunters. As she got out of the cab she heard voices raised, and the sound of people hurrying across the cobbled courtyard.

Instinctively, she moved into the shadow of the trees so

she wouldn't be seen. A couple came through the archway. The woman was dumpy with straw-coloured dreadlocks pulled back into a band; the man was tall, bearded, thick-set, wearing a black leather jacket. "I want the keys to the *van*, Paul!" the woman hissed. "I'm not staying here!"

"Sadie, what the *hell* is the point of doing this if you're going to run the minute anything shows up?"

"And what the *hell's* the point of having all this equipment if we don't believe what it's telling us?" She dropped her voice and Rayne moved closer, still hidden by shadows. "I *knew* that room was the focus, right away. I could feel it."

"Look, we hoped we'd find this," said Paul. "That's why we came here."

"I know. But that energy – it felt *terrible*."

"It was more than I expected. But—"

"More than you *expected*? It was *off* the *scale*! And it was recent, it was *growing* – it really freaked me!"

Paul put his arm round her as three more figures appeared in the archway. Another couple, much like the first, carrying two large cases of equipment, and Mr Stuart, with his hands clasped in front of him, saying, "It seems such a shame! You've only been here an hour or so!"

"I know," the woman said. "But we're clearing out. In seven years of doing this stuff I've never been that scared."

"Oh, come on," said Paul. "What about that time in the old foundry—"

"That wasn't . . . *personal*. This – it was . . . it knew we were there. They way it grew as we moved about the room – it was like it was tracking *us*."

"Oh, dear," laughed Mr Stuart. "I hardly think so. Perhaps your equipment was malfunctioning?"

Paul turned to him. "Has anything happened in that room recently? Anything that could have . . . stirred the energies?"

Mr Stuart shook his head. "Nothing. Just the usual cleaning, the usual guided tours. . ."

"And on these tours . . . could anyone have been allowed to . . . hang back? Be in there on their own?"

Mr Stuart shook his head again. "Ms Barton practically counts everyone in and out. And she takes extra care in Abigail's room, because of the fragility of some of the furniture. . ."

Rayne felt the blood drain from her face. *Abigail's room.* Abigail's room was where she and St John had been, just a few days ago. Heart thudding, she strained to hear what was said next.

"The strongest energy was in a definite line," Paul went on. "It went from that door on the left of the fireplace to the end of the bed, right in the centre. . ."

In her mind, Rayne saw St John turn, smiling, come towards her, steer her towards the bed . . . and her, overcome, wanting him . . . and him pushing her on to the end of the bed, *right in the centre. . .*

She turned and ran through the trees towards the Sty. The night was alive, too alive; the wind was fierce, the trees danced overhead with dreadful warning. She remembered how she felt in Abigail's room, wanting St John one minute, then desperate to get out . . . maybe whatever awful thing they were talking about, maybe it had affected her too. . .

Don't think about it. She ran on.

She reached the Sty, and as she put the key in the lock she heard the sound of the ghost hunters' van driving rapidly down the drive. Mr Stuart hadn't managed to persuade them to stay.

The trees were rearing and bucking like maddened horses. Another storm was on its way.

Chapter
Thirty-nine

As she let herself in, she was shivering. The room was dark and cheerless; she hurried to the kitchen and put the kettle on, then she crouched by the stove and lit the fire she'd laid earlier that day. "You're just spooked, that's all," she muttered. It was like the first night she'd spent in the Sty; she could feel fear growing in her and all around her. "They're nutters, with their stupid ghost machines . . . don't think about it. *Don't think about it.*"

She felt completely alone. There was no one she could call, no one she could phone to give her comfort. She thought of Becky, but she didn't have her number. She didn't want to call St John. It would look like she was checking up on him, and anyway. . . She didn't want to speak to him.

She got ready for bed, and drew back the curtains, just as she had done that terrible first night. She lay in bed trying to calm herself, watching the warm glow of the stove and, through the window, the thrashing of the trees in the strong wind.

Then the storm broke. First a great, sky-tearing spear of lightning, then thunder right afterwards, like hundreds of boulders tipped on the roof. As Rayne huddled under her duvet, her fear left her. She felt exhilarated; braver with each new flash and crash. By the time the huge rain had started, she was half-asleep.

That night, she dreamt that Morton's Keep was burning to the ground, and she was watching from a distance. She didn't go for help, it was too late, the flames were engulfing everything, and also . . . she wanted it to burn. She knew it needed to burn, but she didn't know why, and anguish filled her as she watched.

She stirred into that half-awake, half-asleep state of not knowing what was real and what was still the dream. Her eyelids glowed as though she was watching the great house burn, she could smell smoke. . .

She jerked wide awake, sat up. The fire in the stove was roaring, flames licking up and outside of the half-open glass doors – she could feel the heat on her face. Heart racing, she checked her watch. Four in the morning. *How could it still be going?* The wood she'd laid would have burnt out ages ago. She stared as it flickered and roared, searching for safety, sanity, for a solution. . . Then it came. "It's a bird's nest," she told herself, rolling over, turning her back on it, though she could still hear it crackle, still feel its heat, "it's a nest that's fallen down the chimney in the storm. . ."

She shut her mind to the tiny voice of logic telling her a few shreds of bird's nest wouldn't create all those flames.

Rayne left the Sty the next morning to find that the tall elm at the far side of the medieval garden had fallen. Its roots were torn out from the ground and exposed in a great mushroom-shaped slab that made her think of a door opening into the earth. She went over to it, leant on the bottom of the trunk, and looked down towards the branches.

And was filled with an extraordinary sensation, as though she was rushing towards the top of the tree – as though energy was streaming through from the ripped-out roots to the tips of the branches, taking her with it. It came to her that the soul of the elm tree was leaving, and she desperately wanted to save it, let it live – if she got Ben Avebury to help her stand it upright again, would it reroot itself?

Then she backed off from the trunk. "For *God's* sake, girl," she muttered, "stop being so *weird*. Soul of the tree, honestly. You need to get back to town."

She wandered down towards the lake, and reached it far too soon. The little stream had bursts its banks and the lake had swollen, flooded – all the surrounding land was under water. The three white geese swam towards her; long grass waved like seaweed underneath them.

"This'll take a while to drain off."

She looked up, startled. Ben Avebury had come up noiselessly beside her.

"Two more down in the woods. And did you see the elm?"

She nodded. She was thinking of her idea to get him to help her reroot it, but she didn't say anything.

"They'll all take some clearing, chopping. That were some fury last night."

A memory clutched at her. She turned to him. "*What* did you say?" she asked.

"The storm. It were a real fury."

"*Fury?*"

"Ay. It's our word round here for a storm, a real storm."

Rayne turned away, heart thumping. The memory was with her now. The old mad woman – Patience – in the back room of the Green Lady pub, singing *Fire, flood, fury. She is fire, flood, fury.*

Chapter
Forty

"Sure I'll ask them. It's a brilliant idea. They'd love to come."

St John smiled at Rayne, pushed back her hair, kissed her again. Rayne smiled back, but it stopped short of her eyes.

"It kicks off at about three," she said, "but I wouldn't bother coming till the evening. Not unless you're particularly interested in all the different breeds of English apples."

"No," he grinned. "We'll come when the bar opens."

She'd spent the last few days trying to *keep herself sane*, as she called it to herself. It was as if, inside herself, she'd hauled shut a great door – she was letting nothing through. She worked very hard in the tearoom – she was so chatty and sweet her tips practically doubled. After work she walked fast for at least an hour, so she slept soundly. She avoided the house; she refused to think about all the "weirdness". Weirdness had happened outside too, but somehow, she didn't mind that. She was outdoors for as long as she could be.

After two days she went back to the fallen elm and leaned on the trunk near its great root ball, looking down at the branches. And the extraordinary sensation of speed, of rushing, had gone. It was just a dead tree now. Somehow, she'd known it would be.

It was half-term, and Becky had gone away to stay with her cousins in the North, so she had no one to talk to. Not that she thought she could discuss anything of all this with her. Or with St John. With him, she was "normal". She thought if she acted "normal", she'd *be* normal. She'd said nothing about him staying with Flora at the party, nothing about the ghost hunters, nothing about the fire, flood and fury. They saw each other twice in the week, when he talked seductively of how "Flora was coming to terms with everything". She desperately wanted to believe him. The more she saw of him, the more she wanted him, but it wasn't making her happy. It was like a horrible craving, a craving that couldn't be satisfied.

And now she was suggesting he and his friends turned up on Saturday evening, to the Apple Fair. She said she could get them free hog roast. She was cool, unjealous, relaxed. It was all normal, she told herself, all OK.

The old barn where the Apple Fair was to be held was in a field some sixty metres away from the mansion house, on the opposite side to the Sty. That Saturday, Rayne worked flat out to set everything up. While Ben Avebury and a man hired from the town hauled trestle tables and benches into place, she arranged apples and quinces in towering piles on narrow tables round the barn's walls. Autumn sunlight shafted down through the skylights, illuminating the fruit. The air filled with crisp scent.

The bar at the end was laid out with tea things; crates of wine, boxes of glasses and barrels of beer were stowed beneath, ready for the evening. Mrs Driver kept trotting over from the old dairy with batches of fresh-baked scones. Tubs of thick, crusting yellow cream were in the fridge; jars of glowing home-made strawberry jam lined the shelves behind.

Outside, Ms Barton was in charge. Two large tents were set up for the craft stalls; already a woman with beautiful patchwork quilts, two local cheese-makers and a man with hand-carved wooden toys were setting out their wares. Mr Stuart was wandering around with a clipboard, urging everyone on to make the fair a success.

By three, everything was ready and the first visitors had arrived, and then, steadily, more and more people came, and Rayne was kept busy selling cream teas. The apples and quinces were tasted, judged, discussed, celebrated. At four, they started the hog roast outside; it filled the barn with a rich, savoury fragrance which mingled beautifully with the smell of the quinces and apples.

At ten to six, Rayne sold the last scone. As she was washing the last of the teacups and plates, Mr Stuart came up to the bar, beaming broadly. "Well *done*, Rayne!" he said. "You've been working *so* hard!"

"We had to use paper plates for a bit," she said, "when

the real rush was on, but mostly Mrs D and I kept up with it. . ."

"You did indeed. And just look at that overstuffed cash box." He picked it up and tipped the money into the large leather pouch he was carrying. "It's going splendidly. The craft stalls have done a roaring trade – we'll get twenty per cent of their takings. And there's a new flow of people arriving now, for the evening."

"That's great, Mr Stuart. You're going to clean up!"

"I hope so," he laughed. "OK, I'll take over here now – Ben's going to help me set the bar out. You have a break. Back on at seven-thirty or so to help with the hog roast?"

Rayne wandered out of the old barn. The coal fire glowed under the huge spitted pig; people stood around it in groups, chatting and laughing. The light was fading and the party atmosphere was growing. St John would arrive around seven with Flora, Amelia, Petra and Marcus, and she'd get them free drinks, free food . . . it was *her* thing and it was going to be great. The music, the Morris dancers – it would all be a laugh. Then maybe she'd snaffle some wine and they'd all go back to the Sty – *her* territory – and then everyone would leave but St John would stay so they could have some time alone together. And Flora would just have to accept it.

Back in her room, she ditched her jam-stained white shirt and black skirt, made her eyes up again, dark and dramatic, pulled on jeans and a tight top, and flicked out her hair. In the thin bathroom mirror, she looked terrific. She checked her watch – twenty past six. She should rest, she should lie on the bed for a bit – but she was buzzing too much. She decided to head over to the old barn again, and look around while the stalls were still trading.

She opened the door to find St John standing there, smiling. "Hey!" she cried, startled. "Why didn't you knock?"

"Only just got here," he said.

"You on your own?"

"Of course," he said, moving in close to her. "I parked the bike where I usually do."

"So when are the others getting here?"

"Half an hour or so. We'll see them over there." Then he got hold of her arms and pulled her up against him, and kissed her. All her old suspicion dissolved. He kissed like an angel. Slow, smooth . . . listening to her. She started to draw him back into the Sty.

"Hey," he breathed. "What are you up to?"

She laughed. She wasn't sure what she was up to. "I just want to be with you," she said. "Is that a crime?"

For an answer, he wrapped his arms round her, half-lifted her off her feet, kissed her again. "No crime at all," he murmured. "Hey – it's going to be all right, you know. You and me. It's going to work out." Then he kissed her again, and said, "Let's go for a wander, beautiful. Just the two of us."

Hand in hand, they walked through the medieval garden towards the mansion house. St John gestured with his head towards the ancient archway. "Can we go through there?" he asked. "Take a look at the old courtyard?"

"Why?" she asked.

He laughed. "I want to see where they used to hang people."

Rayne grimaced, and they went through the arch. "It was from up there," he said, pointing. "From that beam, there."

A stubby beam, black with age, jutted from the wall beside a high window. Rayne had never noticed it before; now she wondered how she'd ever missed it. It looked like a decaying finger, pointing obscenely at the sky.

"People make out they had a gallows here in the courtyard, but it's not true," he went on. "That window – it's at the end of the gallery in the Old Stone Hall. Once the death sentence was passed, they'd sling a rope round the prisoner's neck and just shove him out the window. Then they'd haul the body back in."

"Nice," muttered Rayne. "How do you *know* that? Your hidden history stuff again?"

St John laughed. "That's right. Good old Petra and Amelia and their loyal research."

"*Loyal?* Loyal to who?"

"Loyal to. . ." He broke off. Then he laughed and said, "To truth. To *history*."

"Oh, *God*. Come on, let's go. You've made me feel sick with all this stuff about hanging. I've gotta *live* here."

But St John had moved over to the old church-like door. He picked up the strange, severed-hand door knocker and looked down at it intently. Then he stooped and pressed the shining, jagged ring on the middle finger to his lips.

Rayne's spine crawled. "*Stop it*," she breathed.

He turned and looked at her, smiling, then he bent and

kissed the ring again. "My liege lord," he murmured. "I am your bondsman."

"*Stop* it, St John," she snapped. "Stop acting like a prat."

"I follow in your beautiful path!" he crooned, then, still holding the brass hand, he turned and laughed at her.

"Why are you *doing* that?" she demanded.

"Why not?" he said, goading her. He turned back and kissed the hand again. His tongue flicked out of his mouth, slicked over the ring. . . Rayne felt a wave of revulsion. She turned and stamped off towards the archway. He caught up with her as she went through, slung his arm round her shoulder. "What the hell's wrong with you?" he said.

"I think that door knocker's really creepy, that's all," she snapped. "And you *know* I find the house creepy, but you go on about it, wanting to see where people were *hung* and wanting to go in the *bedrooms* and—"

"No, I don't," he said indignantly, taking his arm away. "Hey – calm down. What's up?"

Tension clutched at her. In a few minutes, they'd be with the others. She'd wanted to make it work, she'd wanted to present a loved-up, united front, not this. . . "*Nothing's* up," she said, and she pushed herself back under his arm again, put her arm round his waist. "Come on. Let's go and get a drink."

Chapter
Forty-one

When they arrived outside the barn, they saw Flora, Amelia, Marcus and Petra standing in a line by the glow of the hog roast, as if they were posing for a photograph. Their silhouette against the flames was so dramatic and stylish that people walking by turned to stare. St John called out "Hey!" and the four turned to him, eyes shining in the firelight, and hurried over. Everyone hugged and kissed; as Petra drew back from St John she looked ecstatic, as if he'd whispered magic to her. Even Flora seemed happy – an almost palpable air of pleasure surrounded the group. Rayne felt infected by it, desperate to be a part of it. "I'll go and see if I can get some wine, shall I?" she said. "Or do you want beer?"

" *Wine* will be fine," sang Marcus. "Wine will be *heaven.*" Amelia giggled loudly, and Petra sprang at Rayne and gave her another hug.

"Are you lot *on* something?" she blurted out.

"No," said Marcus. "No, we're just *so happy* to be here, pattering Rayne, gentle Rayne from heaven, summer *Ra-yne* makes me feel *f-ine. . .*"

Everyone laughed at his awful singing, Petra joining in

with him on the last note, and Rayne hurried off to the bar where Mr Stuart was working flat out serving drinks. He let her make off with a couple of bottles of wine and some plastic glasses. "On the house," he said. "After that – cost price."

Ben Avebury was collecting dirty glasses from the trestle tables. She kept a wary eye on him as she hurried past. She hoped he wouldn't spot St John, she hadn't forgotten him warning her off him. The memory made her anxious; there was something else, something else awful to do with all that. . . *Don't think about it.* She didn't want any trouble, not tonight. Tonight had to be perfect. Tonight was going to be the night she was really accepted, the night she joined the group, the night Flora accepted *she* was St John's girlfriend now. Fixing a smile on her face, she drew near the fire calling out "Hey! Look what I got!", and waved the bottles and glasses. St John grinned at her, then he moved in close between her upraised arms and kissed her, gratifyingly slow, on the mouth. The others gathered round, and she handed out the glasses as St John poured the wine. Then she glanced up, puzzled. "Where's Marcus and Petra gone?" she asked.

Amelia let out a shriek of giggles. "They've gone off," she cooed, "to . . . *be* together."

"*What?* I thought Marcus was gay."

"Oh, *God,*" sneered Flora, her eyes flickering with hostility. "Why d'you assume he's *gay?*"

"Er – he *acts* it?"

"No, he doesn't. He's just expressive, theatrical. God, that is so *narrow.* . ."

"*Flora!*" purred St John, and Flora was instantly quiet.

Rayne sipped her wine, shaken. St John put his arm round her. "All right?" he murmured.

"Yeah," she muttered. They stood drinking silently, and she stared at the people round the fire, feeling the weight of his arm round her. Amelia was standing very close to Flora, talking animatedly.

The man in charge of the hog roast had started carving slices from its flank; a queue was forming. "I'd better start helping with the food," Rayne said.

"D'you have to? Can't you stay with me?"

She moved closer against him. "I'll just put in half an hour, then I can get us some free food when the rush has died down."

"Great. That'll be great. I'm *starving*." He smiled down at her, and reluctantly she pulled away and went over to the fire.

For the next forty minutes, Rayne worked hard. She slid slice after slice of succulent pork into fat, floury baps, handed them out, and took the money. In the firelight, the pig's ribs were showing ghoulishly; the queue had dwindled.

She kept hoping St John would come and talk to her, but he was wrapped up in the group again. Petra and Marcus had reappeared and they were all talking together excitedly. *They really are incestuous, like Becky said*, she thought, sourly. Maybe she didn't want to be a part of it, after all. It came to her to make St John choose – *her or them* – but she dismissed it as childish, jealous.

213

"I can manage from now," said the hog-roast man. "You want to take a bap? And one for your boyfriend?"

"Would it be OK to take six altogether?"

He shrugged. "Don't see why not. What's not sold will go to waste. And it's a shame 'cos those scrappy bits – they're often the tastiest." He helped her fill six baps, each in its own thick paper napkin. Then she signalled to St John, who came over and helped her carry them back to the group.

"*Mmmmmm*, thank you, *fabuloso*, darling!" mewed Marcus, sounding even more camp than usual. No doubt Flora had told him she thought he was gay, and he was playing up to it. "We're all so *unbelievably glad* you work at Morton's Keep, *aren't* we, people?"

"Yes, we *are!*" squeaked Amelia, mouth full.

"*Absolutely!*" added Petra. "Thank you *so much*, Rayne!"

Rayne didn't answer. She had the sudden thought that they were mocking her, even though they were clearly loving the pork baps. The night wasn't turning out like she'd hoped. There was this . . . *undercurrent*. She couldn't put a name to it, but it was there.

Everyone chewed speechlessly for a few moments, then Flora said, "We've run out of wine."

"I can get some more, cheap," said Rayne. "Just let me finish eating this, OK?"

While Marcus and Amelia made a show of rummaging for pound coins and five-pound notes to give to Rayne, St John pointed at the fire. "Look," he said. "Look what your creepy gardener's up to."

Ben Avebury, hands and arms wrapped in sacking,

had taken hold of one end of the hog-spit, and the cook, wearing huge oven gloves, had taken hold of the other. Together they lifted the bony remains free of the fire. Then Ben turned to a huge wickerwork basket on the ground, drew out several logs, and threw them on the glowing coals. In the banked-up heat, they ignited and burst into flame; several people cheered.

"Pyromaniac as well as perv," murmured St John.

Ben threw on more logs, emptying the basket, then went over to some nearby bushes and picked up the end of a severed tree trunk. With the help of the hog-roast man, he hauled it over to the fire and heaved it on. They went back and got a second huge log, then a third; soon the flames were burning higher than a man.

And then the drumbeat began.

Chapter
Forty-two

There was something sinister about that single, measured beat in the darkness, like a slow drum roll before an execution. Rayne peered into the night, trying to locate it. It seemed to be coming from a long way away, from the end of the mansion drive, maybe.

"What the *hell*?" she muttered, but St John was silent, a smirk on his face.

Then she saw the torches – ten guttering balls of fire, moving closer. The people round the fire started cheering and clapping. "What *is* it?" demanded Rayne.

"The Morris dancers," said St John. "Lucky *us*."

The ten torches came into full view, each carried by a man dressed in a loose shirt and trousers, some dark green, some dark brown. In their other hands, they held long wooden staffs. One of the men had antlers strapped to his head; another wore a spiky crown of sticks and leaves. An elderly man in a long, tattered-looking cloak followed, beating the drum.

"Otherwise known as the fire festival group," St John

went on, sarcastically. "Didn't you realize they were one and the same?"

She shook her head vigorously, then she said, "Oh, God, of course. Mr Stuart mentioned it, at the posh dinner – when they were all going on about devil worship. But I'd forgotten, and Mrs Driver never said. I thought they'd be. . ."

"What?" he said, putting his arm round her. "Daft-looking old men in pretty straw hats prancing up and down, waving red scarves? Not this lot."

The Morris men lined up in front of the fire. Then with a loud wild shout, they chucked their torches into the flames, and faced each other in a circle. And the "dancing" began.

"*Blimey*," breathed Rayne.

It wasn't dancing. It was like five fights, fights where the opponents kept shifting and changing. There was no other music but the drumbeat. The men leapt at each other, threatening, hostile, and their faces glared in the firelight. They clashed their staffs like weapons, and splinters flew. Six of the men were solid, middle-aged, but they moved with as much force and energy as the younger men.

"*Oh my God*," whispered Rayne, "isn't that—"

"Ethan Sands," hissed St John. "My old buddy. Yes. What an *arsehole*."

The drumbeat stopped, the men bowed, grinning, to a tirade of clapping and shouts of "*More!*" Then the men wearing the antlers and the spiky crown stood to one side with the four other older men, and the four young men stepped forward.

"Here it comes," sneered St John. "Ethan's moment of glory."

217

The drumbeat started again, twice as fast. The dance started; another fight, but wilder and much more savage. Rayne watched open-mouthed as Ethan leapt and twisted, always striking his staff at the right time, landing, springing, always in time . . . but even so he jumped higher, leapt further, than all the others. She thought he looked beautiful, primeval.

Then, just as suddenly as it had started, the dance finished. "Go and get the wine, will you?" drawled St John, above the clapping. "I need alcohol if I've got to watch this."

"*No*," hissed Rayne. "I want to watch." The arm he'd laid casually about her shoulders slackened in disapproval, but she didn't care. She didn't even care when he took it away, and turned back to talk to the rest of the group. She stayed watching, enthralled.

For the next dance, there was music. The man with the antlers produced a mouth organ from his pocket, the crowned man a kind of pipe; two other men were handed fiddles by the elderly drummer. Then, with the ease of long practice, they started playing together. The high, joyful notes carried loudly on the night air. The next dance was more like a dance, the six men turning and jumping high and jigging, then coming together to forming a star shape with their sticks. "*See*," hissed St John, back at her shoulder. "The pentagon. Black magic symbol."

"No, it isn't," Rayne hissed back. "That's got five points, they're doing six."

"Whatever," snapped St John. And he stalked off again.

Two more sets followed, to louder and louder applause. Rayne was entranced. She'd never seen anything like it.

218

Sheer animal energy drove through the strict forms of the dance, always threatening to break out and cause chaos, but always staying within the forms. The stag who'd disturbed them in the woods came into her mind – the power of him, the amorality. That was what this dancing was like.

As the fifth set came to an end, Mr Stuart appeared with a huge tray with eleven brimming glass mugs of beer on it, and the men bowed to enthusiastic applause and took a break. They each took a mug of beer, then like dark crows they descended on the cooling pig skeleton, tearing off strips of meat and devouring them, laughing and joking together.

Rayne found herself watching Ethan. Now that she'd seen the power in him, she could see it in every move he made. She wasn't sure what she felt about it, but she couldn't stop staring. Then suddenly he looked up, and saw her. He stopped chewing. He said something to another young man standing next to him, and together they put their beer mugs on the ground, and started walking towards her.

She froze, waiting. But it wasn't her they wanted. Ethan planted himself right in front of St John and snarled, "What are *you* doing here?"

"None of your business, dancing boy," replied St John. His voice was tense, defensive.

"And what if we make it our business?"

"Then you'll look like an idiot. An even bigger idiot than you looked five minutes ago, prancing round in circles."

Ethan and his friend grinned like wolves, teeth gleaming in the firelight. The insult hadn't even flicked them. "You try it," said Ethan's friend. "When we start up again – *you* try it."

"We'd love to have you join in," said Ethan, menacingly, and he took a step closer to St John. Marcus and the others had come up behind St John and were standing in a protective semicircle behind him. But they weren't nearly as close as Ethan Sands. "You'd better leave here," Ethan went on. "*Now*. We don't want your sort here."

"I'm here by invitation," said St John. "I was invited by my girlfriend."

St John was trembling with the effort of standing his ground. Rayne could sense it. *Don't you move!* she urged, silently, and she stepped forward, half-barring Ethan. "Who are *you* to say who can be here?" she demanded, glaring at him. "I work here. I *live* here. If I invite him, he's allowed."

Ethan didn't so much as glance at her. His eyes were fixed on St John's face. "Oh, yeah. And Mr Stuart knows he's here, does he?"

"Of course he does."

"Like hell he does."

It was one of the older men who'd spoken, the man with the strange, spiky crown. He'd come up behind Ethan and his friend, and behind him was Ben Avebury.

"I think we'd better go and get him, don't you?" Ben said. "Let Mr Stuart himself decide who's a guest at his feast?"

Rayne opened her mouth to speak, but nothing came out, because the night was torn by the sound of a police siren screaming up the main drive.

Chapter Forty-three

The police car headlights flashed through the trees, harsh and searching, blinding out the firelight. In an instant, the mood of the crowd switched from relaxed enjoyment to strident curiosity. As the police car screeched to a halt before the walls of Morton's Keep, Rayne started running towards it, but it wasn't until she reached the forecourt that she realized it was Ethan Sands and not St John who was keeping pace behind her.

She barely had time to react to this before Mrs Driver hurried up, face twisted with anxiety. "Someone's broken into the glass case, the one halfway up the grand stairway," she said. "I noticed it when I was going up for a cardigan . . . the glass lid was hanging down below the curtains. . ."

Rayne put her hand on Mrs Driver's arm. "What was taken?" she asked. "Everything?"

"No. Just a few bits and pieces. Jewellery mostly, the stuff that can be sold, I suppose. . . Anne Boleyn's comb's still there, thank God."

"The daggers?" asked Ethan, sharply.

"Yes – one of them's gone. Oh, and those strange gloves. They'd smashed the bolt to get in. . ."

Mr Stuart was standing by the ivy-choked fountain, involved in an energetic discussion with two policemen and another man. Nervously, Mrs Driver looked over at him. "He'll be angry, because we called the police," she said. "Right after I'd discovered the case had been smashed I bumped into Mr Laker – he's one of the trustees – and he *insisted* on phoning—"

"Well, of course he did!" said Rayne. "Why wouldn't you call the police?"

Mrs Driver shook her head. "Mr Laker's not from round here," she muttered, and moved closer to the four men. Rayne and Ethan followed.

"With respect, sir," one of the policemen was saying, "that was not the information Mr Laker gave us over the phone. He admitted the alarm was off, as guests were staying and coming in and out of the property during the evening, but he insisted all the guests would be scrupulous about locking up if they popped back for anything."

"Well, clearly, one of them *wasn't*," snapped Mr Stuart. "One of them left a door unlocked, and some opportunist from the fair wandered in, and as I said, I don't want to make a great song and dance out of it."

The policeman stiffened. "It's your property, sir. But as we've been called, we have to make a report. My colleague and I will need to examine the property to make sure there are no signs of forced entry, no window-catches broken. . ."

"You won't find anything," said Mr Stuart. "Waste your time if you want to."

"Charles, what's going *on*?" erupted Mr Laker. "Those artefacts have been in your family for centuries!"

222

"They're not particularly valuable."

"Perhaps not, but they're irreplaceable! And you're refusing help from the police?"

"I'm just refusing to waste my time," Mr Stuart gritted out. "That's all." Then he took hold of Mr Laker's arm, and walked away with him, still talking.

Rayne stared at the house. A wraith of smoke was coming from one of the chimneys – the huge chimney over the Old Stone Hall. "I don't know where they could've got in," Mrs Driver said, mournfully. "It was all locked up. I hope he doesn't think it was me who left a door open."

"Of course he doesn't," soothed Rayne. "You're extremely scrupulous about locking up." *Excessively so*, she thought.

"I think I'll get to bed, dear. I'm shattered."

"I would. If Mr Stuart wants it dropped, the police won't need to question you. . ." She watched as the housekeeper plodded off. Then a voice behind her said, "Have you got keys to the house?"

She spun round to face Ethan Sands. "Yes," she said, angrily. "Two keys, to the kitchen door. And if you think I—"

He shook his head. "No, not you. What about your *boyfriend*?"

"Look – what the *hell* have you got against him?"

"I'll tell you one day," said Ethan. "Right now I'm going to find him." And he turned and ran back towards the barn.

Rayne watched him go. Her heart was pounding. She thought of phoning St John, to warn him, and then an image of the keys, nestled in the cutlery drawer, came into her head, and she remembered going to the bathroom and leaving St John on his own for a few minutes, just before they'd left the Sty earlier that evening.

She was running back to the Sty almost before she knew what she was doing, bursting through the door, into the kitchen, yanking open the cutlery drawer . . . the keys were there, alongside the teaspoons, where they'd always been. She felt relief and guilt pulse through her, guilt because she'd doubted St John. She pulled out her phone.

He answered after four rings.

"You'd better make yourself scarce before that idiot Ethan Sands gets hold of you," she said, urgently. "He's on his way now, he's—"

"I'm on the bike now. Just about to leave."

"You're on your bike?"

"Thought I'd better clear off. With the fuzz arriving and everything, the party seemed to be over."

"St John, I'm at the Sty! Don't go, come here!"

A pause, just a bit too long. "Love to, Rayne, but – I dunno. I'd better make myself scarce, OK?"

"*No!* Don't be daft, don't—"

"Oh, *shit*—" The line went dead. In her mind she saw Ethan lunging at him, grabbing him off his bike . . . she ran outside, across the ancient garden towards the bushes where he always parked his bike.

Then she heard it, roaring down the drive. She started running down the drive after it, and she was just in time to see its silhouette disappear through the great gates. There was someone riding pillion behind him – someone slim, with her head resting against his back.

Chapter Forty-four

Twenty-five minutes later, St John called Rayne back. "Sorry about that," he said. "Ethan came racing up through the trees – I decided to make a dash for it."

"Really?" she said. "I didn't see him. I came out – when you cut me off."

"Yeah, he was there. He must've doubled back when he saw me go."

"Who was with you?"

"On the bike? Amelia. She needed a lift home. The others went with Marcus."

His voice was smooth and easy. But she didn't believe him. Ethan had been nowhere near, and the girl on the back was Flora, she knew it was Flora.

"Come back," she said, her voice raw. "Come back now, *please*."

"Rayne, I'm knackered. I'll see you tomorrow, OK?"

She lay down fully clothed on the bed and went off to sleep thinking – *It's over. He's going to finish with me.*

She woke just before dawn, full of grief. She knew she'd

dreamed horrible dreams, but she couldn't remember them. She made tea, then paced around the Sty, back and forth into the empty room on the other side, trying to convince herself it was all OK. Maybe it *had* been Flora on the bike, but that didn't mean anything – he'd tell her it was Amelia in case she did *just this* and got all jealous for no reason. . .

But she couldn't comfort herself. Grief – *dread* – was still lodged inside her, heavy, immovable. She knew he'd changed. Or – she was beginning to realize something, *know* something that had always been there in him, between them. . .

She couldn't stand her thoughts. No idea what she was doing, where she was going, she let herself out of the door, and started walking in the eerie grey light of dawn. She went down past the lake, and walked along a little track beside some fields, away from the house.

No birds were singing. The silence was fearful, as if something was waiting in it.

She climbed over a stile into a field, and started crossing it, heading towards the woods on the other side. And then she realized that she'd been there before, in a storm – Ethan Sands had shouted at her to get out from under the great tree, the tallest in the line. . .

She walked over to it. It looked spectral, sinister, in the grey light. A black cloud of crows rose up at the edge of the field, and flew high, cawing bleakly. She thought of battlefields, with nothing but the crows left alive, gorging on soldiers' flesh.

She went on into Fleet Woods.

*

"Come and get me," she muttered, as she walked on through the trees. "Come and get me, *devil* worshippers." She felt as though she couldn't care less what happened to her.

The trees got thicker, denser, as she walked on. She knew she was nowhere near the weird altar St John had torn apart, the day she'd seen the stag – maybe she'd stumble on another one. She didn't care.

She thought of the stag, the way it had looked at her. She wished she could see it again. She walked on, deeper and deeper into the silent woods, and the first streaks of daylight filtered through the branches above her.

Then there was a movement some way ahead of her, to her right. She stopped, stood silent, and stared ahead. In a space in the trees, there were dark shapes, moving. . .

Men. Men gathered in the clearing. The devil worshippers. Her skin crawled; fear invaded her. She stepped behind a thick tree trunk to watch as they formed a circle, the circle of dark ritual. She thought of Mrs Driver, anxious about locking and bolting the house, telling her to always lock her door at night . . . afraid of these men.

One of them raised his hands; she could see the antlers on his head. And the spiky crown on the head of another. She counted – there were eleven of them. They must have come straight from the dancing. They were chanting in a low, ominous murmur. . .

Horrified, but mesmerized, she leaned forward to hear and as she did, a twig cracked under her hand. Two of the men turned to face her, but in the half-light their faces were featureless. They started coming towards her.

And she heard, "It's her . . . it's *her*!"

The words liquefied her with terror. She broke cover and ran. She had no idea if the men were following – the cracking, crashing noise of her flight covered any sound they may have made. She hurtled on, arms out in front, shielding her face from the branches whipping at her, running anywhere there was a path through the trees, running, running, doubling back on herself, her breath coming in great gasps. . .

Ahead of her was a hollow tree. It had a great crack in it, like a sideways-on mouth. She stopped, wildly considering it as a bolt hole – and heard them behind her, crashing through the trees, shouting, "*Wait, girl! Wait!*"

She'd be trapped, wouldn't she, a rat in a trap, if they saw her climbing into the tree. . . But she couldn't keep running in mad circles. The shouting and crashing were getting louder, closer, there was no *time*. She clambered up on the gnarled roots, thrust her foot through the crack, began to push her way in. It was tight, oh *God*, too tight . . . she was stuck, she'd be wedged there like a rag doll . . . frantically she forced her way, and the ancient wood pressed into her breasts and her back and she eased forward and then at last with a slither full of pain like being born, she fell into the belly of the tree.

Only it wasn't like being born, it was like going back to before birth.

A feeling of intense enclosure surrounded her.

She breathed, slowly, let her heart thud back to normal. It occurred to her that she'd never get out of the tree again, but this thought didn't frighten her. No one and nothing could harm her here. All she could see was the inside of the tree, its brown, intricate texture – her senses were full of it. The smell of bark, the rough warmth under her hands. Suspended in wood like a fly in amber.

Then she heard the men go by, searching, still calling. They were after her but she was unafraid; she was still. She remembered St John; it seemed odd that she'd been so upset about him. He didn't seem to matter now.

There was a hole in the trunk, at head height, where a branch had fallen off. It was letting a soft light into the tree. She waited until the men had gone so far past that she couldn't hear them any more, then she put her face to it and looked out.

Her eyes refocused. The outside world was still there.

She smiled, and thought she must look like one of those stupid seaside photo things, where you put your face through a cut-out of a strongman or a ballerina. What would she look like from the outside . . . a tree spirit? A girl turning into a tree? Didn't some girl get turned into a tree once, rather than be raped?

And then, stalking calmly through the trees, came the stag. It stopped in front of the tree and gazed at her poked-out face steadily, as if it knew who she was and why she was there.

Then it turned and walked off.

Ten minutes later, Rayne reached the edge of Fleet Woods again. It had been easy to slip out through the slit in the tree again, far easier than getting in. She'd slithered through head first, loving the feel of the breeze on her face, the way everything opened up again, grinning at how absurd she must look. Except there was no one there to see her, now the stag had gone. She'd got her arms through, pulled hard, and landed in a handstand on soft moss and bracken, unhurt. There was no sound of the men, but anyway she wasn't afraid of them now. She felt weirdly invincible.

She walked through the woods, and set out across the field to go back. As she passed the tall tree, someone stepped out from under it.

"Hello, Ethan!" she called.

Chapter
Forty-five

"That was a good trick," Ethan said. "Hiding in that tree. I used to play in that one, when I was a kid."

"So you were with them, were you?"

"Yeah, I was in front."

"Why didn't you tell them where I was?"

He shrugged.

"Would they have hurt me?"

"Of course not. Just—"

"Just *what*?"

"Just wasted time, that's all."

"What were they up to? That creepy group, in the woods?"

"Watching. Trying to protect."

"Protect *what*?"

He shrugged again. She took a step towards him – if she reached out now, she'd touch him – and said, "Look, Ethan, don't you think you'd better start explaining things to me? There's something weird going on at the house, isn't there, and Mrs Driver thinks it's *you* lot, she—"

"No, she doesn't. She knows what's what, even if she

won't admit it to herself. She's with us. So's Mr Stuart. We're all together."

"Together? Together against *what*?"

He smiled, aggressively. "It's your *boyfriend*, now. I know it's him. The others aren't sure. Only old Ben Avebury, I know he's sure. Especially after the break-in last night. But he won't talk about it."

"Look, I know you've got it in for St John, but he didn't take my keys. Trust me – I checked. They were still there, in the drawer where I keep them."

"Maybe. But it's not just about that."

"What *is* it then? Tell me!"

"You wouldn't believe me if I did – sometimes *I* don't believe it. You know what? You should go and ask your Mr Stuart. You should go and get it out of *him*."

Rayne stared at him, and he stared back, unblinking. The birds had started singing now, all around them – the sun was out. "OK," she said. "I will."

When Rayne let herself into the Tudor kitchen, Mrs Driver was laying out breakfast things on a large wooden tray. "Hello, dear!" she exclaimed. "You're very early!"

"So are you," Rayne said.

"I couldn't sleep. All that to-do last night. I've told Mr Stuart to have a lie-in, I'm bringing his breakfast up to him. . ."

"Let me take it," said Rayne, and she took hold of one of the strong brass handles of the tray.

"What? Oh, I don't know if he'd like that. A young girl . . . he'll be in his dressing gown. . ."

"Mrs Driver, *let me take it*. Please. I've got to talk to him."

Rayne was expecting more, another refusal, a demand for an explanation, *something*. . . But Mrs Driver just looked at her and said, "All right, dear." Then she put another mug on the tray.

Mr Stuart's bedroom was in the modernized section of the manor house, near Mrs Driver's room. Carrying the heavy tray, Rayne went steadily up the grand staircase, past the glass case halfway up. It had its curtains firmly drawn, and the lid must have been fixed because it no longer hung down beneath them. She reached the top just as the old Dutch clock struck seven. The doors to the Spanish room, the Red Queen's room and Abigail's room were shut, like always – she felt a flick of fear at the sight of them. She turned down the long, window-lined corridor and hurried towards Mr Stuart's room. Balancing the tray on one arm, she knocked on the door and heard "Come in, Mrs D!" She turned the door handle and went in.

Mr Stuart was standing at the window looking out, wearing a long, formal dressing gown with a monogrammed pocket. He turned at her entrance, exclaiming, "Rayne! Is Mrs D all right?"

"She's fine. I – I asked her if I could bring up your breakfast. I need to talk to you."

"At seven o'clock in the morning?"

"Yes, if it's OK. I've been up for hours. I went to Fleet Woods. I saw these men . . . they were the fire festival group. They were doing something, some ritual. I've heard all these hints and rumours and stuff, ever since I first arrived. I thought it was about them, but now I'm not so sure. I've been told they're watching – *protecting*. And now there's been that burglary, that you won't involve the police in." She paused, took in a breath. "Mr Stuart – what's going on here?"

Mr Stuart exhaled, long and low. Then he indicated the elegant gate-legged table in the bay window and said, "Put the tray down there. You'd better join me for breakfast. Mrs D always does enough for two. I see she's provided another mug for your tea."

Rayne sat down, and without being asked, started to pour the tea. It hit her that she was dying for a cup, and the normality of this felt good to her. As did the fresh autumn air blowing in through the half-opened window. Mr Stuart sat opposite her, lifted the cover on his plate, then loaded scrambled egg, bacon and tomato on to a slice of thick brown toast, and handed it to her on a napkin.

The first mouthful she took tasted wonderful. She was amazed how hungry she was.

"Who told you the fire group is 'watching'?" he asked.

"Ethan Sands."

"Ah. I suspected as much. He's young, impatient. . ."

"He thinks the . . . *weirdness* has got something to do with my boyfriend." She paused. It felt wrong, calling St John her boyfriend now.

"St John Arlington. I wonder. He was poking about a while back, asking questions – some silly website they've set up, trying to find out about the hidden history of Marcle Lees, make contact with people far away who might know the place . . . I made it quite clear I had nothing to tell him. And then we had a break-in. In the library."

Rayne nodded. "Mrs Driver told me. She warned me to keep the windows closed."

"No reason to think it was Mr Arlington, but something made me think that whoever broke in knew what they were looking for. . ." He trailed off. "They didn't find it, of course. I've had it all locked up in a safe in one of the attics for the last thirty years."

"Mr Stuart." Rayne sat back in her chair, and put her mug down. "*Please*. Please stop all this skirting round stuff. *Please* start at the beginning. Tell me what you know."

Mr Stuart took another mouthful of toast, chewed it slowly and swallowed. Then he said, "Very well. You remember the dinner in the Old Stone Hall?"

"Yes."

"The questions? About the history?"

"Yes. Yes, of course. And I remember you changing the subject, you seemed *uncomfortable*. . ."

"Yes, I was. I wasn't being fully honest. I knew a lot more than I said about Sir Simeon Lingwall." He pushed the name from his mouth like poison.

"The lord of the manor who ran the hellfire group," prompted Rayne. "The one who abducted girls, or something. . ."

"It was worse than that, Rayne. It was worse than anything you can imagine. I found. . ." He passed a hand through his hair, raked it back off his forehead. "Years ago, I found some old papers, in the library. I'd just come back from university, I was bored, I was rummaging about . . .

God, often I wish I'd just left them there, on that shelf, behind the. . ."

"Mr Stuart!" Rayne croaked. Her mouth was dry. "What . . . what *were* they?"

"Records that . . . they were accounts of Sir Simeon Lingwall's 'experiments'. That's what his group was about. You know the old idea of hell? Being tortured for an eternity, fried on a burning griddle for aeons, on and on and on, never-ending terror? This group wanted to achieve it on earth. They'd . . . abduct young people. Mostly girls, but boys too sometimes. They'd be tortured . . . unimaginable things, sick things, vile things. Then 'saved' . . . given a soft bed, made well again, looked after, befriended. Told it had all been a nightmare, or they'd been rescued . . . the torturers wore masks, these poor young people were disoriented and of course they *wanted* to believe they'd been saved. They'd join the grand dinners, the parties, the dances, they'd laugh and make merry and then – they'd be taken down to the dungeon again. It's clear from Sir Simeon's writings that it gave him an acute thrill to pretend to be an avuncular friend to a young girl, just hours before he'd be . . . well."

Hand trembling, Rayne put her slice of toast down on its napkin. The feeling of invincibility she'd had ever since climbing out from the hollow tree had seeped away, gone entirely. She felt sick now, sick and alone and scared. "That's what you heard, was it?" she whispered. "When you were a boy?"

Mr Stuart frowned. "What? What do you mean?"

"When you first met me – in the library corridor in front

of the portrait of Sir Philip Musgrave – you said you heard ghosts dancing. You said it was weird because it should have been happy, but the feeling was . . . it was horror."

Mr Stuart was staring at her. His face had gone fixed and white. "Good God, I'd never made the connection," he said at last. "You're right, I'm sure you're right. I was hearing one of his . . . one of his monstrous parties."

There was a silence. "Go on," muttered Rayne, at last. "Go on with Lingwall's records."

"Yes. Yes, of course. Well, he set himself a challenge to see how many 'cycles' – as he liked to style it – he could get through. The highest was four, with one Annie Ayslip. Before she died in the torture room. Poor brave little Annie. In the end she'd have been mad, purely mad, of course. They'd all try to die, try to jump from windows, dash their brains out against walls . . . they'd be stopped. That was all part of the vileness. Giving them hope, then destroying it and . . . stopping them die."

"Like Nazi doctors," Rayne mumbled. "The ones who used to revive people to get tortured again."

Mr Stuart shook his head, as if warding such horrors away. "He was the puppet master," he went on. "It was total ownership. Torturing someone's mind, their emotions . . . that's more fun, more subtle, more sophisticated than just breaking up their bodies. Although of course he'd do that too."

There was a silence. Mr Stuart picked up the large eggshell blue teapot. "Would you like a refill?" he asked, politely.

Silently, Rayne held out her mug. She wanted to crawl

back to her bed, sleep to escape the images in her mind, escape from hearing what was going to come next. "But this all happened . . . what, three hundred years ago?" she whispered.

"Yes, thereabouts. But the thing is, Rayne, there have been . . ." he leant forward and pronounced the word carefully, "reoccurrences."

Something about the word made Rayne feel grief, deep inside herself. "How do you mean?" she said.

"Ever since it was built, nearly a thousand years ago, this house has been associated with cruelty and death. People used to say its walls ran with blood. Myths, stories, legends abound. Sir Simeon Lingwall is simply the most . . . extreme." He put his knife and fork down. Silence vibrated between them. Rayne could hear the wind outside, the trees moving.

"I found two other papers," he said.

Chapter
Forty-six

"They were with Sir Simeon Lingwall's writings, in the library," Mr Stuart went on, heavily, as though it hurt him to speak. "One was dated some sixty years after his death, the other a hundred years after that. It's clear that the authors had read Sir Simeon's accounts and they'd placed theirs by his for a purpose. They describe . . . they describe *reoccurrences*. The first was written by the elderly mother of the young lord of Morton's Keep and it talks hysterically about a kind of copycat group, run by her son. If my understanding of her euphemisms is correct, it had a more *sexual* nature. The poor old lady goes on and on about 'bad blood' – a postscript at the end in different handwriting says she 'died of shame and grief' a few months after penning it. The second account, the most recent one, is far more literate. It's dated 1865 and it was written by the then-steward of Morton's Keep, who must have been a remarkably educated man for his time. I believe I'm the first to have seen it after it was placed in the library. I had to unpick a weighty wax seal on some black ribbons to gain access—"

"What did it *say*?" croaked Rayne.

"It talks in grisly detail about monstrosities carried out by the lord of the manor. No need to go into them here. Again they didn't quite reach Sir Simeon Lingwall's heights – or depths, rather. The interesting part of the paper is when it goes on to theorize about Morton's Keep being built on a site of ancient evil. Hence the ghastly things that went on here – the hangings and slaughterings. The steward surmises that it was all kind of *contained* until Sir Simeon Lingwall came along. Sir Simeon was fed by the old evil – but at the same time he made something new. One feels that if the steward knew about viruses and their ability to mutate he would have seized on that as an image for what happened." Mr Stuart sighed, and took a sip of his tea.

"And it's the *something new* . . . that caused the reoccurrences?"

"He thought so. So do I."

"And these papers – they're what you think the library break-in was about?"

"Yes, I do. Someone learnt of their existence. They knew where to look – on the philosophy shelf. All the books on that shelf were scattered, some of them ripped apart."

There was a silence. Then Mr Stuart said, "The steward finished his account by expounding his belief that this mutated evil waits in the house, a kind of residue here, waiting, growing year by year, until someone arrives and aligns himself and the next time of horror begins. . ."

"D'you think he's right?"

"Unfortunately, I could say I *know* he's right. That was the end of the written reports, but there have definitely been more *reoccurrences*. There are old people still alive who remember their parents and grandparents talking of horrors here in their lifetimes. And there are rumours and stories from times before that."

"*Jesus*. Why didn't someone just burn this place to the ground?"

"I don't think it's about bricks and mortar, Rayne. Who knows what might have happened, after a fire – what might have been released? We felt it was . . . *containable*. After all, with the rise of the rule of law, it became impossible to perpetuate atrocities like Sir Simeon Lingwall's."

"Did it?" said Rayne, and looked out of the window. It was a fine October morning, and blackbirds and thrushes were pecking on the lawn for worms that had come up with the dewfall. She felt she could barely begin to process what she'd been told. The knowledge that St John might be caught up in it all was like something terrible waiting behind a door. She couldn't let it come out.

Mr Stuart pushed the plate with his half-eaten breakfast on it away from him, and said, "I was a boy when it last happened."

"Oh God. *You've* lived through one?"

"It was a smallish scale, then, just a couple of girls going missing from Marcle Lees. . ."

"Who was it? Not your *father*?"

"No. No, thank God. The abductor's name was Peter Saul, and he used to do odd jobs around Morton's Keep, before he went off to fight in France. Long after World War Two was over, we discovered he'd come back to us. We found him in the tower. You know, the dovecote. He'd been living there."

Rayne thought of the eleven black candle stubs on the flat stones that seemed to point at the tower. "And no one realized?"

"Morton's Keep was a lot more derelict then, my father was in the process of doing it up . . . the tower garden was completely overgrown. We think Saul had been there for months."

"And he brought the girls there."

"Yes. No one would have heard a thing."

"How horrible."

"Everyone tried to make out to me he was still shell-shocked from the war, but . . . I overheard conversations. People muttered about something terrible that had happened in the same tower during Victoria's reign. There are three grave markers in the garden—"

"I've seen them," Rayne broke in. "Laid out like an arrow, aimed at the dovecote."

"They're apparently the graves of three murder victims. I never learned the details but I heard enough to know everyone thought it was something to do with . . . *something* in the house, some influence, and that everyone felt it had happened again. I kept hearing that word – *again*. Then years later I came back home as a graduate and found those terrible papers. I didn't tell anyone. I had a strong instinct not to discuss it openly." He took another sip of tea; his hand shook as he lifted the mug.

"Mr Stuart, why didn't you just *leave*? How can you live here like this?"

"Oh, you'd be surprised. I live very well. Months go by when I don't think of Morton's Keep's evil past at all. And as every year goes by, my conviction that I'm personally safe from it deepens – and that's a tremendous boost."

"It must be. You're – you're a good man."

"Oh, I don't know about that. Just not open to . . . well. It's a beautiful spot, as you know. The woods, the fields . . . and I also stayed out of duty, I suppose. I felt it was my role to watch with the others."

"The others?"

"Yes. Gradually I learned that there were people . . . *monitoring* it all. Watching it. Tales were handed on from father to son and mother to daughter . . . there's a kind of . . . *balance* that exists. You know the pagan fireplace in the Old Stone Hall?"

Rayne nodded. She could picture the two goat-legged men standing on severed heads very clearly. "It's pretty powerful," she said.

"We hope so! Some people say that it was put in as a kind of altar, a source of power to balance out the evil. . . This watching has been going on for centuries."

"It's the fire festival people, isn't it? They're the watchers."

"They tend to be. We don't discuss it. We don't want to name it. In fact I've never spoken about it to anyone as openly as I'm speaking to you now." He paused, and smiled at Rayne. "That's interesting, isn't it?"

"And Mrs Driver?" asked Rayne, quickly.

"Mrs D, bless her, won't even admit to *herself* that there's something amiss, though I think deep down she knows."

"Yes, I think she does."

"But we all try, in our different ways, to . . . *contain* it. And then it dies down, for decades, maybe half a century. I've made

243

it my life's work to watch this house, to map the energy, check it when I can. I hoped not to see another . . . *reoccurrence* . . . in my lifetime. The last batch of ghost hunters—"

"I saw them leaving. They were terrified."

"I knew something was up then. And the theft last night – that was a terrible shock. The gloves that went missing – do you know them?"

"Yes. Embroidered flowers that, when you look closer . . . they're faces in agony."

"They were *his* gloves. Sir Simeon Lingwall's. So was the dagger."

"God. Why did you keep them?"

"Well . . . a bit like the house, we were scared to destroy them. Not knowing what we might unleash if we burnt them, say. And like the house – we felt we *contained* them. We *watched* them."

Rayne thought of the red velvet curtain drawn on them, night after night. She turned to stare out of the window again, at the beautiful green lawns. "What about the girls?" she asked. "The girls in the dovecote? Were they killed?"

"One of them was never found, not even her body. The other, Patience . . ."

"Patience," echoed Rayne.

". . . she wouldn't speak when they found her. There were no marks on her, but she wouldn't say what had happened – she wouldn't say anything. I saw her soon afterwards, in Marcle Lees – it gave me bad dreams for weeks. Her eyes . . . eyes that could bore right through you, that still seemed to be seeing . . . I didn't want to think what they'd been seeing."

"Didn't anyone find out what had happened?"

"No. Peter Saul confessed to murder, but gave none of the details. They hanged him. One of the last men in England to be hanged, as it happened. After that, Patience started talking . . . but it was all nonsense. She spoke in these strange little sing-song rhymes. Her mind had gone."

"*Fire, flood, fury,*" sang Rayne, softly. "*She is fire, flood, fury.*"

Mr Stuart sat back, horrified, as though she'd uttered a curse. "That's what she sang! Oh, God – I never thought I'd hear that again. It . . . it isn't something you want to hear, not the way she sang it. Where did you. . .?"

Rayne shrugged. "I've met her," she said. "I've met Patience."

"You've *met* her?"

"She was in the Green Lady inn. I got the impression she practically lives there."

"And she's still singing. . .?"

"Still singing."

Mr Stuart shook his head, wondering. "I've never been to that pub. Never fancied it. But Ben Avebury's talked about the green lady. It's one of the myths of the area that have grown up with this . . . this ancient pattern of turmoil. She's supposed to watch too, she's supposed to protect. Maybe poor old Patience feels she's being protected, in the pub. I hope so."

Rayne stared down at the table. She thought of her stove roaring with flame when there was nothing to burn. She thought of the stream bursting its banks, the lake flooding. She thought of the storms – the *furies* – thrashing the trees. And something else . . . something her mind had cut out. . .

"One last question," she said. "The door knocker, on the old part of the house, that weird brass hand with the ring. . ."

"Ah. Yes. It dates from the early eighteenth century. Some say it was linked to Sir Simeon Lingwall. Some say it was actually modelled on his hand."

An image of St John kissing the brass hand, promising his allegiance, slid into her mind. Abruptly, she stood up. "Thank you for what you've told me," she said. "I think I'd better get back now. Shall I take the tray?"

"It's all right," said Mr Stuart, gently, tiredly. "I'll just finish that toast."

Chapter
Forty-seven

Rayne hurried back to the Sty, locked the door behind her, and crawled into bed fully clothed. Then she slept long and deeply, and when she woke, she'd forgotten any dreams she'd had.

She checked her mobile, and found two missed calls from St John. She didn't call him back. She lay on her bed staring at the low ceiling. Processing, processing.

The things she'd been told – they were ludicrous, unbelievable. Yet somewhere deep inside her she was starting to believe them.

She got up, and took a shower. As she was dressing, she got a text from St John saying, *what's up? what u up 2 2day? xxx*

The thought came to her that she had to put him off her scent, and that thought scared her but she didn't hesitate to act on it. She texted back: *have 2 help clear up xxx.* Then she got dressed, and headed over to the old barn.

The clearing up from the Apple Fair was well under way. She helped sweep and bag up litter and carry leftover boxes of apples over to the kitchen.

Ben Avebury was there, shifting out the trestle tables and benches. It seemed to Rayne that he wouldn't meet her eye.

Over the next few days, Rayne got on with her work in the teashop as usual, and spoke only to Mrs Driver. They talked about the weather and the customers and the takings and not much else. St John texted her a couple more times, and she fobbed him off with excuses. Which he accepted, despite their lameness. He didn't come out to see her.

She felt suspended, dazed. She wondered when she'd have any energy again. She missed Becky. She kept thinking about leaving, packing up and going home, but this strange kind of inertia had got hold of her, and she did nothing.

Then on Thursday she got a text from St John saying: *fancy a laugh 2moro nite? first fire festival march, town centre. C U there 8 pm?*

No offer to pick her up. No kisses. She didn't reply. But she knew she'd go.

"It's time," she thought. "Time to find out."

As she left the teashop on Friday afternoon, it was raining. A stream of water from the roof was forming a huge puddle by the door. Rayne stepped her way round it, then looked up. The water was coming from the mouth of a gargoyle she'd never noticed before. The gargoyle was hideous, leering, as it spewed out water on to the ground. It was crowned with leaves that half-covered its face.

It was ten past eight and dark by the time the bus drew

into Marcle Lees market square, and quite a crowd had gathered. Rayne got off the bus and wandered round, trying to enjoy the festive atmosphere. Stalls selling mulled wine, punch and beer vied for trade with hot dog and hamburger stands; a small band with an excellent fiddler played stomping folk music. A few people were dancing already, laughing at themselves.

She tried phoning St John but it went straight to answerphone. So she bought herself a paper cup of mulled wine and walked about looking for him.

"Hey – *Rayne*!"

She spun round to see Becky, waving frantically, hurrying towards her.

"Becky, hi! D'you enjoy your trip up north?"

"Are you *joking*? It rained the whole time, and my aunt is one of the most boring women in existence! She never shuts up! It's made me almost glad to get back here!"

Rayne smiled. It surprised her, how glad she was to see Becky. "Did you hear about the Apple Fair?" she asked. "The break-in and everything?"

"Oh, yeah – Mrs D told my mum. Not a big deal, she said. All she could talk about was the *huge profit* they made this year – they were so pleased! Did you enjoy it? Did you like the *fire boys*? They'll be here tonight, in the procession, I'm gonna make sure I'm at the front of the crowd. . ."

Rayne looked at Becky as she rattled on about how fit the fire boys were, and thought about telling her about being chased in Fleet Woods, about her interview with Mr Stuart and the terrible things she'd discovered about the house.

But she couldn't. She didn't know where to start. It was too dark, too immense, too private, too . . . *real*. Becky knew all the stories and rumours about the place but this was . . . *real*.

"Becky! *Becky!!!*" Across the square, a group of girls were waving and shrieking her name.

"I better go," said Becky. "Hey – you here on your own? You wanna join us?"

Rayne shook her head. "I'm supposed to be meeting St John," she said.

"Oh." Becky's face hardened – her dimple disappeared. "Well, have fun. See you!" She hurried off.

Rayne paced on, all the way round the square, and her phone stayed silent. Then some young kids at the north end started shouting, "They're coming, they're coming!" The crowd surged over and Rayne went too, easing her way through everyone.

From some distance away, snaking its way upwards (the market square was at the top of a low hill) was a procession of torches. The fire-shapes in the dark night were thrilling – there were forty or more, flaring, burning. Rayne's pulse quickened as they came closer, grew bigger. She thought it looked like the avenging mob heading for Frankenstein's castle. Soon she could hear the drum they were marching to, and see the faces of the men and women carrying them.

They came marching into the square, right through the centre, laughing and calling out to their friends. Ethan Sands was there at the front, grinning at something the boy to his left was saying. He shoulder-barged him and for an instant their torches merged, flaring off each other. Rayne stared, hoping he'd see her. But if he did he made no sign of it.

The fiddler from the band jumped to the end of the procession, playing wildly in time with the drum, and then half the crowd tagged on to the end, and walked out of the square with them, faces shining in the firelight. Rayne turned to the robust-looking elderly woman who was standing beside her. "Excuse me," she said. "What happens now?"

"They go to the south of the town, then east. They go to all the boundaries, you see, to protect us – they've been west and north. They'll be back here in half an hour for a party."

"To *protect*. . .?"

"Oh, it's an old tradition, protecting the boundaries from what's without. Goes back to before Christianity came to this island."

"What do they do with all those torches, when they come back here?"

"That's what those are for." The woman nodded towards several tall braziers, logs half-filling them. There were groups of them all round the square. "They dump their torches in those baskets. And they burn up and *they* protect us from what's within."

Chapter
Forty-eight

Rayne turned to stare at the old woman. She was about to ask her to explain what she meant by *what's within*, when a familiar shape caught her eye. Tall, long-legged, elegant. With his back to her.

St John. With his arm round Flora.

Who, as Rayne watched, craned up and nuzzled him passionately on the neck. He pressed his cheek down on the top of her head.

Hurt hit Rayne like a blow to the solar plexus. Her heart thudded. Her mind told her: *But you knew this. You knew it already.*

She waited for the turmoil inside her to die down a little, to be replaced by something harder. Then she walked over to confront him.

"Hi," she said coldly, to his back.

He spun round, his arm slipping from Flora's shoulder.

"*Rayne!* You didn't text me – you didn't say you were coming!" He made a move towards her, face dipped to kiss her, but she stepped back.

"Which is why you're here with Flora," she said.

He stepped back too, and smiled at her. There was something new and harsh and naked about his face, as though he was saying – *OK, the gloves are off now.* "Ah, Rayne," he said, in a purring, teasing tone. "Hidebound, convention-bound Rayne."

"You never finished with her, did you?" she demanded. "You had two of us on the go."

She turned furiously on Flora. "What's *wrong* with you, you *stupid, passive* cow? He lied to me but *you* – you knew all along he was two-timing you. Why the hell did you go along with it?"

Flora's eyes sparkled. "He's great in bed," she said. "But you didn't get round to finding that out, did you?"

Rayne sprang at her before she'd finished speaking, and hit her, hard, on the face. Then she spun round on St John but he grabbed her, twisting her round and holding her tight against him, pinning her arms to her sides.

"*Let me go,*" she snarled, tears of rage coming into her eyes.

"No," he said, calmly. She could feel his breath on the back of her neck. She was filled by a vile mixture of old desire and new hate.

Then she heard the drumbeat and the music from the fiddle. It grew louder – the marchers were coming back. She turned her head and saw the torches coming like a snake of fire towards them.

"*Please* let me go," she repeated. "I can't *bear* you to touch me."

"Apologize to Flora," he said. She could tell from his voice that he was smiling. Flora stood right in front of her, rubbing her cheek where Rayne had hit her, smirking as though being hit was a kind of triumph.

With her right foot, Rayne stamped down, hard, aiming for St John's instep, but he anticipated her and side-stepped and she only caught the end of his shoe.

"*Ouch!*" he said, ironically. Then he kneed her, hard, on the back of her right leg.

The pain made her gasp, made her collapse like a puppet, but she didn't fall because he was gripping her arms painfully tight. "Why can't anyone see what's going *on*?" she thought, anguished. But the crowd were all focused on the procession of fire. "I'll scream," she thought. "I'll fill my lungs and *scream.*"

But before she could, out of the crowd came Amelia, Marcus and Petra. They walked up and stood next to Flora.

"*Amelia,*" Rayne begged. "Marcus. Make him let me go. *Please.*"

"Rayne, we can't make him do anything," drawled Marcus. "No one can. Haven't you learned that yet?"

"What's wrong with you?" she gasped. The four faces in front of her were smiling, serene. "Petra, what's going on?" Petra didn't answer. The three of them moved closer, surrounding her, so that she was shielded from view.

"You're sick," she sobbed, "you're all *sick*. You all knew what was going on. What was your game, what was the *point* of it?"

"You know, if you weren't such an unimaginative little prude, you could have been in on it too," said St John, into her hair. "There's nothing wrong with having two girlfriends. Or even more. But it's over now, isn't it? Now you've found out."

"It's over anyway," said Flora. "We don't need *her*. We've got what we want."

The marchers had arrived. All round the square, braziers were flashing and sparking as the flaming torches were thrown into them.

Rayne filled her lungs and opened her mouth and screamed. St John slammed his hand over her mouth, and she bit down, hard. "You *bitch*!" he spat, hitting her viciously on the side of her head, shoving her away from him. She staggered against Marcus, who grabbed her, and as she yanked herself away she saw Ethan Sands.

He was throwing his torch into the air. It spiralled, flaring, then nose-dived with beautiful accuracy into a brazier several metres away. "*ETHAN!!*" she screamed.

He'd spotted her and was in front of her in seconds. "*What's going on?*" he demanded. He squared up to St John, fists bunching.

Rayne tried to speak, but to her horror burst out sobbing. The words couldn't find their way out.

"It's OK," Ethan said. He put his arm round her, but his eyes didn't leave his enemy's face. "You're OK now. Right, *St* John, what's been going on? What's your game?"

"*Game*, again," sneered St John. "You're both very keen on *games*."

Ethan smelled of burning petrol. Rayne could feel the muscles of his arm and chest tensing, ready to fight. "He – he hit me," she muttered. "He's. . ."

"*Did you hit her?*" demanded Ethan.

"None of your business," drawled St John. His mouth was open as though he was going to say more, but Ethan lunged and landed a punch so hard that St John flew backwards and fell, blood spurting from his nose.

A kind of wail went up as Amelia, Marcus, Flora and Petra gathered round their fallen leader like acolytes. Flora pulled her cotton cardigan off and held it to his nose to staunch the blood. "*Get the police!*" howled Petra.

"Yeah, you do that," growled Ethan. "You call the police. You see what they say when it all comes out."

"You'll regret that, *Ethan Sands*," snarled St John. He got hold of Marcus's arm and pulled himself to his feet, his other hand holding the bloodstained little cardigan to his face. "You'll regret that *very* soon, *very* seriously."

"The only thing I regret is not laying you out like that months ago," said Ethan, then he put his arm round Rayne again, and steered her away through the crowds.

"Can I get you a drink?" he asked. "You need a drink."

"Yes, please," she muttered. Now that they were away from St John and all the drama, she was starting to feel awkward, overwhelmed, but she was sorry when he let go of her to buy mulled wine for her, beer for him. They stood opposite each other, drinking, not really looking at each other. "So," he said. "Are you going to tell me what happened?"

"I feel like an idiot," she muttered. "He's a complete bastard. He . . . told me he was finished with Flora, but he wasn't. He's been seeing both of us. She doesn't care. They were both . . . they were *all* gloating about it. He's a shit. They're *all shits*!"

"They're more than that," Ethan said. "Did you talk to Mr Stuart?"

"*Look*," she snapped, "I've just been *hit* and *humiliated* – I'm not exactly in the mood for your theories about Morton's Keep right now."

"OK," he said, defensively. "But I warned you. I warned you about St John."

"Yes, you did. And, *yes*, you were right." She clamped her mouth shut, hating herself for sounding so waspish. She realized she felt ashamed in front of him. As well as so grateful she didn't know how to deal with it. "Look," she said, "thank you for stepping in back then. I mean it – thank you – you were great."

"S'OK. Anyone would've done it."

"No, actually, they wouldn't. But look – he was still sort of my boyfriend up until about twenty minutes ago. I feel really. . ." She broke off. She couldn't explain. All she wanted to do was crawl into bed and pull her duvet over her head. "I can't . . . I can't talk now," she mumbled. "I'm going to get the bus back, OK?"

"Sure," said Ethan. "You take care." Then he put his hand in his pocket, and pulled out a crumpled piece of paper. "My number," he said, handing it to her. "In case you need it. Just tell me – *did* you talk to Mr Stuart?"

"Yes," she said, bleakly. "He told me everything. And I think . . . I think you're right about St John. But I can't talk now, OK?"

"No. No, all right. You call me, OK?"

She turned and started to walk away, then she heard, "Did he say anything about the dungeon? The dungeon in the house?"

But she didn't look back, she didn't answer him. She

felt as though a great weight was on her, like she'd never feel good again. She crossed the square towards the bus stop. A group of three braziers, flaming away, was in her path and as she made her way round them she noticed a strange-looking figure almost dancing in front of them. A thin, slightly bent woman with wild, white-grey hair.

It was Patience.

She was jigging from side to side, an ecstatic look on her face. Her mouth was moving, although there was no one next to her to hear what she was saying.

Or – what she was singing. Rayne didn't want to get closer, didn't want to hear her song.

The storm started as she was halfway back to Morton's Keep – a gust of wind so strong that the bus rocked on its wheels. Hailstones cracked against the windows. "Blimey, that came out of nowhere!" said the driver, slowing right down.

Chapter Forty-nine

"Is something the matter, Rayne, dear?" asked Mrs Driver. She was lifting line after line of little coconut cakes from a huge baking tray and laying them neatly in a big Tupperware box. "You've been . . . well . . . *off*, for the last few days."

Yes, thought Rayne. Ever since Friday night.

"Did something happen over the weekend?" Mrs Driver went on.

"Um – you could say that. I was . . . er, seeing this boy."

"St John Arlington. I know."

"Well, it's over."

There was a silence. Rayne, polishing water glasses, waited for Mrs Driver to say something along the lines of "good riddance", but she didn't. She lifted the kettle and filled it, muttering about making a nice cup of tea.

Rayne couldn't remember ever feeling so alone in her life. And worse than that, she felt . . . crystallized. Turned to stone. Nothing going on in her head or her heart.

She hadn't phoned Ethan, and she hadn't talked again to Mr Stuart. She knew she ought to, she knew she should face the things they'd told her, but it was all too weird and overwhelming. It was easier to do nothing. It was easier to go back to the Sty and pull the duvet over her head and sleep. She'd done a great deal of sleeping, over the last few days.

In despair, she'd called home. She'd thought of leaving Morton's Keep – packing up and going back to Jelly and her mum. Maybe even to Damian, if he'd have her. But her mum had been in a sour, resentful mood, accusing her of abandoning them. "What d'you think it's been like for me," she'd moaned, "these last weeks, dealing with Jelly all on my own? And you haven't been to see us *once*. Don't you care any more?"

"Yes, of course I care, Mum, but I've got my own life, haven't I? And I want to help with Jelly, but that's not all I'm *for*, is it?"

"What d'you mean – all you're *for*! That's a nasty thing to say. You had your friends, Damian – I never stopped you."

"I know, I know. But I used to feel . . . what you mainly wanted me for was Jelly. Looking after Jelly."

She was amazed at the ease with which it came out of her mouth, amazed at how true it felt to say it. Her mum slammed the phone down on her and she knew there was no going back home, not for a long time.

"Here, dear," said Mrs Driver. "Here's your cup of tea."

"Oh, thank you, Mrs D. That's lovely."

They went through into the tearoom and sat together in silence, drinking tea and eating the bits of broken coconut cake that Mrs Driver had put into a dish.

"Would you do me a favour?" asked Mrs Driver, suddenly.

"Of course."

260

"It's only putting the tearoom scraps out for the birds. They expect it, now, at dusk. I get quite a crowd of them turning up. Only I've got . . . I've got a couple of letters to write. I must get down to it, I keep putting it off."

"Of course, no problem. You feed them on the main lawn, don't you?"

"That's right, dear. It's a nice thing to do – it's relaxing, watching them. It might even cheer you up a bit."

They finished their tea and stood up to go. "That's why she wants me to feed them," Rayne thought gloomily, picking up the large paper bag of leftover cake and scone from the corner of the kitchen. "It's got nothing to do with her writing letters. It's all she can think of to cheer me up."

She went outside, on to the main lawn. Dusk was gathering behind the great black wrought-iron gates at the bottom, settling down into the woods beyond. She picked out a handful of stale cake and scone, and tossed it, and almost immediately, the birds appeared.

Rayne knew about birds – she could recognize the types. She'd had a real thing for birds when she was ten; she had a pictorial chart of British birds up on her bedroom wall. The only birds you saw on Cramphurst Estate were tired pigeons with twisted feet, but *here*—

The starlings were the first to arrive, a great gang of them, swooping down to forage. Then a cock and hen blackbird joined in, after the sultanas from the scones. . . She threw down another handful. A cloud of sparrows arrived, jostling with the starlings – then a robin, three chaffinches, and a couple of huge wood pigeons. Rayne smiled. Mrs Driver was right, it was relaxing just to watch them as they fluttered down and hopped about, pecking eagerly at the crumbs on the grass. . .

Something was happening. The blackbirds, sparrows and others fed on undisturbed, but the starlings had risen in a cloud, and were hovering a couple of feet above the ground, crying. She threw some cake down, fruitcake fat with cherries, but they ignored it. The blackbirds each seized a cherry and flew away. The sparrows fled, chirping, followed by the other birds. But the starlings still hovered, in a screaming, nervy cloud. The noise they made was other-wordly, full of panic – she'd never heard a noise like it. It made her uneasy, as though she was sharing their fear.

There was a sudden gust of wind through the trees at the edge of the lawn; the sound of the leaves mixed with the crying of the birds. Then suddenly the starlings wheeled round as one and flew towards the gates, as if they were on the attack. She peered into the gloom, expecting to see a cat slink along the ground – she'd heard that starlings could mob a cat if there were enough of them.

But there was no cat there.

The starlings were flying at the iron gates, screaming, claws out, flying at the same spot, then retreating all together, swooping away and then returning again, always to the same place. . . Rooted to the spot, Rayne watched and terror settled over her, stopped her breath.

The birds were forming a huge shape, the size of a great tree. The space where they didn't fly was the shape of a head, a human head. And there were shoulders too, and an arm uplifted, pointing. . .

Pointing at her.

Chapter Fifty

Back in the Sty she told herself not to be so absolutely bloody stupid and filled and switched on her little electric kettle. More tea, tea with two sugars, that's what was needed.

What had it *been*, though? When she'd seen the shape of the head, it had looked exactly as if the birds were attacking someone, swooping in on eyes and forehead, a thick cloud of them . . . and the arm, too. The upraised arm.

Stop, it, stop it! Stop thinking like that.

She took a slurp of her tea, too hot – it scalded her throat.

And dropped the mug on the floor, where it shattered into pieces.

She'd remembered.

She left the Sty, walking fast, heading for the greenhouses. When she reached them she stared up at the shattered one, at the tall palm tree breaking its way through the glass roof.

She could see her, still, in the long, waving leaves. The giant woman with her green hair flowing, her arms flailing in warning, in fury. . .

The same woman that the starlings had made.

The green lady.

Chapter Fifty-one

It was quite dark now. Rayne hurried back to the Sty, heart pounding. When she reached the steps to the medieval garden, she looked back at the house. White-grey smoke was coming from the Old Stone Hall chimney again.

She no longer felt tired or depressed. All her instincts and senses were on high alert, like a fox in the night. She felt as strong and wild now as she'd felt when she'd pulled herself up and out of the hollow tree – slithered out like being born again.

"I'll phone Ethan," she thought. "I'll phone him *now*, arrange to meet him – I've put it off long enough."

The wind was blowing up strong again. *Fire, flood, fury*, she thought, and it didn't scare her now. *Fire, flood, fury.*

Something flashed deep in the nearby bushes. She turned – it had gone. But as she peered closer, she caught the hard shining outline of a motorbike mudguard.

She crashed her way through the shrubbery, heedless of scratches. And as she expected found St John's bike hidden there, like he used to park his bike when he visited her. But this was deeper in the bushes, much deeper, well hidden from view.

Except the rising moon had hit on it, just for that second.

She raced back to the Sty, seized her mobile, seized the slip of paper Ethan Sands had given her. She'd been so down and lethargic before she hadn't got round to adding it to her phone – now she punched it in at top speed.

After four rings, Ethan answered, guardedly.

"Ethan!" she barked. "It's me, it's Rayne. He's in the house. St John. I'm sure he's in the house."

"OK, OK. You saw him?"

"No. Just his motorbike. Really well hidden. Something else happened too, something. . . Oh, God. You'll think I'm mad if I tell you. But look – I know you're right about him, we've got to stop him. We've got to get him *out*."

"OK, I'll come. I'll try and get hold of some of the others. If I can't get a lift I'll be twenty minutes, max. . . Look – have you told Mr Stuart? Is he in the house?"

"Yes, he's here. I'll go and tell him, I'll tell him now. Keep in touch. Call when you get here."

And she rang off.

Rayne let herself into the Tudor kitchen. It was in darkness except for a small lamp glowing on a shelf. Mrs Driver had told her that she always left a light on for Mr Stuart, who tended to stay up a lot later than she did and often liked to make himself a milky drink before bedtime. He'd put the extensive burglar alarm system on, too, when he went to bed.

The alarm wasn't on – he must still be up.

Rayne took in a deep breath, and hurried down the stone-flagged corridor, through the heavy green curtains, and into the Great Hall. A solitary lamp was alight here, too, on the long side table. She was sure Mr Stuart would be in the library – Mrs Driver had mentioned he often spent the evening there, reading, sometimes playing the piano. She sped across the hall and into the library corridor.

The door behind her swung shut; she was in pitch-blackness. She put her hands out either side and let her fingertips guide her along the narrow, curving corridor; they brushed across the arrow-slit windows and framed pictures; she imagined with a shiver them brushing over Sir Philip Musgrave's ghostly face. Then she saw the sliver of light ahead of her, under the library door.

She knocked, much harder than she meant to, and heard an indignant, "Come in!"

She stepped inside. "Mr Stuart," she said. "I'm sorry. I'm sorry but your house is under threat."

Chapter
Fifty-two

Mr Stuart was sitting on one of the sofas in front of the fireplace with a large, leather-bound book in his hand. A morose fire burnt in the grate. He eyed Rayne warily as she crossed the floor towards him. The candles had been lit in the holders on the two mirrors nearest to him; the strings of glass teardrops glittered and scintillated magically, but Rayne barely glanced at them. "It's St John," she said. "His motorbike is here. I think he's got into the house."

"It's all locked up," said Mr Stuart. "You've got your keys, haven't you? He hasn't stolen them?"

"No, I've got them. But – I think it was him who got in before, and broke into the glass case. He's found a way. His *bike's* here. Mr Stuart – where's the dungeon?"

Mr Stuart slammed his book shut with a bang. "Dungeon?" he echoed. "Who've you been talking to?"

"Ethan Sands. He mentioned a dungeon."

"Old myths. Old hearsay. There's no dungeon here."

"A cellar, then. An outhouse. *Somewhere.* Where would St John go? Where would. . ." She paused, took in a shaky breath. "Where was it Sir Simeon Lingwall did his experiments?"

"I don't know and I don't want to know."

"Look, Mr Stuart – St John's in this house, now. He's in here and it's a . . . a *reoccurrence*, I'm sure it is, just like the ones in the old papers you were telling me about. He's got his little group, they all worship him, they'll do whatever he says. . . Look, you should call the police. They'll find him. They'll bring dogs – they'll track him down."

"I'm not calling the police."

"Why *not*?"

"Because we have to keep it private! You don't know what damage you'll do, confronting it. Sometimes these things just have to . . . they have to work their way out."

"So we just sit back and do nothing, do we?"

"Not nothing, no."

"No? What are you doing, Mr Stuart?"

"I'm watching, I'm monitoring."

"Tamping it down, damping it down, until the next time, until the next generation of people get hurt? You talk about myths, hearsay. It's more alive than that and you know it. It's *dangerous*."

He hung his head. There was a long silence. Exasperated, Rayne turned and marched over to the door, then with her hand on the handle, she turned back and said, "I don't think the green lady is a myth, Mr Stuart. I think she's *real*. And I think she's angry. I think she wants action. I don't think she wants things to be just *watched* and *monitored*. I think she wants someone to kick off. That's why *she's* kicking off. Fire, flood, fury. OK?"

And she walked out.

*

When she reached the Great Hall, the door to the Old Stone Hall was opening. Ben Avebury came out with his huge wickerwork basket on his shoulder. "Just going for some more logs," he said.

"Why are you lighting a fire in there, Ben?" she demanded. "Why have you been lighting one in there every night, for weeks now?"

He shrugged, then he muttered, "It's all I can think of to do."

"You know it's happening again, don't you?"

"I'm afraid of it."

"Where's the dungeon, Ben? *Where's the centre?*" He wouldn't look at her, wouldn't meet her eye.

And suddenly she knew where it was.

Chapter Fifty-three

She put one foot on the bottom of the grand staircase and looked up ahead, fearfully. "Come with me, Ben!" she begged. But all she heard was the double doors to the hall thudding shut and the huge key grate as Ben locked them behind him.

She faced the flight of stairs ahead of her, and started to climb. The only light was from the lamp on the long side table. Shadows pressed in on her, clots of darkness were all around her, corners disappearing into blackness – anything could be crouching in them, waiting, *anything*. . .

She took another step up. Everything in her told her to wait for Ethan, to go after Ben and plead with him to come with her. . .

But she kept climbing, step after step, up into the darkness ahead, as the one-handed clock ticked in pace with her. She reached the half-landing, hurried past the glass case with its curtains drawn. She reached the top landing, and then – ludicrously, absurdly in the ancient silence – her phone went. She snatched at it, hissed, "*Yes?*"

"It's me, it's Ethan. I'm at the bottom of the drive, it'll take me three minutes—"

"Oh, thank *God.* D'you know the door to the Tudor kitchen?"

"The one up those steps? Yes."

"I left it unlocked. Go through – no one's about. Turn left down the corridor, through the green curtains and you're in the Great Hall. I'm at the top of the stairs."

"Is Mr Stuart with you?"

"No."

"OK. Wait there."

"Have *you* got anyone with you?"

"They wouldn't come. They've gone off to Fleet Woods again. *Useless.*" He rang off.

She took a slow step towards Abigail's room. Her heart was wrenching with terror. She put out her hand, put it on the handle. Maybe it would be locked.

But it wasn't. The door creaked open. She could see the horrible shadowy shrouded shape of the four-poster bed, the massive, cold fireplace, the dismal dark portraits lining the walls.

She stood back, to wait for Ethan. And then. . .

Something was behind her, urging her on. Pushing energy and power into her. She knew who it was. She felt her anger. Willing her to act, giving her the strength to act.

Rayne didn't dare turn, even though she was sure if she turned she'd see nothing. She stepped over the threshold, into Abigail's room. Then, step by step, she crossed the floor, towards the door to the left of the fireplace. The door with a lock, but no handle.

It was standing slightly ajar.

She couldn't tell now if the power and force was still behind her, or inside her, or both. Her mind was screaming *Ethan, hurry!* but she had to go on. She pulled the door further open.

Rank, stale air filled her nostrils. A thin series of worn wooden steps twisted down ahead of her.

This was it, she was sure of it. The core of the evil, the entrance to Sir Simeon Lingwall's experiment room. This was why St John had wanted to get into Abigail's room. This was why the ghost-hunters' machines had gone off the scale.

It was *here*.

She stepped on to the first stair, and started to go down. After seven steps, the door above her creaked to, cutting out the light, so now she was climbing down into absolute blackness. With her hands out on either side she went down ten more steps, another ten; then another. She thought she must be underground now. What air there was was dank, oppressive.

At first, she didn't realize it was a sound. It meshed with the thudding of her heart, with her soft steps downwards – a terrible, rhythmic whimpering. She held her breath, horrified. Then she heard a voice – St John's voice.

She couldn't hear what he was saying, but his voice was changed. It was steel-thin, cruel.

A thin band of yellow light crept up the narrow stairs towards her. It was coming from underneath the narrow door ahead of her. She stopped, filled with dread at the thought of going through the door.

Then a noise on the steps behind her startled her, but

before she could turn a voice whispered, "*Rayne!* Why didn't you *wait*?"

She stared silently at Ethan's face in the yellow light. She'd forgotten he was coming.

"I . . . I had to go on," she muttered. "*God*, I'm glad you found me. How did you find me?"

"The door to the bedroom was open – and *this* door – I knew where you'd gone." He sped down the last few steps to join her. "Is he down there?"

"Yes. I heard his voice. And . . . can't you hear it?" She held up her hand; they waited in silence. But the whimpering had stopped. Then the sour yellow light swam up, filled the stairwell. The door at the bottom had opened.

"Welcome," said Flora, sarcastically, as she leant against the door frame. "Come in."

Flora had the same harsh, naked look to her face that St John had had on the night of the fire festival in the market square. As if everything hidden had come out now, and she was glad.

Rayne took in a deep breath, and walked down the last few steps, with Ethan right behind her. She pressed herself against the far side of the door frame, keeping as far away from Flora as she could.

"Go on in," Flora smirked, and as Rayne did, Flora leaned towards her and poked her forefinger hard against the top of Rayne's arm.

"*Don't!*" snapped Rayne, repulsed.

"We're sisters," Flora breathed, into her face. "I minded at first, about you, but now I don't. Why can't you accept that we're sisters?"

"*No, you're not!*" said Ethan, fiercely. "You're not anything to do with her. Go on, Rayne."

They went through the door.

It was Amelia who'd been whimpering. Her mouth was red, blood-vivid like a vampire's. As Rayne looked closer, she saw that it was bleeding. Her eyes met Rayne's and she whispered, "Help me!" Rayne felt faint. She looked down and saw that Amelia's clothes were blotched with red.

"What have you *done* to her?" Rayne choked out. Flora giggled. Nothing was restraining Amelia, but she didn't move an inch. Marcus stood beside her, staring straight ahead as though he'd been mesmerized.

The room itself was unexceptional: a brick cell half the size of the bedroom above it, with a low ceiling supported by thick struts of wood, and no windows. But the feeling in it was hateful – it vibrated with fear and malevolence. Black candles were set all around, on every available surface; a table, the seats of two wooden chairs, a huge iron-bound chest, the shelves on the back wall. In the flickering shadows near the shelves, Rayne saw St John.

"Well," he said, stepping forward. "What a lovely surprise!"

"What have you done to Amelia?" Rayne croaked.

"*Amelia* is a stupid bitch. She committed herself – she came *here* – in *here* – then tried to back out."

"She's *bleeding*."

"It's just a few nicks. We were playing, weren't we, Amelia? Cruelty is beautiful."

"You're *sick*. Where's Petra?"

"Petra – show yourself."

Petra too stepped out of the shadows at the back. She had the same blank, drugged expression that Marcus had.

"See?" said St John. "We're all here. And now you are too. With *Ethan*. How sweet."

"What have you done to them? Why are they looking like that?"

"It's the air down here," smirked St John. "It has that effect on people."

There was a silence, no one moving. The candles burned steadily, the shadows loomed. Then Ethan said, flatly, "You're the one, aren't you."

St John said nothing, but his smile didn't waver.

"I knew it," Ethan went on, "though they said there was no proof. I knew it all along. You're the last of the line."

"Oh, I hope not," said St John. "Not the *last*. I want lots of babies."

"You're a Lingwall."

"Yes!" St John lifted his head proudly. "People said the Lingwalls died out – what nonsense. You can't kill *us*. The name died out, that's all. The female line – through Sir Simeon's wonderful twisted niece, Selina – lasted. It lasted on and on and nothing could destroy it and now – there's *me*." He raised his arms, mockingly; grotesque shadows danced on the walls.

"Selina," said Ethan, bleakly. "I've heard horrible stories about her."

"I'm sure you have. We discovered loads of marvellous tales about her. A source in Italy was particularly helpful there. One of my favourites is the one that tells how Sir Simeon seduced her when she was fourteen. Then seduced her into his ways. Brought her down here to show her his work."

Rayne stared at the walls, thought of the screams and blood and terror their brickwork had soaked up. She felt weak, nauseated. Ethan, too, looked white. She knew he was fighting it, like she was – fighting the choking sense of dread, like poisonous air all about them.

"Selina followed her every desire," said St John, triumphantly. "She had her will. Absolutely. And that's how I plan to live. It's all over – all the waiting, and planning. I've done it. I'm here."

"Mr Stuart knows you're here," Rayne croaked. "I told him."

St John grinned. "That doesn't matter. He can't do anything now. I'm here." He exhaled triumphantly, and looked all around, as though he was standing in a palace. "It was worth all the trouble it took."

"By trouble, you mean me," said Rayne.

"What else, darling? All that time I had to put in making up to you – *God*, you were demanding! And jealous! But you liked my kisses, didn't you?"

Rayne stared at him, hating him.

"And I was prepared to put in the time on you because you were my key to the house. We got into the tower often enough, that was easy, but it wasn't enough. His energy was weak there, and all mixed up with the gross vibrations of Peter Saul. What a disappointing disciple *he* was!"

"It was you who lit the candles," said Rayne. "Black ones, like these. Eleven of them, in the grass, on the gravestones."

"Eleven," muttered Ethan. "Trying to get at us, were you? Trying to harm the watchers?"

St John waved this away. "That, the website, trying to contact people who knew about the past, breaking into the library when the papers were already gone, sniffing round after old stories and half-remembered facts – that was all just the start. Just kid's stuff. *This* is all that matters now."

"And the glass case?" Rayne demanded. "Was that kid's stuff?"

"Not exactly," St John grinned. "Petra and Marcus did well, there."

"You used my keys to get into the house, didn't you? You stole them the night of the Apple Fair. Then you got them back into the drawer in the kitchen. . ."

St John laughed, his mouth all twisted and sneering. Rayne hated it, that she'd kissed that mouth. "Really, Rayne, you're not very bright, are you? If I 'got them back into the drawer' – how did I get in tonight? I saw where you kept them that day you took me up to Abigail's room . . . when I tapped on the door to *here*. God, that was a beautiful moment. I knew it hadn't been blocked up, annihilated, it was still *here*, waiting – do you remember that?"

Rayne remembered. She was full of shame at the memory. St John kissing her, lifting her up, steering her back towards the hideous bed. . .

"Once I knew you kept the keys in your kitchen," he went on, "it wasn't exactly SAS stuff to find them in the cutlery drawer. I got hold of them the night we had that *sweet* little supper together, just after Amelia and Petra had been telling you you *had* to join our group because you were so *wonderful*. I was so excited that I took myself off on a little walk, while you slept – do you remember?"

Rayne flinched. She remembered the fear she'd felt when she'd seen him coming through the trees in the thin light from the new moon. With his wide skull's grin.

"You thought I was excited about *you*, of course. God, the *lies* we all had to tell! We prayed you wouldn't take it into your head to do your laundry, and discover the keys were missing, but you were getting so spooked by the house I thought we were safe. Petra got them copied and I put them back the night I picked you up for that party. When I told you I had to have you *all to myself* for a while, and we had a beer. You never noticed they'd gone."

Ethan at her side didn't move. Amelia stared out blankly; the other three acolytes stood behind St John, expressionless and threatening. And Rayne could feel rage build in her, beside the fear. "Why did you wait till last Saturday?" she demanded. "Why not break in before?"

"The *alarm* system?" he said, sarcastically. "Either people were about, or the alarm was on. On the night of the fair, I let myself into the kitchen. The alarm was off but everyone was out at the barn. So I gave Marcus and Petra the go-ahead. It was as easy as taking candy from a baby."

Rayne stared at him, remembering how the group had greeted him that night, all excited and ecstatic. "Right," she muttered. "As easy as taking the keys from me."

"You said it, darling. And all the time you thought it was *you* I was after."

It seemed to Rayne that she'd actually hit him – slapped him with all her force round his sneering face – before she knew she was going to. He snarled, clutching his face, but made no move to hit her back. "You'll regret that," he said.

"No, *I won't*. I hope you *rot in hell*. I *loathe* the fact that you've been anywhere near me. I wish I could spew it all up, tear it out of me, I hate it, I can't bear it that I let it in, *you* in, your *vampire kisses*—"

Flora let out a high-pitched giggle. Ethan moved closer

to Rayne. "You wanted Lingwall's dagger," he said. "From the case."

"Yes," answered St John. "And his gloves. But most of all – *these*." And he drew out of his pocket a ring with five dark, ancient-looking keys on it, all different sizes, and jingled them smugly. "More keys, Rayne darling. I saw them when we looked into the case together, under an old watch chain and a particularly ugly Victorian mourning brooch. Of course I didn't know that they were the *right* keys. I could only hope. And we could have broken in but – how much better to come in like the rightful owner, hm?" He swaggered towards the great iron-bound chest. "One key to the outer door. The lock only works from the outside, which is why you two were able to . . . *join* us. Two keys to the inner door, at the bottom of the stairs. And two keys – for this."

Then he lifted the black candles off the chest, one by one, and handed them to Flora and Petra.

Chapter
Fifty-five

St John unlocked the huge padlock on the clasp of the chest, and opened the clasp. Then he inserted the smallest key into a keyhole underneath, turned it, and swung the lid open.

Rayne stared into the chest. There, lying on the top, were the long yellow-brown gloves with their agonized-flower faces. "Aren't they wonderful?" St John purred. He picked one up and slid his right hand into it, flexing his fingers, smoothing it to fit over his wrist and lower arm. "I'd heard about their existence from one of our website contacts. And then you told me they were in the glass case on the grand stairway. And then I saw them, on our little tour – saw them for myself." He shut his eyes and sighed, smiling. "I've wanted them to be mine for so long. I feel so much stronger, somehow, when I'm wearing them."

Flora, carrying her black candles, took a step closer to him, her face alight with adoration. St John put out his gloved hand to her hair and stroked it, gently. Then suddenly he turned to Rayne, reaching for her face.

She jerked back, nauseated. "There, you see?" he said. "You feel their power, too."

Heart hammering, Rayne looked down into the chest. Beneath the other glove were sheaves and sheaves of parchment covered in black writing, all tied up with red and black ribbons and heavy wax seals.

"I hadn't thought beyond finding this room – the centre," St John went on, as he reverently pulled the glove off his hand and laid it, with the other one, in the lid of the chest. "And then we found all *these*." He gathered up bundle after bundle of papers and laid them lovingly in the lid, too. "We'd heard there were papers of my ancestor in the library – they were gone when we got in, of course. No doubt Mr *Stuart* has them in a bank vault somewhere. Well, they don't matter any more. They were for . . . *general* consumption. This is the real stuff. This is *poetry*. It made Amelia quite faint when she read some of them, didn't it, darling?"

Amelia continued to stand there, like a doll, unmoving, her mouth drooling blood. Rayne looked at her, looked at Marcus, and at Flora and Petra, standing there like mesmerized votaries with a black candle in each hand, and she tried to ask them why they were doing this, why they were here with this madman – but she couldn't frame the words.

St John leaned towards her, smiling, and murmured, "He's strong here, isn't he? Can't you feel him all around you?"

It seemed to Rayne that she could feel him, waiting, watching. Growing. The sense of him filled the cell. The green lady had no power here.

"And more than the poetry," St John went on, "I

discovered that this house is mine. *Legally* mine. Marvellous, isn't it? I'd planned to enter by the back way – Sir Simeon leads me in through the front. *Here!*" He lifted up a thick wad of paper festooned with dark seals and ribbons. "This is his last will and testament. Sir Simeon died childless, but he willed this house to his niece Selina, and all her descendants, male or female, after her. You should like him, Rayne, darling! He was an early feminist! He definitely preferred women! Legend has it that two of Selina's feckless nephews stole it from her young granddaughter. Guff about inheritance through the male line. I can *prove* my inheritance through the female line. I'm going to take this to court and challenge ownership."

"You're mad," croaked Ethan. "All that happened over two hundred and fifty years ago. No court in the land would uphold your claim."

"Wouldn't they? We'll see. I'm the rightful heir, and *he* wants me to inherit. Do you really think there won't be a way? He's got me this far, hasn't he? He helped me with Rayne, didn't he, my *sweet*? He made me . . . *irresistible*."

Rayne stared at him. She couldn't speak.

"These papers have been lying here, untouched, since Selina died. The keys were waiting for me, in the glass case. It's meant. It's *meant*."

There was a silence. No one moved.

"Two generations after the thieving nephews," St John went on, "it was sold off to *outsiders* to pay debts . . . sold off like some semi-detached box. To outsiders like your hopeless Mr Stuart with his *Apple* Fairs and musical evenings. It should be in Lingwall hands. And it will be."

Rayne's head was swimming. *Stay strong*, she urged herself. *Stay strong*. But second by second she could feel herself weakening.

"Rayne?" groaned Ethan. "We've been down here too long."

"Doesn't it suit you down here?" gloated St John. "Funny, that's what Amelia said. And yet it's just a plain little cell. They cleared out all the equipment when Selina died. Not that one needs *equipment*. And as I said to Amelia – I can't let you leave here. Not now you've been down. That's the last thing *he'd* want."

His hand went to his pocket. In the flickering light from the candles, Rayne saw the dagger blade glint.

She felt as though the ground under her feet was dipping, sinking, leaving her falling – her mind swam in terror.

Then there was a sudden noise, and the door to the dungeon flew open.

Chapter Fifty-six

Petra screamed; its noise echoed round the dank walls. All Rayne could see was a huge flame half-blinding her, coming towards her. She stared at it in fear and hope. And then, behind the fireball, she made out Ben Avebury's face.

"Another guest," said St John, his voice tight with anger. "*Aren't* we busy tonight? What do you want, Mr Avebury?" His eyes flicked sideways, at Marcus. Together, he and Marcus came forward, moving in on Ben and his torch.

"*Throw it!*" yelled Ethan.

The fireball arced wildly through the air. Ethan leapt and caught the torch. Then, just like in the market square, he hurled it up and it flew across the dark space, then it spiralled down and dropped with perfect accuracy into the middle of the open iron-bound chest.

St John screeched, flung himself towards it. Ethan charged and brought him down and the brass-handled dagger shot across the floor. Then Ethan landed a punch full of fury to the side of St John's head. He lay still.

The ancient papers exploded into flame. Ethan leapt up and with three huge kicks he shoved the burning chest up against one of the wooden roof struts, then he picked up a wooden chair and threw it against the chest. The wooden strut caught alight; fire licked at the ceiling. Ben seized one end of the long table, Rayne the other, and together they tipped it forward on to the flames. The black candles flared up; fire was snaking along the ceiling, reaching the other struts.

And all the time Flora, Marcus and Petra stood there dazed, as if they couldn't move without the direction of their leader. "Time to get out!" Ben shouted at them. "*Now!*" The three turned and ran, straight for the steps.

"What about St John?" roared Ethan. "You just gonna leave him to *fry*?" But they'd gone.

Rayne seized Amelia's hand and dragged her to the stairs. "*Ethan!*" she screamed. "Come *on!*" Second by second, the fire was building. The table cracked into flame.

"*Leave him!*" shouted Ben. "*Leave* that bastard!"

"No," muttered Ethan. "I can't."

Chapter Fifty-seven

Ethan took hold of St John under the arms and started dragging him towards the stairs. Ben, swearing, picked up his feet, and together they lifted him on to the stairs. Ben slammed the inner door shut just as the dungeon exploded into flames. Together they heaved his body up the stairs towards Abigail's bedroom. "What you have to hit him so hard for?" Ben groaned.

As soon as they were through the door, Rayne slammed it shut behind them. Ben and Ethan let go of St John and he crashed to the floor. Below, the fire was booming – soon it would be surging up the stairs. "The whole house'll burn!" wailed Ben.

"Let it!" snapped Ethan. But Ben was racing for the hallway. Seconds later, they heard a small smash of glass, and the fire alarm screamed out.

"We'd better get out of here!" said Rayne. She let go her grip on Amelia, who shivered like someone coming round from a bad dream, and tottered to the door.

Ethan stirred St John – none too gently – with his foot. "Wake up, you shit. I'm not carrying you any further."

Then Ben's anxious face appeared round the door. "The fire brigade's on its way," he said. "Mr Stuart says to get out on the back lawn *now.*"

St John moaned. He was coming round. Ethan dragged him to his feet and, with Rayne's help, frogmarched him out of the bedroom and down the grand staircase, into the open air.

The local fire brigade arrived within fifteen minutes, just as the fire broke through the door into Abigail's room. The worst damage was caused by the firemen smashing the ancient bedroom windows to get the huge fire-hoses through. The firemen were puzzled by how slowly the fire had climbed upwards. They reckoned it had something to do with downdraught and the damping effect of the dungeon air.

Mr Stuart, Mrs Driver, Ms Barton and the other staff stood on the back lawn and watched as Abigail's bedroom was doused. While St John lay slumped at their feet, Rayne and Ethan gave Mr Stuart an account of what had happened in the dungeon. Ms Barton listened avidly, but Mrs Driver wandered off, humming to herself.

"When I was a child," said Mr Stuart, slowly, "I asked my father about that door without a handle. He told me it was just an old cupboard, all bricked up inside."

"And you never wanted to check?" asked Rayne.

Mr Stuart shook his head. "No," he said.

There was a noise at their feet. St John was coming to, looking all around, wide-eyed, silent. "We should call the police," said Ethan, standing over him. "You should have him arrested."

"And what exactly would they arrest him for?" asked Mr Stuart.

"Breaking and entering?" erupted Ethan. "Sadistically attacking Amelia? Plotting to take over Morton's Keep? Being a mad, power-crazed lunatic?"

"Nothing that would stand up in a court of law. Apart from Amelia, and she's not likely to say a word against him. No, the firemen were making noises about *arson*. And that, my lad, is *you*."

"Oh, *what*?"

"Don't get on your high horse. I'm very grateful for your arson attack. I *think*. I also think we don't want this whole affair . . . given too much oxygen. Let's . . . just let sleeping dogs lie."

"If we'd let sleeping dogs lie, Mr Stuart," said Rayne crisply, "St John would still be in the dungeon. With his acolytes. Being fed by . . . whatever's down there."

Mr Stuart dropped his eyes. "I know," he murmured. "And I know you had to act and I'm grateful. I'm just . . . nervous, too."

St John moaned, and got to his feet. Ethan made a move towards him, but Mr Stuart put a restraining hand on his arm. "Let him go," he said. "We can always catch up with him later, if we need to."

They watched as St John stumbled off towards the bushes, where he'd left his bike. "Aren't you even going to warn him never to step foot on your property again?" demanded Rayne.

Mr Stuart shrugged. "What's the point?"

"What's going to happen to the dungeon?" Ethan said.

"I've been advised that the safest thing for the house – to strengthen the foundations – is to fill it in with hard core and concrete."

Ethan let out a crowing laugh. "Well, that'll stick it to Sir Simeon!"

Mr Stuart smiled in a pained fashion, bowed slightly from the hips, and walked away. Ms Barton followed him. "Ungrateful git," muttered Rayne.

"He's not," said Ethan, "he's just . . . scared. He thinks that not even fire can purge Lingwall completely. Maybe he's right. Maybe there'll be a . . . I dunno. A *residue* left."

Rayne pulled a face, and looked up at the pall of grey smoke that was still hanging above the roof of Morton's Keep. It was strangely elongated and tall above Abigail's bedroom. "Ethan," she said, "can you see a shape in the smoke?"

"A bit like a person?" muttered Ethan.

"Yes. Look – there's the head, the arm. . ."

"Yes. D'you think it's him, d'you think it's *Lingwall*. . ."

But Rayne was smiling at it. "It's not him," she said. "It's *her*."

Chapter
Fifty-eight

A week after the fire, the whole affair had died down, just as Mr Stuart hoped. The local paper gave it a half-page spread where it was put down to "careless use of candles while exploring a cellar room". No one but Mr Stuart was mentioned by name in the article.

Night after night, Rayne saw Mr Stuart sitting in the library window, writing on thick sheets of paper. She was sure he was writing up the next *reoccurrence*, to be placed in the safe in the attic with the other accounts.

St John and his acolytes were keeping a very low profile in the town. Rumour had it that the group had split up, that Flora had stayed with St John but the others were having nothing to do with him. Amelia had left, to stay with relatives in Wales.

Morton's Keep carried on as if nothing had happened. Mrs Driver, of course, refused to mention the affair; but she seemed lighter, less anxious about the coming winter. She talked about how glorious Christmas was at the house. "We put holly everywhere," she said. "It looks a treat. So traditional."

292

It was a beautiful October. The weather was calm now and still quite warm. When she'd finished at the teashop, Rayne would walk along the lanes and in the woods. Burnished leaves dropped gracefully from the trees and caught in her hair like confetti.

She didn't feel lonely, although she was more alone than she'd ever been in her life. She'd had one text from Ethan, the day after the fire, asking her if she was OK. She'd replied that she was, and that was the end of any communication between them.

And yet there was so much they'd shared, so much for them to talk about. She thought about suggesting they meet up, but couldn't bring herself to do it.

The day before the workmen were due to arrive to fill in the fire-gutted dungeon with hard core and concrete, three cars drove up to the house at twilight. Rayne heard them as she heated up a tin of soup in the Sty for her supper.

Curious, she ran out and made her way along to the forecourt. She stood back in the trees and watched as eleven men got out. Peering through the half-light, she recognized the Morris dancers from the Apple Fair – the men who'd chased her in Fleet Woods. Then with a lurch of her stomach she saw Ethan Sands. He had his head lowered, his shoulders hunched. He had an air of not wanting to be there.

Hidden in the trees, she watched as Mr Stuart came out through the ancient arch to the courtyard and greeted them quietly. Then they all trooped into the house, and Rayne went back to her soup.

But she was too curious to leave it there. Fifteen minutes later, she was back staring up at the house from the shelter of the trees. Through the broken windows of Abigail's bedroom, she saw candles moving in a circular procession, into the far corner of the room where the door to the dungeon was, then one by one they disappeared, as though extinguished.

She stayed in the trees, watching. There seemed to be no reason to go. Then Ethan came stomping through the arch. He had something white in his hand. She watched as he walked over to one of the cars and leant up against it – then he lifted the white thing to his mouth, and started eating it.

She laughed. It seemed so incongruous, to be eating a sandwich. She stepped out from her hiding place, and walked over towards him.

"Hey, Ethan!" she called.

His face opened up when he saw her. "Hey!" he called back.

"What's been going on?"

"Oh – a watchers' thing. A ritual."

"Wow. What – to tie Sir Simeon down in the dungeon?"

"Something like that. They wanted to *clean* the place before it gets filled in tomorrow. Consecrate it. It's a pile of shite. It won't work. Just makes them feel better."

"So why go along with it?"

He shrugged. "They needed eleven. That's the number. And . . . they said I should be there, because. . ."

"Right. You burnt it."

"I couldn't let them down. Plus I was curious to see the place again."

Rayne shuddered. "God, I'm not. Was it . . . was it . . . was the *feeling* still there?"

"Kind of. It's all burnt out and collapsed, we had to drop down the last twelve feet by rope. But it's still a nasty place."

"And the sandwich?" She smiled at him, and he smiled back.

"Mrs Driver laid on refreshments, in the kitchen. I had a beer then decided I'd had a bellyful of all their talk, so I—"

He broke off. Voices were coming from the other side of the wall, growing louder – the men were returning.

Rayne felt a kind of desperation fill her. If he went off now, just got in one of the cars and went off – she leant towards him. "Ethan," she muttered, "d'you wanna talk some more? I mean – will you?"

He shunted himself off the car he was leaning against. "Come on," he said.

Chapter
Fifty-nine

As if acting on instinct, they walked fast, side by side, straight into the trees. A half-moon low over the woods lit their way. They reached a small clearing made by a tree uprooted in one of the recent storms. Ben Avebury had started to saw it up into firewood; two hefty logs made convenient seats. They sat down, not quite opposite each other, and Rayne realized she had no need to ask him anything, she understood it all, his impatience with the watchers, and with Mr Stuart – she felt the same.

"Will they wonder where you've gone, the men?" she asked.

He shrugged. "They'll think I just took off. They knew I was pissed off."

There was a silence, just the rustling of small night creatures in the undergrowth. Then Ethan looked up and said, "You've seen her, haven't you. I mean – *really* seen her."

"Yes," said Rayne. "Once in a palm tree, once as birds. Then in the smoke. Didn't you, in the smoke?"

"Kind of. Once you'd said. Not like you did. I mean – I didn't *know*. Look – can I say something here?"

Rayne smiled, nodded. It seemed an odd question to ask as they half-faced each other in the moonlight.

"The men – the watchers – they've got wind that you're . . . they think you're special. Here for a purpose."

Rayne thought back to the chase in the woods, the men shouting, *It's her, it's her!* "Why do they think that?" she asked.

"Well – I'm afraid it was partly my fault. When we were all in the pub, Patience was on about the 'sweet dark wet girl' who was a friend of the green lady. I said I thought it might be you – and they took it seriously. And now they know you were the reason we burnt out the dungeon, they're sure of it. Look – don't tell them you've seen her. They'll turn you into some kind of icon."

"What?"

"I'm serious. They'll have you starring at all their rituals, they'll have you stuck up on top of a maypole with a big crown on. . ." Rayne laughed, and he went on, "When I was younger I thought the watchers were brilliant, I was dead excited by it all. But now . . . now I know more of what's going on. . . Their fight, it's not *real*. Their rituals and everything, they're like comfort blankets. Smoke screens. And if they find out you've seen *her* – they'll mess it up. Oh, shit. I don't know what I'm saying here. I just—"

"Don't worry. I won't say a word. I want it all to just go away, actually. It's been so weird. Terrifying."

"So why are you still here?"

She shrugged. "Nowhere else to go. And I love it here. These woods – the silence – everything."

There was a pause. Rayne looked at him. She thought of the incredible thing that had happened to them, that bonded them. She was longing for him to say he hoped she'd stay, but he didn't. He shifted on his log as though he was about to stand up and go. She thought about asking him back to the Sty for a coffee, but the words sounded so lame when she ran them through her head that she couldn't say them.

If he gave her one sign, one clue that he liked her, she would, but. . . "I wonder why I saw her," she said, abruptly. "Just because I was here? On the spot?"

"Partly. But also. . ."

"What?"

"Remember that time I caught you outside, in the storm, under that huge tree? I saw your face. You loved it. You were part of it. You're *like* her. Patience saw it too. It's in you, like it's in her."

There was a pause. Rayne felt moved, flattered, by what he'd said. Then she murmured, "You were out in the storm too."

He shrugged. They were facing each other now, twisted towards each other. "It must hurt," he muttered. "What happened with St John."

"Yes, it hurts. More than anything it's so *humiliating*. I look back and I think – how could I have been that *abject*? I'd just got out of one controlling relationship and then I let *him* walk all over me."

"I don't think you had a lot of choice."

"What d'you mean?"

"Remember what he said – that Lingwall was helping him? St John had this weird power. That's why he had that group of – *slaves*. That's why I hated him. I hated him even before I found out the rumour about him being the last of the Lingwall line. I saw how he used his power. You weren't the first. Just the most . . . *deliberate*."

"Vampire kisses."

"That what it felt like?"

"Yes. He was amazing. Urgh. Don't want to think about it."

"Then don't."

"No. It's over."

"You've learnt your lesson, right?"

"Yes. No more men for me . . . not for ages. *Years!*"

Ethan turned to her, grinning, and said, "That's a shame."

Rayne met his eyes for as long as she could, then she jumped to her feet. "I'm getting cold out here," she said. "D'you want to come back for a coffee or something?"

And coming soon…

At Morton's Keep, the darkness has receded. St John has gone to ground and Miss Skelton, the bright new manager, is full of money-making ideas for the old place.

So why does Rayne feel so uneasy all the time? She's afraid of the fire festivals. She'd like to get closer to Ethan, but she can't help being suspicious of him, and why he wants to get closer to her. Even the ghosts seem to be warning her.

And then something happens that's so shocking she knows she was right to be afraid.

The saga continues next year.